All This Belongs to Me

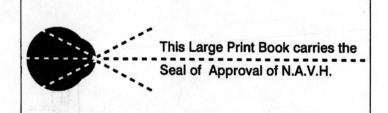

This Large Print Book carries the
Seal of Approval of N.A.V.H.

All This Belongs to Me

Ad Hudler

Thorndike Press • Waterville, Maine

All This Belongs to Me is a work of fiction. Names, characters, places, and incidents are the products of the author's imagination or are used fictitiously. Any resemblance to actual events, locales, or persons, living or dead, is entirely coincidental.

Published in 2006 by arrangement with The Ballantine Publishing Group, a division of Random House, Inc.

Thorndike Press® Large Print Americana.

The tree indicium is a trademark of Thorndike Press.

The text of this Large Print edition is unabridged.
Other aspects of the book may vary from the original edition.

Set in 16 pt. Plantin.

Printed in the United States on permanent paper.

Library of Congress Cataloging-in-Publication Data

Hudler, Ad.
    All this belongs to me / by Ad Hudler.
        p. cm. — (Thorndike Press large print Americana)
    ISBN 0-7862-8607-5 (lg. print : hc : alk. paper)
    1. Edison, Thomas A. (Thomas Alva), 1847–1931 —
Homes and haunts — Florida — Fiction. 2. Administration
of estates — Fiction. 3. Museum curators — Fiction.
4. Museums — Fiction. 5. Psychological fiction. I. Title.
II. Thorndike Press large print Americana series.
PS3608.U33A44 2006b
  813'.6—dc22   2006006185

For **Grandma Muriel,**
in this life and others

Acknowledgments

I thank Leah Barr and Drew Sterwald for their fine and friendly editing; my mom and dad and the staff of the University of Nebraska's Love Library, both of whom offered me writing refuge during a turbulent hurricane season; Maureen O'Neal for her enthusiasm, support, and friendship; John Yape, who keeps my computer healthy and productive; the staff of the Lee County library system; Wendy Sherman, who sells Ad Hudler to a decreasingly reluctant world; and the Pink Ladies Book Club of Sarasota, Florida, for their support and help in critiquing and planning the novel. (They are: Mary Jane Hartenstine, Nancy Bailey, Sue Benjamin, Sara Bailey, B. J. Creighton, Kay Hall, Judy Nimz, Brenda Cannon, and Elaine Bustard.)

I could not be happier with my publisher, who has seen me through three novels. At Ballantine Books I thank the sales and marketing staff for all their hard work and vision. Also, thanks goes to Ingrid Powell and Allison Dickens, a dream of an editor, insightful and helpful.

I consulted many books for research, and I am thankful to Neil Baldwin (*Edison: Inventing the Century*); Robert Conot (*Thomas A. Edison: A Streak of Luck*); Margaret Cousins (*The Story of Thomas Alva Edison*); Olav Thulesius (*Edison in Florida: The Green Laboratory*); Peter M. Nichols and the movie critics at *The New York Times* (*The New York Times Guide to the Best 1,000 Movies Ever Made*). Also thanks to *The News-Press* of Fort Myers.

And, of course, heartfelt thanks to Carol, for her patience and guidance through the storms of fiction writing.

Thomas Edison spent the last several weeks of his life drifting in and out of a coma, surrounded by his doctors and children and his wife, Mina. It is said that on his final day of life on this earth, he pulled himself into consciousness one last time, looked at his wife, and said to her, "It is very beautiful over there." Then he closed his eyes and died.

Part One

Chapter One

Welcome to Kansas, *Land of Ah's!*

Though Geena Pangborn was just sixty-two miles from Barry and his family, crossing this invisible line felt like shutting and locking a door behind her. As she sensed her anxiety ebbing, Geena released a deep breath and finally popped open the forgotten can of Diet Cherry Coke that had been warming between her thighs for the last hour.

She scanned the flat landscape. Western Kansas really looked just like eastern Colorado, less hilly but still brown and crispy, field upon field of the freeze-dried remnants of last summer's corn and wheat crops. When there was a light dusting of snow on the ground, as there was now, it reminded her of breakfast cereal awash in milk.

There was not a tree to be found, save the occasional grayed, sun-bleached exoskeleton of an elm near a dry creek bed that had surrendered long ago to the bitter winds and drought of the High Plains. Born and raised in the anonymity of an apartment complex in one of Denver's older, leafy neighborhoods, Geena had really never grown accustomed to this feeling of being exposed and vulnerable. It was unnatural to not have trees and water on the surface. There was no place to hide. Why were humans the only large mammals dense enough to call this terrain home?

In her years with Barry, Geena had tried to quell this vastness; she'd planted a birch, two maples, three blue spruce, a line of poplars along the fence. All but two of them died. From her favorite vantage point of the kitchen sink, looking into the backyard, it had been hard not to run an ongoing tally of mortality.

Geena now looked over at the Rand McNally road atlas spread open on the passenger seat of her Ford Excursion. It was a map of North America's freeway system, a network of blue lines that spread across the white continent like varicose veins on a pale leg. She would have ventured west, to the safety of the mountains, but a storm had been brewing along the Front Range, and she most likely would

14

have been forced back home. The winters of eastern Colorado were formidable, with the winds of the prairie and the snowfall of the mountains, and several times each year the highway patrol had to shut down the interstate and set up cattle gates at the entrance ramps so people wouldn't wander out, get lost, and perish in the blizzards. Geena had lost count of the times in the past eighteen years she'd been called upon to make a pan of beef enchiladas or seven-layer salad to help feed the stranded tourists spending a night on cots in the Armory downtown or in the high school gymnasium.

Eastward, she now drove. Behind her was Goodland (AMERICA'S FIRST HELICOPTER!) and Colby. On the horizon, Oakley and Hays (BIRTHPLACE OF U.S. ASTRONAUT BRAD FELDHOUSEN) . . . and then Salina (HOME OF TONY'S PIZZA). Sometime after that, Geena knew she would have to get off of I-70 and find some lesser-traveled two-lane road. Nine hours would have passed, and by then Barry surely would have canvassed every street of Sublette. Yellow Roof IGA Grocery . . . Rhonda's house . . . the Gibson's Discount Center out by the interstate . . . Mode O' Day and Renee's Wearhouse and Daylight

Donuts on Leonard Street . . . there were only so many places to hide in a town of two thousand three hundred inhabitants.

She passed two Kansas State Patrol cars, parked side by side, the troopers in dark glasses chatting from their front seats like teenagers who had flagged each other down on a Friday night. In her rearview mirror, Geena watched for reaction as she passed by, and she wondered: How long would a man search for a woman he no longer loved?

Geena pulled into the parking lot of a Wendy's outside Junction City and stopped in to buy some coffee and stretch her legs. She opened the back of her Excursion to search for a Yanni CD that had been sliding around the floor for the past week and was thrilled to rediscover a dark green lawn-and-leaf bag stuffed with a schizophrenic collection of clothes she'd meant to drop off at the Goodwill Dumpster behind Pizza Hut.

Geena smiled — "I came prepared after all," she said to herself — as she opened the bag.

It was mainly Barry's clothes. Like most men his age, he'd been gaining two pounds a year, most all of it in his stomach. Geena

16

pondered now the unfairness of how
women always had to hide their stomachs
with loose clothing or a forearm self-
consciously draped across the fleshy rise,
yet men displayed them with pride,
perched atop their belts like some trophy
on a mantel.

Geena pulled out dress shirt after dress
shirt before coming to a T-shirt from The
Stratosphere in Las Vegas . . . pairs of his
athletic tube socks that he wore beneath
his boots, the elastic now tired and
limp . . . a red Polo shirt, a yellow one,
too . . . a man's silk tie with tiny blue
Viagra pills on a red background, a phar-
maceutical freebie given to him by their
friend Dr. Eberhart.

Suddenly Geena stopped. With utmost
care, as if it were a piece of formalwear
losing sequins, she pulled out the navy
blue V-neck sweater that had been Nathan's favorite.

"You bastard," she whispered.

There were spans of days, sometimes up
to a week, when Geena would wear this
sweater every day, much to Barry's dismay.
She would come into the kitchen, and he
would look up from his *Rocky Mountain
News* and give her a look of feigned concern tinged with judgment, the same look

he employed when she ordered dessert in a restaurant.

And then suddenly the sweater vanished. And here it was. Geena shook it out and pulled it over her green blouse. She began again to rummage through the sack.

"There you are," she said.

It was still in the box, and it was a stroke of luck — fate? — that after all these years she had waited so long to get rid of it. Geena had received Safe-T-Man as a gag gift eight years ago at a surprise birthday party given to her by her girlfriends. ("Just in case Barry can't satisfy you," Deanna Wisehart had joked.)

She read the box: *Safe-T-Man — Your escort for security on today's dangerous roads. Life-Size. Realistic beard stubble!*

With a rubber head, Safe-T-Man was a handsome fellow by Euro-American standards, with blue eyes and brown beard shadow painted on and the parted acrylic hair of a conservative soap opera actor. Beneath this head dangled the body, limp like a long, expired balloon. He reminded Geena of the Resuscie Annie from the CPR class she had taken at Mile High Red Cross as a teenager.

Geena looked for and found the nipple on the upper back. And then, facing the dining room of Wendy's, she sat on the backseat, door open, and proceeded to blow. In the next five minutes a six-foot-two stranger with painted-on white Jockey briefs and a T-shirt materialized before her. His skin was bronze. He appeared to be about a size-eleven shoe.

A married couple emerged from the restaurant and approached their car, next to Geena's.

"I wish my husband looked that good without his clothes on," the woman said.

"Better watch it, baby," he said, smiling.

"Does he talk?" she asked Geena.

"No."

Cocking her head, she put her hands on her hips and drank him in. "Then he just might be about the most perfect man I've ever seen."

They laughed, got into their car, and drove away. Geena looked at the tag (Tennessee) to help her place their accent. She then held Safe-T-Man at arm's length and looked him over. He did have a nice build, broad shoulders that tapered down to a cute little butt. They'd even given him nicely rounded biceps, and for this reason Geena chose for him a clinging white T-shirt from the Muscular Dystrophy 5K run.

Geena set Safe-T-Man into the passenger seat and buckled him up. She then stood back, trying to gauge what was wrong, the way she did when she rearranged the furniture at home. It was the posture — that's what bothered her. No one sat up that straight. It was unnatural.

Geena let out some air, then reclined the seat forty-five degrees. In the backseat she found a Pioneer Seeds baseball cap, which she slipped over his hair, then tipped it forward, over his eyes, as if he were using it to shield his face from the sun.

Sleeping, Safe-T-Man accompanied Geena as she drove south on U.S. 77, out of Junction City, to someplace warmer and farther away.

Chapter Two

A special meeting of the museum docents had been called for 7:00 a.m., and Ellis, who was usually plugged into the buzzing undercurrent of administrative happenings, had no idea why.

Hoping to find out something if he arrived early, Ellis decided to take shortcuts in his morning work-preparation ritual. Usually Ellis fried one lamb chop for breakfast each day, which he ate with a piece of rye toast with butter and one cup of black coffee. This morning, he decided to forgo the meat.

The arthritis in Ellis's right shoulder was flaring up, so he was slower than normal as he put on his clothes: khaki Bermuda shorts with elastic waist, black support hose, and white tennis shoes, his official, city-issued baby blue Polo shirt with EDISON WINTER ESTATE embroidered on the breast in navy blue thread. Everything

21

but the shoes had been washed the night before and laid out on the empty side of his queen-size bed.

On the way out the door, he grabbed his broad-brimmed, white straw hat, the very same style worn by the famous inventor himself. For years Ellis had searched for such a hat, and then, on one fortuitous morning during his walk to work, down McGregor Boulevard, he found precisely the hat he'd been looking for. Clean and new-looking, it sat atop a pile of rubbish set out on the curb for trash pickup. Thinking it too good to be true, like a piece of fresh cheese on a mousetrap, Ellis looked over his shoulder . . . right . . . left. Surely this handsome hat belonged to somebody.

Right . . . left.

Surely they did not mean to throw it away.

Right . . . left.

Perhaps it had flown out of a passing car, and a pedestrian set it on top of the heap so the rightful owner could spot it later on.

Reluctantly, Ellis left it alone, but three hours later, during his coffee break, he returned and was thrilled to find it untouched, now warmed from a morning in the Fort Myers sun. Yes, he was certain this hat did belong to someone, but as he heard the whine and banging of the approaching sanitation truck farther down the boulevard, Ellis realized it was he and only he who could save this hat from an early, undeserved demise in the Lee County incinerator. He plucked it from the top of the trash pile, put it under his arm, and walked briskly back to work. With the help of some duct tape and a smashed, empty toilet paper roll, it fit him perfectly.

As he anticipated, Ellis arrived at the historic Edison home before anyone. The chairs had been set up in the break room in a manner he had never seen . . . in straight rows and at an angle, facing, of all things, a podium in the corner.

A podium! Where did such a thing come from?

It was oak and appeared to be new, with the seal of the City of Fort Myers on the front, which featured a shield in the shape of a U.S. interstate sign, segmented into three pictures: a thrashing silver tarpon hooked on a fishing line, a beach scene with palm tree, two oranges hanging from a branch.

The bulletin board was bare. Gone were the work schedule, and the take-out menus for Sub and Pub and Wings 'n' Ribs, and the list of local young men and women who'd been nominated that year for king and queen of Edisonia at the Pageant of Light. Gone was the photograph of Mary Ellen's new granddaughter in Dayton. Gone was Ellis's new handwritten suggestion that docents carry in their pockets a bag of tissues for runny-nosed guests unaccustomed to the prodigious amount of pollen from the subtropical flora on the grounds.

As Ellis absorbed the blankness, the door swung open and in walked a moderately plump woman dressed in a tailored black suit and very loud heels. She looked to be about thirty, and she wore the strangest glasses Ellis had ever seen . . . lemon yellow plastic frames in the shape of perfect ovals. She'd pulled her dark brown hair into a tight bun on the back of her head. Ellis thought this unbecoming; it accentuated her somewhat fleshy chin.

"Good morning," said the woman.

"Good morning," Ellis answered warily.

"You must work here."

"Yes, madame, I most certainly do."

She nodded her head, saying nothing.

"I am the senior docent," Ellis continued. "I have worked here longer than anybody. Except Larry."

"Mr. Livengood?" she asked.

"Yes. Larry Livengood. The director of the museum."

She leaned toward him to read the white plastic, lightbulb-shaped ID pin on his chest.

"It says your name is Edison. Can that be right?"

"Well, that is not exactly my name. Not my real name."

"Oh?"

"You will notice Edison is in quotation marks. That is so people realize it is only a nickname."

"And how did you get to be called Edison?" she asked.

Ellis suddenly was distracted by a sound outside, the clatter of the rakes and hoes and other gardening tools jostling about on the back of Mike Rathbun's golf cart, which was passing outside the window.

"May I be of some assistance?" Ellis asked. "Are you looking for somebody?"

"Actually, no," she answered. "I'm new here. I start today. I'm running the meeting at seven." She offered her hand. "I'm Judith Ziegler."

"Does Larry know you are here?"

She paused, looked at the floor, then finally met Ellis's stare. "Mr. Livengood is no longer with the Edison estate."

"I beg your pardon?"

"It was in *The News-Press* today. Did you not see it?"

He had not. Ellis had let his mother's subscription expire after she died nearly twenty years ago. The only thing he missed was Dear Abby and Hints from Heloise; both columns were still featured in the newspaper, though they were now being written by the women's daughters. If there was anything important about the museum in the paper, Ellis read it during lunch break from the copy in the museum's employee lounge.

"Larry has left the museum?"

"Yes."

"But why?"

"I'll talk more about it at the seven o'clock announcement."

She looked over Ellis's shoulder, toward the kitchenette. "I came in to make coffee before everyone got here."

"I make the coffee," Ellis said.

"You make the coffee?"

"Yes. I make the coffee every day."

"Every day?"

"Yes."

"Who makes it when you're gone?"

"I am never gone."

She gave him an amused, crooked smile. "Then . . . would you mind? I need to run across the street for something."

When the door shut behind her, Ellis hurried to the window and watched her walk across the parking lot. She first retrieved a manila envelope from the backseat of her bronze Saab sedan, which had Virginia tags and a Wellesley sticker in the back window. She then stopped to chat with Frank McComer, smiling and offering her hand. It was Frank who sat on the stool along the white picket fence and controlled the stoplight over McGregor so the docents and their gaggles of tourists could cross from the ticket office to the estate. Sometimes, when Frank had a doctor's appointment, Ellis would sit in for him, and while he much preferred to be educating visitors about the greatest inventor in American history, he did find great satisfaction in watching hundreds of cars stop and go at his command.

Ellis went to check Larry's office but found the door locked. "This door is not supposed to be locked!" he said, out loud. On the wood were the two square, cushiony, sticky white pads that once held the nameplate.

Ellis's face grew flushed. His eyes began

to blink twice as often as normal, as they were wont to do when he became agitated or challenged by a skeptical tourist who did not believe something Ellis had said on a tour.

He went back to the lounge and found the newspaper on the white Formica table. Through the clinging, clear plastic bag, Ellis could read the headline above the fold: EDISON HOME GETS NEW HEAD: NEW DIRECTOR HOPES TO TAKE MUSEUM TO 'WORLD-CLASS LEVEL.'

"World-class level, indeed," Ellis said.

At the press conference, the front row of chairs was filled by members of the greater Fort Myers media . . . and Ellis, who had firmly but politely insisted to a young female reporter from WFMY that she was, indeed, sitting in his chair.

Dick Moody, the mayor, stood up to speak, telling of how the city was committed to turning the winter residence of Thomas Edison into a Smithsonian-caliber institution, with a research library and annual symposium on American creativity. Just as the mayor was introducing the new director, Ellis raised his hand.

Dick Moody looked at him, quizzically. "Yes?"

Ellis stood from his chair and smoothed out the wrinkles on his thighs where his pants had gathered while sitting. "Your Honor," he said. The mayor smiled. "Did you know that the Edison home is one of the most-visited historic homes in all of the United States?"

"Yes," he answered. "I'm not sure about the exact numbers, but, yes, I certainly know it does well. We're very proud of the job y'all have been doing here."

"Well, then forgive me for being forward, sir, but then why would you want to change such a lucrative, famous landmark when such changes obviously are not warranted?"

As if on cue, three TV cameramen hurried to the front of the room and turned toward Ellis. One by one, they clicked on the lights atop their cameras, instantly bathing him in bright whiteness.

The mayor looked over his shoulder at Judith Ziegler, then spoke. "As good as things have been here at the Edison home, we think there's always room for improvement," he said.

Judith stepped forward and gently grabbed the mayor's upper arm. "Of course, we want to build on all the wonderful work that's already been done here," she added.

A TV reporter in a salmon-colored suit — Ellis recognized her as Stefanie Maddox from Eyewitness NewsCenter 4 — held a microphone up to Ellis's face. They had met before . . . three years earlier, when someone stole three of Mina Edison's historic wicker chairs off the porch in the moonlight and escaped by motorboat down the Caloosahatchee River. Viewers that night watched Ellis Norton make an appeal for twenty-four-hour FBI surveillance of the historic site.

Ellis lifted his chin twenty degrees and looked into the camera, not straight on but obliquely, the way Gloria Swanson did at dramatic moments in her silent films.

"Larry Livengood's job has been terminated," he declared with punctuated force. "The man who made this museum into what it is today has been fired from this institution!"

Muffled banter rose from the group of blue-shirted docents, many of whom had not heard the news. The mayor, recognizing that he was now riding in rapids, motioned for Judith to take over. She stepped up to the podium, smiled, and authoritatively grabbed the edges with her hands.

"That's correct that Mr. Livengood will

no longer be directly involved with the museum," she said. "After a long and proud tenure he has decided to retire, and I am replacing him, effective today. I'm an archivist specializing in the Industrial Revolution, and I've been brought on board to help organize the museum collection into what we hope will become a resource not only for researchers worldwide but for this community as well."

"Where did you come from?" Ellis asked. "What are your credentials?"

"I was the associate curator of collections at Monticello. I have a PhD in material culture."

The mayor leaned into the microphone: "And we had to pay a pretty penny to snag her away, too."

Ellis, who was now holding Stefanie Maddox's microphone himself, continued to stand. "Did you know, madame, that Larry used to deliver the *Tropical News* to Mr. and Mrs. Edison? He personally knew the inventor and his wife."

Judith fought to contain a smile. "Mr. Livengood contributed something very . . . unique to this institution," she said. "But he was ready to move on and do something different. . . . Next question?"

The cameras and their lights abandoned

Ellis, and he suddenly felt cold and anemic. He wished he had brought his cardigan with him.

Ellis had never had another boss. Larry hired him when he was twenty-four. The only other job Ellis had had was as a stock clerk at the old American Department Store, which was now a climate-controlled storage facility for snowbirds who migrated south with too many material possessions.

It was Larry who let him playact as Edison every Saturday afternoon, walking the grounds like a ghost.

It was Larry who gave Ellis a key to every lock on the estate.

It was Larry who discovered him one time lying in Thomas Edison's bed, eyes closed, dressed in a pair of the inventor's pants and shoes.

"Oh, hello, Ellis," he said at the time. "Are you feeling all right?"

Ellis sat up, as if just woken from a nap in his own home on Wilna Street. "Fine, Larry," he replied. "Thank you for asking."

Chapter Three

In three generations' time, the Pangborn family of Sublette, Colorado, built the largest real estate empire in the tristate region. If someone had to sell his ranch or farmland or home in the northeastern quarter of this expansive, rectangular state, his list was short: Centennial Realty, with headquarters on Leonard Street in Sublette, and thirteen satellite offices stretching from Julesburg in the north to Cheyenne Wells in the south. The company's trademark yellow-and-brown for-sale signs with a small yucca plant at the bottom seemed native in the landscape that was northeastern Colorado.

The family included Geena's husband Barry and his four brothers, all of them realtors; their mother Dot and father Brit; and Daltry, grandfather and founder of the company. They all lived in sprawling, modern, brick ranch-style houses with expansive concrete driveways. All their kids had horses. The entire family traded in their cars and trucks every year, taking turns with the dealers who did business with them. On what they called "D-Day" — for Detroit Day — usually in November, they arrived en masse at a dealership, test-drove all the models that had even marginal appeal, then departed in a convoy, their old cars shed and left behind like the useless skins of rattlesnakes. Geena pushed perennially for a Toyota — in fact, she specifically wanted the hybrid Prius for its earth-friendly mileage — but she never got her way because there wasn't a Toyota dealer in the region, and Brit insisted that they buy their cars locally.

Once or twice each week, all or most of the family could be found eating at a long table at Prairie Pines Golf and Country Club west of town, usually on Thursdays, which was prime rib day. It was not hard to spot the Pangborn clan . . . the women with their expensive Denver haircuts and clothes they'd bought at Cherry Hills Mall . . . the men by their black leather coats, custom-made Stetson hats, their six-foot-plus height, their strong, square faces with high cheekbones and ruddy complexions.

Between them all, the Pangborns shared two full-time housekeepers. When they went to Denver to shop, they always stayed at the historic Brown Palace Hotel downtown or, if that was full, the Westin. And when any of the Pangborn families went on vacation, they always said they were visiting relatives out of state, and then they'd fly business-class to London or Miami or New York or Las Vegas and stay in a Four Seasons Hotel.

For a while, after marrying Barry, Geena felt guilty about her new trappings, particularly the bit about not having to clean her own toilets or iron her own shirts anymore. After they'd been married for a month, Barry walked in one day and found her clipping coupons from the Sunday newspaper and organizing them in a cardboard accordion folder, just as she used to do for her and her mother.

"What in tarnation are you doing?" he asked.

"What does it look like I'm doing?"

Barry smiled, then reared his head back and laughed at the ceiling.

"What?" she asked, snipping the last edge of a coupon for Miracle Whip.

"I can just see my momma's face right now."

"What? What, Barry? Tell me."

He shook his head, still smiling. "If Dot Pangborn knew one of her daughters-in-law was passing coupons at Safeway, she'd probably lay down and die."

Before she knew it, Geena was tossing items into her cart without looking at the prices . . . even expensive cuts of beef. She started wearing high-end Nocona boots, as did all the other Pangborn women, and found herself strutting in and out of the stores on Leonard Street, emboldened by the respect with which she was treated. For the first time in her life, she did not know the current price of gasoline.

Gas, Geena thought to herself now as she drove south, crossing into Oklahoma. *This frigging gas-guzzler is going to take every cent I have.*

She had told Barry she was going to visit Lisa Bass, her friend in Fort Collins. Geena packed a small overnight bag and brought along just more than three hundred in cash. Any more than that and they would have thought she'd run away, which would have handed him and his family the final bullet they would need to assassinate her already moribund character.

At 5:20 in the afternoon, hungry and wanting to get out and move around,

Geena spotted a granite-and-glass high-rise Hyatt just north of Tulsa. She pulled into the lot, parked her car along a line of yew bushes, then refreshed her lipstick and brushed her hair.

Carrying her big purse made from a kilim rug, which she'd bought at Harrods in London, and wearing a new brown leather coat from Nordstrom, she strutted into the lobby in her black cowhide boots. God, she loved these boots! It was impossible to walk in boots without exuding a sense of ownership of all that you tread upon. The entire Pangborn clan wore spendy cowboy boots, and Geena was certain this had unwittingly created at least one-half of the family's mystique and perceived omnipotence.

She nodded at the check-in staff behind the counter — "Good evening!" — as she passed them, toward the bar . . . which, this being a Hyatt . . . had to be . . . yes . . . up there on the mezzanine level to the left . . . and the elevators were . . . she listened for the chime of doors opening . . . yes! . . . behind the corner, there on the right. Geena had been a guest in many Hyatt hotels over the years . . . just not this one.

As she expected, it was happy hour in

37

the bar. Geena ordered a glass of chardonnay, set it on a table in the corner, then went to the buffet. Standing behind a fleshy, balding businessman who reminded her of Bob Pack, the president of Kit Carson County First National Bank back in Sublette, Geena studied the food. The crudités would be perfect for keeping overnight, as would the mini–egg rolls. Oh . . . and the triangles of flaky spanakopita. The smothered meatballs for now . . . and some of those cheddar cheese cubes on toothpicks . . . okay, some more meatballs . . . oh, and shrimp . . . definitely shrimp.

"You've got quite an appetite," said the man.

"I've been in meetings all day," she answered without hesitation. "I had two bites of a stale bagel at eight o'clock this morning and nothing since."

"You here for the swine convention?"

Geena smiled and looked up from her plate. "You're insulting me, and I don't even know you."

Embarrassment and surprise flashed across his face. "Oh! . . . No!" he said. With his free hand — the other held a plate of food — he instinctively reached out to touch her back but stopped short. "I mean, there's some kind of convention

38

going on. Oklahoma swine breeders. Or something like that."

"No," she said. Geena dropped a dollop of cocktail sauce on the rim of her white plate. "I'm in town on business."

"What do you do?"

"I'm an architect," she answered. — *Architect! Where did that come from?* — "I design restaurants for Wendy's."

Wendy's!

"No kidding? So you're based out of Columbus then? I'm from Akron."

"No," she answered. "The construction services division works out of Atlanta. I live in Atlanta."

Construction services? Geena!

"Do you mind if I join you?" he asked.

Geena hesitated.

"I'm not some pervert," he said. "Really. I just want some company."

He followed her to her table and they sat down. He was a dental supplies salesman from Ohio, and curious. Geena soon was surprised at how easily the misinformation about her new life poured from her mouth, as if she were a news anchor wired to her producer in some far-off dark booth who was feeding her words: ". . . We're going to bring back those historic-newspaper-print Formica tables from the seventies . . . Do you remember those? The tables we had when Clara Peller was on TV with those 'Where's the Beef?' ads . . . We're also thinking of redesigning the signage. . . . Oh, no, we'll keep little Wendy in there — in fact, we're thinking of making the entire sign in the shape of her head . . . really large and hovering over the entrance. You know, like the clowns on the old fun houses. . . . There's a prototype going up in Orange County. . . ."

Geena was amazed at how this new reality was being put together, details from her own real-life experiences (last year's vacation in Southern California) mixed in with childhood memories (Elitch Gardens Amusement Park in Denver) and things she'd read while sitting in the waiting room of the doctor's office (an article from *Psychology Today*, revealing how retailers used color to evoke emotions in their customers). Geena wondered if this was what it was like to be a screenwriter, creating fictional lines and characters. She was surprised at how good it felt telling so many lies, as if each one separated her farther and farther away from Sublette and Barry and Dot.

"Would you excuse me?" said the man, named Ron. "I need to go to the men's room." In their half hour together, he had drunk two vodka tonics compared to Geena's one chardonnay, largely because she was the one doing most of the talking.

"Then I'll go on up and check my e-mails," she said.

"Meet you back here?" he asked.

"Okay."

She watched him get up to leave, and when he was out of sight, Geena quickly wrapped three spanakopita and four egg rolls in a napkin and stowed them in her purse. She set a five-dollar bill on the table and made a hasty exit for the bell captain's stand in the foyer.

Geena approached an older gentleman in a burgundy Hyatt Windbreaker. "Excuse me, do you have a screwdriver?"

"Is there something wrong in your room?" he asked. "I can call maintenance."

"Oh, no," Geena answered. "It's just something loose on my car."

"Can I help you with it?"

"I can do it, but thanks. Do you have one?"

He disappeared into his little room off the foyer.

"A Phillips, please!" Geena yelled after him. "Big one if you've got it."

Back at the car, she reached beneath the seat and pulled out a Kansas license plate.

She had found it in an urban neighborhood of Wichita, by trolling the streets until she came upon a bungalow-style house shaded by overgrown trees. A washing machine sat on the porch and three cars were on cinder blocks in the front yard. The hood of the yellow Impala was open, the engine gone. It surely was not going anywhere soon. After ringing the doorbell to make certain no one was home, Geena found a pair of pliers in a toolbox beneath one of the other cars, unscrewed the plate from the chrome bumper, then slipped back into her car and drove away.

In the dark of the Hyatt's parking lot, as Ron was hurriedly brushing his teeth in Room 614, Geena removed her Colorado plate and replaced it with the one from Kansas. She then peeled off the current year's sticker from her own tag and pressed and smoothed it over the expired '99 sticker on the Kansas plate. A corner continued to peel away and, like a stubborn cowlick, resisted all attempts to keep it in place. Geena reached for her purse — God, how she loved this purse! So expansive. So useful! — and fumbled around until she pulled out a tube of Super Glue, which she used to reattach the obstinate corner forever.

And then, as if she were throwing a Frisbee, Geena winged the old Colorado plate into the triangular, man-made lake on the edge of the Hyatt property. It hit the water with a slap. For a moment the moonlight reflected off its silvery aluminum back, but this began to fade as it slowly sank toward the mucky bottom.

Chapter Four

Cloudy, cool days always brought the frustrated, bored tourists in from the beach, up McGregor Boulevard, and into town, where they toured the home and laboratory of Fort Myers's most famous resident. On the mornings that Ellis had to bring his cardigan to work with him, he knew he could expect a less interested crowd, visitors who considered the rich lives of Thomas and Mina Edison more a consolation prize because they would rather be sorting through the shells on Sanibel Island or drinking Budweiser and frozen cocktails beneath the coconut palms at the Lani Kai resort on Fort Myers Beach.

Two young men at the back of Ellis's 11:30 group had proven to be a problem from the get-go. Hecklers, both of them. They had new, first-degree sunburns and eyes reddened by beer consumed somewhere along the way, probably at Hooters,

Ellis thought to himself, noting on one man's chin the dried orange sauce he assumed came from buffalo wings. One of them wore a faded, red Indiana Hoosiers tank top with a bleach stain on the front, the other a baseball cap with a small embroidered Confederate flag and the saying IT'S NOT HATRED, IT'S HISTORY. And they both had tattoos, those rings around the upper arms that look like bracelets of magnified blue-black barbed wire. Ellis had hoped that the recent admission price increase from nine dollars to twelve would winnow out such specimens, but, alas, here they were, belching beneath the shade of the towering mango trees outside the Edison children's bedroom.

Like overindulged, domesticated parrots, the two men retorted nearly every time Ellis stopped talking.

On the mention of Edison's deafness: "What? Can't hear you!! Whazzat again?!"

On Edison's Madagascar rubber vines: "Rubbers! Hey, dude, do those come ribbed? You got 'em in magnum size?"

Ellis ignored them, but he did begin to use his bullhorn in hopes of exerting more authority and perhaps intimidating them into submission and silence. Every docent at the Thomas Alva Edison Winter Estate

45

was equipped with a bullhorn attached to a navy blue strap, which they suspended from their shoulder in the same manner a student carries a light backpack. Plugged into the side of this was a black spiral cord that ended in a mike like the ones on citizens band radios. Ellis preferred not to use his bullhorn; he prided himself on his strong, concise voice. In fact, before incorporating some new bit of information into his tour, he would first practice at home in front of his bedroom mirror with a tape recorder, the television volume turned up high to replicate the sound of passing traffic and distracting chatter on the real job.

Suddenly from the corner of his eye, Ellis saw one of the two men pull an opened Butterfinger from his pocket and take a bite. As quickly as he could, he pointed the head of his bullhorn directly at him as if it were a cannon.

"Young man!" he fired, his dam of frustration finally bursting. "We do not allow food or beverages on the estate. This is a national historic treasure, and droppings of anything would attract rats and mice and other unsavory creatures who might then decide to inhabit this lovely home."

The man shrugged his shoulders and

gave an incredulous look. "It's just a candy bar, man."

"Put it away right now. You and your companion have been nothing but trouble on this tour."

A sudden, violent sound yanked everyone's attention toward the street. They saw a compact Hispanic man on the side of McGregor Boulevard feeding a crispy, dead frond from a royal palm into a roaring shredder pulled behind a blue City of Fort Myers pickup truck, a common sight this time of year. Expired fronds, some of them ten feet long and weighing up to fifty pounds, would frequently drop to the ground, heavy and fast, like some large mammal falling out of a tree to its death. Just the previous week, Judy Teten, one of the docents, witnessed one of them crash through the windshield of a passing Buick LeSabre from Minnesota. With bloodied faces, the silver-haired driver and his hysterical wife were escorted into an ambulance. Shortly afterward, before traffic was restored, Ellis had emerged from the caretaker's cottage with a broom and dustpan to clean up the sparkling confetti of tempered glass from the street.

"If you do not put the candy bar away, I will have no choice but to summon the authorities and have you escorted from the grounds."

"You gotta be kiddin'."

"I am not."

"Oh, yeah?"

As if it were a cigarette, the man threw down his Butterfinger and ground it into the redbrick walkway with the toe of his flip-flop. "Well, fuck you. Fuck this shit . . . your stupid little museum, you old shriveled dick . . . Come on," he said to his partner. "Let's get the hell outta here."

Ellis watched as they swaggered back toward the white picket fence, their shoulders drawn back in anger, dangling but tensed arms pumping at their sides like the boys in *West Side Story* when they had to retreat, outnumbered, but still wanting to look strong and in charge. "Get a life, freak," one of them yelled over his shoulder.

Ellis returned to the front of the group and clipped the microphone back onto the elastic waist of his khaki shorts.

"Very impressive," said one man.

"Thank you," Ellis replied. "I have dealt with adversity before."

Ellis raised his chin and blew out a shallow, punctuated sigh, the type that is akin to changing the channel of a televi-

48

sion and starting anew. "Well, then," he said. "This whole candy bar issue reminds me of an interesting story about our esteemed inventor, Mr. Edison. . . . Thomas Alva Edison, who was called 'Al' in his earlier years, ate like a bird . . . a very disciplined eater, as you can imagine. Most lunches included nothing but a single lamb chop, two tablespoons of fresh peas, and a dish of applesauce. . . . Do I hear some stomachs rumbling?"

Small smiles sprouted on the faces of his group, and Ellis, emboldened once again, continued.

"On occasion, Edison's daughter Madeleine would have friends over for lunch. The inventor would join them and read throughout the meal, looking up every now and then to survey the situation. As Edison nibbled on his modest meal, the girls gorged themselves on a feast fit for princesses of muffins and four-layer cake and salad and fruit and cheese and, let me see, there was steamed salmon.

"When the meal was over, Edison would stand up and say, 'Well, ladies, who is ahead now? I, who fed my body the spare nutrition it needed and then fed my mind? Or you, who have been digging your graves with your teeth?' "

★ ★ ★

Drained from his stressful encounter, Ellis retired to the employee lounge for his hourly glass of water. In all his decades as a docent, Ellis could count on one hand the number of times he had had to call in sick, and he attributed this to two things: the seventy-two ounces of water he drank each day and the fact that he walked everywhere he needed to go. This was one point on which he and Edison disagreed. The inventor believed in exercise only for the mind, not for the muscles or heart. He saw the body simply as a vessel to carry the brain.

Though they both were five feet, nine inches tall, Ellis noted with pride that he did not share the same penguin profile. His cheeks were not as cherubic, his legs thinner and, probably, much stronger.

Ellis had never driven in his life — he had no need to. Before his mother died, she would take him everywhere. In the years that followed her passing, he fashioned an intimate world navigable by foot that fulfilled most every need, except for visits to his urologist on Summerlin Road, and he could always find one of his docent friends to take him. For groceries, he pulled a two-wheeled cart to the Publix at

Ricardo and U.S. 41. Though the character of his neighborhood had changed over the years, Ellis could still find his cornflakes and frozen Lean Cuisines among the cassava root and salsa casera and frozen head of goat. (Once, he had to return some plantains that he'd mistaken for bananas.)

But at this moment he was thinking of Larry Livengood, with whom he'd had a disturbing encounter the previous night. Over the past ten days, since Larry had disappeared, Ellis had left sixteen messages on his answering machine. Finally, Ellis decided to walk the eight blocks to his house on Passaic Avenue.

Ellis rang the doorbell three times. Having no luck, he put his ear to the door and heard the television going inside.

He began knocking. "Larry? . . . Larry! . . . Larry, are you in there?"

Finally, the door slowly opened.

"Larry!"

"Oh, hell, Ellis, what are you doing here?"

He was wearing a pair of brown polyester slacks unfastened at the waist and a white tank top T-shirt with a smudge on the chest of what appeared to be yellow mustard. Normally clean-shaven, the lower

51

half of his face was covered in white beard stubble. Ellis had never seen his boss with so much exposed skin, and he could not help but stare at the preponderance of white hair, which seemed to flow from the neck and armholes of his shirt like the bubbles of agitated champagne, climbing then cresting his shoulders, then sheeting down his arms and back, thinning as the journey from chest to limbs progressed. Ellis suddenly realized that in all his research of Thomas Edison, he'd never once seen a picture of him in his underwear or even a swimming suit, and he wondered now if Edison, too, was a hairy man and thus self-conscious about his appearance. He did, after all, have those prodigious wild eyebrows that reminded Ellis of unmanicured bougainvillea.

"Larry, why aren't you answering your phone?"

"I don't want to answer my phone, Ellis."

"Why not?"

"I'm pissed off — and I'm drunk."

"What's going on at the museum?"

"You tell me. I got fired."

"But why?"

"I'll tell you why. Susan Freeland, that's why."

Susan Freeland was a relative newcomer to Fort Myers from Binghamton, New York, and she'd been elected to city council that November. One of her main platforms was to reform the tired Edison estate, a world-class historic site that, she said, was being run with the nonchalance of college kids working a miniature-golf course during summer break.

For fodder, she hired a historic-building inspector from Charleston, South Carolina, who presented to the council and a *News-Press* reporter an engineer's report that read more like a postmortem. Hiding behind frequent coats of white paint and sprawling bougainvillea bushes were rotten and termite-infested floorboards and joists, support beams, and stairs. The paper ran a six-part series detailing all the decay.

Thousands called the mayor. Hundreds wrote letters. Greater Fort Myers had nearly a quarter million retirees with time on their hands, and such en masse activism really wasn't that unusual. When *The News-Press* was planning to redesign its comics page, editors debated canning Mary Worth to make room for the more contemporary Get Fuzzy. Wanting feedback, they ran a story divulging their plans. The next day they got sixteen hundred phone calls, most of them from seniors promising that, if editors should make such an unwise deletion from their comics page, they would drop their subscriptions. The next day's front page proclaimed MARY'S WORTH IT!

"Oh, hell, Ellis," Larry said. "Come on in." With help from his cypress-wood cane, he slowly turned and began walking into the darkness.

The house smelled like fried meat and Mentholatum and something sour, like curdled milk or dirty socks. The shades had been drawn, and the only light came from a floor lamp beside the slate-colored La-Z-Boy, making it look as if a spotlight were trained on the chair, a scene from a one-man play.

Ellis sat down on the edge of the couch and rested his hands in his lap, nervously patting his thighs as if inviting a dog to jump up and join him.

"You want something to drink?" Larry asked. "I'm drinking bourbon."

Ellis started to speak again but stopped short. A quote from the teetotaler Edison dropped into his consciousness: "As a cure for worrying, work is far better than whiskey. I always found that, if I began to worry, the best thing I could do was focus

54

upon something useful and then work very hard at it."

Ellis had memorized the entire *Quotable Edison* sold in the museum gift shop. He thought it his duty to do so as an expert on the man, and he often bought his peers copies of the book as birthday gifts so they would do the same, though nobody did, not even Jessica Nusbaum, the youngest and, in Ellis's mind, most promising docent he had met in decades.

Frequently, almost daily — and not just on his tours — Ellis would pull such Edisonisms from his memory bank as he saw need. And each time, because he had watched hours upon hours of scratchy, black-and-white film clips of the inventor being interviewed, Ellis could hear and see him speak anything and everything he needed him to say in that raspy, monotone voice of an obsessive deaf man who had no regard for the spoken word, and words impatiently would tumble from his mouth as if they were a handful of unwanted pennies being tossed on the floor. Ellis possessed a knowledge bank of every sound the man uttered. Every vowel. Every consonant. Every diphthong. If needed, Ellis could hear and picture him saying, "Don't forget to buy fish sticks."

"Oh, no, thank you," Ellis answered. "I do not drink alcohol."

"I sure do this week," Larry said. He sat down with his plastic Tervis tumbler of bourbon and ice, took a drink, and sighed.

"Did you know she made me change my name tag?" Ellis offered.

"How's that?"

"My name tag. She said it could not say 'Edison' anymore. She called it unprofessional. She made me change it to 'Ellis.' "

Larry swallowed and shook his head.

"She said it was unprofessional," Ellis repeated.

It had not been Ellis's sole nasty encounter with his new boss. To check the accuracy of her docents' tours, Judith Ziegler had planted what she called fact-checkers — Ellis referred to them as spies — in randomly chosen tour groups, and Ellis had thus grown suspect of any unfortunate tourist who exhibited more than an average amount of curiosity.

After she audited three of Ellis's tours, Judith called him into her office.

"Have a seat, Ellis," she said.

"I hope there is not a problem."

He noted that Larry's old wooden, slatted chair had been replaced by something black and looming and curvaceous

56

with wheels and lots of knobs for making various adjustments. It looked as if it could fly.

"Tell me about Mrs. Edison," she said.

"Mina."

"That's correct."

"What would you like to know?"

"Everything you find interesting."

Ellis reared back and squinted his eyes in skepticism. He turned his head, raising his chin.

"Go on."

"She was born in Akron, Ohio . . . a socialite . . . a noted soprano . . . well, there is not that much interesting or remarkable about her, really."

In truth, Ellis despised the woman. He remembered her coming in to shop at his mother's store on Hendry Street, Irene Norton Fashions, and was enthralled at the way every clerk would flitter toward her like moths to a lightbulb. His mother said Mina was uppity, a gold digger. She did, after all, marry the rich thirty-nine-year-old inventor when he was twice her age, somewhere between father and grandfather. And before the sheets of his deathbed were cool, she married another wealthy inventor, and when he died just four years later, she dropped his name like a hot pan and resurrected the former husband's because, of course, it carried more cachet. Nobody knew Mina Miller Hughes. The entire world had heard of Mina Miller Edison.

Ellis's mother thought Mina vulgar. She allowed live peacocks to roam the estate. She bought a dry sauna for her dressing room at Seminole Lodge, one of those large, square boxes filled with mirrors and bright lightbulbs that you sat inside to burn off fat born of indulgences.

Judith stood up and began to pace behind her desk. "History is a slippery thing, Ellis," she said. "It can be bent and molded to fit any ideology or purpose. I expect docents to stretch the truth a little. It makes things more interesting, and it's human nature to do so. Innately, we worry that others will not be interested in what we say, so we make the story better."

"Yes?"

"But we are the ones responsible for educating the next generation about one of history's most dynamic, important families."

"Yes?" Ellis repeated.

"And we have a responsibility to be good stewards of reality . . . of the facts, Ellis. Do you understand?"

"I have a tour in ten minutes, Miss Ziegler."

"Okay . . . I'm extremely frank. You've learned that by now, I'm sure."

"I have indeed."

"Ellis." She leaned on the desk with the palms of her hands. "Is it true that you have told your visitors . . . on numerous occasions . . . that Mina Edison killed both her husbands?"

"No," he answered. "I did not say that."

"That's not what I heard."

"I merely present the facts, Miss Ziegler. I let visitors make their own decisions."

"But you have intimated as much."

Ellis had not encountered such strength and confidence in a woman since his mother. While he did not feel crippled by Judith Ziegler, he certainly felt as if she frequently tied his shoelaces together. Ellis did not like to watch her, just as he did not like to see a movie with Bette Davis or Joan Crawford.

"Are you okay, Ellis?" she asked. "Your eyes are closed."

Ellis opened his eyes. "You must admit," he said, "that the fast death of Mr. Hughes was quite unusual."

Judith had sat down, but again she shot out of her Herman Miller chair.

"My God, Ellis, you can't do this! You've got no evidence to back such a claim. You realize you're calling this woman a murderer? Sweet, plump Mina Edison?"

"Mr. Edison's death was questionable as well."

"How so?"

"No one really can explain why he died."

"Let me help you: diabetes . . . Bright's disease . . . old age. He was severely malnourished. The man drank more milk than an elementary school."

"She should have prepared more nutritious meals," Ellis said. "In the end, it was her fault. . . . So you see."

Ellis had decided not to share this with Larry or anybody. He felt that being written up by Judith Ziegler was akin to an actor getting interrogated by Joseph McCarthy; even if you were innocent, just the fact that it happened cast a glowing red light around an otherwise ivory persona.

The two men sat in Larry's living room, watching Shirley Temple in *Baby Takes a Bow* on Turner Classic Movies. Ellis had caught him in the last half hour of the movie, and it didn't take long for him to realize that Larry would not want to talk much until it was over. He accepted a

Cherry Coke in a purple aluminum glass, which he wiped occasionally to keep the rivulets of condensation from dripping onto his pants.

When the movie ended, Larry got up with his empty tumbler and shuffled off to somewhere in the back of the house. A few minutes later he returned, carrying a Johnston & Murphy shoe box.

"I've got something for you, Ellis," he said.

Larry set the box down on the end table, then lowered himself into his recliner, loudly expelling gas on the way down. He slowly leaned forward, toward Ellis, and rested on his cane.

"You've got to swear by all that's holy that what I'm about to give you will be our secret. No kidding here, Ellis, this is one to take to the grave. . . . Do you promise?"

Ellis stared at the lid of the box, saying nothing.

"Ellis? You've got to promise me you won't say nothin' to nobody. . . . Damn it, Ellis! I'm talking to you!"

"Yes, Larry! Yes, yes, of course."

"Okay, then. You promise?"

"I promise."

Larry slowly removed the lid to reveal a dirtied white rag cradling two test tubes whose cork tops had been sealed with white paraffin. He took one out and held it up to the light.

"It is empty," Ellis said.

"No, not empty," Larry replied. A sly smile formed on his lips. "You know what this is, Ellis. I don't need to tell you."

Like recipes, stories change with the passing of decades, people tweaking the ingredients, adding or subtracting what they like or dislike. In short, the fragile truth is recast with each generation. Yet Thomas Edison had not been dead seventy years, so the famous "last breath" story about the Wizard of Menlo Park had not yet lost its purity.

In the final days before Edison's death, someone set eight open test tubes in a rack beside the bed, and barely a minute after the great inventor passed on, Edison's son, Charles, asked the attending physician to quickly seal the tubes with paraffin, thus capturing Thomas Alva Edison's final breaths on earth. One of the test tubes went to Henry Ford, who put it in his Michigan museum. It is labeled "Edison's Last Breath," and it sits there today. The other seven inexplicably disappeared.

"Larry!"

"I've had them all along, Ellis."

"How do you know they are real?"

"Oh, they're real all right. Clarence gave them to me before he died."

Though he had never met him, Ellis knew that Clarence Oshby had preceded Larry Livengood as caretaker of Seminole Lodge, and rumor had it that the solemn transferal of power between the two men was conducted some night in a ceremony involving beer and blood on the end of the Edisons' fishing pier. If there were secrets to be known of the Edisons' lives in Fort Myers, these men were the holders.

Using his index finger, Ellis reached out and stroked the glass tube as if it were a butterfly wing. And then suddenly, he jerked it back, a realization dropping into his consciousness.

"But Mr. Edison died up north," Ellis said. "How did these get here, to Fort Myers?"

"Christ, Ellis! Do you want it or not? I'm offering you a remarkable piece of history. You loved that man more than his children did."

"But . . . it is stealing," Ellis said.

"It's not stealing. It's preserving heritage."

Ellis shook his head. "I cannot do this, Larry. It is not right."

Larry shook the test tube at Ellis as if it were the chastising finger of an elementary school teacher. "If you don't take this, I'm gonna have to kill you, Ellis, because they'll come throw me in jail, and I am too damned old to be sittin' in the Lee County jail."

"You would not kill me, Larry."

"I just might. Now take the goddamn test tube, Ellis."

Again, Ellis gently touched the glass. He imagined that it hummed ever so slightly, like the pump on his aquarium at home but even more subtle. The final breaths of the greatest man who had ever lived! Right here! In Larry's living room!

Toward the end of his life, Thomas Edison had grown preoccupied with inventing a machine that could communicate with the spiritual world. He said spirits were nothing more than electrical energy, and when one died this energy rose from the body like heat waves from a highway in July, into the air around him. Edison was certain that if someone could harness and give form to this energy, well, then, the great chasm between the living and dead would be closed.

My Dear God, Ellis thought. What is the great and invisible thing that dwells inside this tube?

As if receiving Communion, Ellis cupped his hands and reverently held them out to his friend.

Chapter Five

Geena washed and brushed her teeth in McDonald's bathrooms. She slept in the well-lit parking lots of Wal-Marts, near the safety of retired, wanderlust-stricken couples who had parked their RVs for the night.

Outside of Arab, Alabama, she finally rented a Super 8 motel room for the night so she could dye her blond hair red and take a long, hot bath. And though she had restricted herself to just two meals a day, she was surprised at how fast her money was melting away. It did not help that she had rediscovered garage sales along the way. For the first half of her life, Geena and her mother had spent Saturday mornings canvassing the affluent environs of south Denver, Geena guiding them from sale to sale with a map and the classified section of the *Rocky Mountain News* open on her lap as her mother drove and chain-smoked Virginia Slims.

In Mena, Arkansas, Geena bought a box of used romance novels, a paring knife, and a Dallas Cowboys–themed Igloo cooler. In Clarksdale, Mississippi, she found three blouses and some blue jeans, which she supplemented with a ten-pack of cheap panties from a nearby Target. And then there were the pure indulgences: the half-empty bottle of Bijon perfume . . . the throw made of sewn-together rabbit pelts . . . a copy of *Buddha in Your Backpack,* a book that Nathan had read and shared with her when he was in high school . . . the blue baseball hat from the Gore-Lieberman campaign of 2000. (Geena had decided that jewel-tone blue was Safe-T-Man's best color.)

At a library in Indianola, Mississippi, four days after she'd left Sublette, Geena found a public-access computer and typed her name into the Google.com search engine. Two stories popped up, one from the *Denver Post,* the other in the *Greeley Tribune.* Geena clicked on the hotlink to the former.

SUBLETTE — Authorities continue to search for a Kit Carson County woman who has been missing since Thursday.

Geena Marie Pangborn apparently drove from Sublette to Fort Collins to visit a friend but never showed up, according to Ray Faddis, spokesman for the Kit Carson County Sheriff's Department. No note has been found, and there was no sign of struggle. Pangborn was last seen shopping at Merit Drugstore in downtown Sublette on Thursday.

Pangborn is married to Barry A. Pangborn, executive vice president and part owner of Centennial Realty, one of Colorado's largest rural real estate firms.

Friends in Sublette experienced sadness and shock that tragedy could strike the same family in such a short time. Last year, the couple's only child, seventeen-year-old Nathan Allen Pangborn, perished in a house fire.

The family declined to comment.

Geena stewed over the last line, running the cursor from one end to the other and back again, as if fanning a flame.

The family declined to comment?

The family DECLINED to comment?

Fine! Here! Let me help you fill in the blanks. Let me tell you about how a mother tried to raise a good son in a paralyzing macho family that thinks drinking and driving and mean pranks are okay — "Boys will be boys, Geena," they always said — and that any mother who tries to reign him in is basically cutting off his balls and turning him queer.

Let me tell you what happens when young testosterone runs wild with no parent to tame it. Let me tell you how a sweet but out-of-control and angry seventeen-year-old boy comes home one night when his mom and dad are out of town, and he is so drunk he can't even wake up when the house is on fire.

Let me tell you about a conspiracy to assassinate a mother's character . . . the story of how she takes the battery out of the smoke detector so she can use her new meat thermometer she got for Christmas because she's expected to make the fucking pot roast her husband wants every Sunday night.

Let me tell you how her husband wonders why the smoke alarm didn't wake him, and she tells him the truth, and instead of standing by his wife he sides with his parents, and the whole family starts treating her like pig shit, warm as can be in public but cold as ice in private.

Let me tell you how Barry refuses to make love to his wife ever again.

And then — and this is what finally pushes her out of town — when this grieving mother decides to buy an Irish setter, her mother-in-law says to her in a voice that no one else can hear, "Are you sure you should get a dog, Geena? You might kill it."

They think something awful has happened to me? Perfect. Let my blood be on their hands just as they smeared my son's on mine. That family took the best years of my life and turned them into nothing. I hope they imagine me dismembered and lying in the rotten sunflowers and rag-weed in some ditch in Weld County or someplace. I will haunt them every time they look at a picture of Nathan. They will see my chin and my eyes and my blond hair. People in town will mention my name with respect be-cause they'll think I'm dead, and every member of that arrogant, nasty family will have to lower their chins

70

and feel guilt and remorse . . . or at least fake it.

I will be more powerful now than I ever was in person.

Revenge that will never end — I love it!

Oh, and for the record, Nathan was a sound sleeper, even sounder after drinking. If he didn't wake up when the china cabinet fell off the wall in the hallway, then he sure as hell wasn't going to wake up with a smoke alarm.

I didn't kill my son — they killed him. If I played any part in Nathan's death, it's only because I didn't take him away from that family soon enough and save his character. I could have changed him if they'd let me. So screw you, Barry and Dot and Brit. . . . How's that for comment?

Chapter Six

When Judith Ziegler first came south to interview for her job at the Thomas Edison Winter Estate, she felt like Howard Carter discovering King Tut's tomb. The house was just as Mina Edison had left it after her death in 1947. It was as if she had said, "Fine! Take it! It's yours. I want nothing of it," and got up and walked out forever.

On the secretary in Mina's bedroom lay the genesis of a letter on Seminole Lodge stationery with a pen lying beside it: *"Dear, Dear Edward and Bob . . ."* Beneath the bed, Judith found a bone corset, lying there like some decomposing carcass trapped in a cave. Soiled, monogrammed hand towels hung from the racks in the bathrooms, the water stains now the color of dried, diluted tea.

In the inventor's spartan bedroom upstairs she found Thomas's false teeth on the nightstand beside a sterling silver denture holder inscribed with his initials. In the laboratory was an army cot, the pillow dented by the inventor's head, and a pair of his abandoned shoes on the floor.

And then, after the thrill of discovery . . . panic! Judith saw overweight tourists resting upon the fragile wicker furniture on the veranda. She watched docents pick up and handle artifacts — a book, one of the inventor's famous oversized handkerchiefs, a small elephant constructed by Mina and the children from delicate Sanibel Island seashells and glue — and pass them around their tour groups. In the living room of the main house she saw a cleaning woman moving and rearranging artifacts without wearing the museum-requisite white cotton gloves to keep damaging skin oils off the priceless items.

In the laboratory, Judith witnessed one child pick up a test tube of dried, amber-colored material and accidentally drop it to the floor. "Now be careful when you're handling those things, son," the docent said. *Handling those things?* Judith thought. *How dare you handle those things! And how dare you let him! Where are the proper barriers to separate patrons from artifacts?*

And then, after beginning the job, more

surprises. She discovered one office worker using Mina's mother-of-pearl letter opener. She found Charles Edison's bronzed baby shoes being used as a pair of bookends. Soon the situation began to remind her of her summer dig in Belize, where the locals, having lived atop precious Mayan ruins for generations, thought nothing of using found artifacts in their everyday lives. One man's priceless stele was another's kitchen tabletop.

Mina Edison had willed Seminole Lodge to the City of Fort Myers, wanting to memorialize her husband with a museum, and indeed there appeared to be a community-wide feeling that the estate belonged to the people. Lovers married on the veranda. Kids in the neighborhood fished for tarpon and catfish from the rickety pier and came over to swim in the historic concrete pool. (Judith internally winced when she envisioned this, imagining the now-brittle diving board snapping in half like the femur of a ninety-year-old man.)

Though the archaeologist in her was mortified by all this, the anthropologist in her was intrigued. As history goes, this was modern history, and there were still people alive in Fort Myers who had socialized with the Edisons, even more who remembered roaming the grounds as children during garden parties or the bird-watching seminars Mina used to organize. It made perfect sense that they would treat the estate like a YMCA.

Yet perhaps Judith's biggest surprise came when she first explored the old caretaker's cottage. She discovered, upstairs in the attic, a room with a door that felt as if it were being blocked by something soft and springy. Judith pushed and pushed, and the door slowly inched open, and when she could finally stick her head inside she discovered the obstruction. The room was bursting with at least a hundred artificial Christmas trees, lying on the floor, leaning against the walls. And stuck in between these, random and everywhere, like hairpins in a giant, evergreen bouffant, were painted plywood snowmen and elves and penguins and carolers with Cheerio-like mouths.

"Holy Christ," she whispered to herself. "I hope this isn't what I think it is."

But it was, and no one had told her about it. And intuitively she knew just what an explosive situation this could turn into.

Every Christmas season, the Lee County Women's Club, of which Mina Edison was a founding member, decorated the fourteen-acre estate for the annual seven-week-long Holidazzle celebration. And in addition to wrapping palm tree trunks in 4 million lights and setting up the plywood characters in yuletide vignettes around the grounds, the women transformed the interior of the home with the energy of little girls playing dress-up. They tied red bows to chandeliers and toilet-flush handles and drooped Christmas-theme towels over the basins of sinks and fake garland along the banisters and mantelpieces. They set up dioramas of teddy bears having tea. They lay out a plate of sugar cookies with a fake note from Mina, asking Santa if he had any "bright ideas" for her husband's gift list.

Judith also didn't know that the founder of this tradition was none other than Ellis Norton's mother Irene, and that she annually would dress her boy up to be a living character — something that grew increasingly embarrassing with each year.

At Christmas his eighth-grade year, when Ellis was tall and lanky with a whisper of a soft, brown mustache, Irene instructed her son to dress as an elf. She smudged black mascara on his cheek and forehead and posed him by the fireplace with Santa Claus, hoping to convince the youngsters in attendance that they had just, in fact, wriggled down the chimney. After just minutes, two boys from school saw Ellis and teased him, and he ran out of the house, toward the river, the bells on the toes of his green felt boots jingling in the darkness. Ellis did not emerge from beneath the Edisons' dock until one o'clock that morning, and he ended up in the hospital with pneumonia.

"Serves you right, Ellis Randall Norton," said his mother.

"I am sorry," Ellis replied.

Logan Simmons set Ellis's brown mug of steaming tea with a wedge of lemon on the table, then bent down to kiss him on the cheek as she always did.

"Hello, you sweet man." (She said this every time he came in.)

Ellis feigned surprise, then said in a scolding voice, "Young lady, what would your husband say?" (He, too, said this every time. It was a script they had not strayed from in three years.)

"Oh, I'm not married. I'm still waiting for the right man to come along. You don't know one, do you?"

Every night of the week except Sunday, when it was closed, Ellis ate dinner at the

Banana Leaf Café on McGregor Boulevard. After work, he would walk the eleven blocks from the Edison home and take his table at the window, reserved each day from 5:15 to 6:15 with a foreboding, plastic-oak ELLIS SITS HERE! sign that Tom Poenbrook, the owner, had had specially made at Office Depot.

Each and every night, Ellis ordered the same thing — a grilled tuna salad sandwich with yellow mustard and sliced tomato, and French fries cooked so long they were closer kin to chips than to a baked potato.

It was Logan who usually drove Ellis to places outside his walking world, and once or twice a month he and she and her six-year-old son Brendon would go to the movies. Be it Reese Witherspoon or *Finding Nemo*, it never mattered to Ellis, though he always preferred something with a story of romance. Afterward they would go to Love Boat Ice Cream and Ellis, who loved movies and indeed had memorized several hundred scenes by heart, would tell his young friends about plots and characters from older films, and how everything nowadays was copied and tired. He'd said more than once, "The last true masterpiece of the cinema was *The African*

Queen with Katharine Hepburn."

On the first Saturday of every month the three of them would drive out to Fleamaster's Flea Market on Martin Luther King Jr. Boulevard, and Ellis usually came home with something: a framed print of a large amaryllis blossom, a resin gargoyle lawn sprinkler, an unusual lamp of some kind that he would add to his collection of illuminating devices in the Edison Room back home, on Wilna Street. His closets and the cavities beneath the beds were stuffed with such items.

Ellis carried a balance on five credit cards. He had memorized the minimum payment on each one and was careful never to look at the numbers inside the total-amount-owed box. Like Edison — who referred to the "humbuggery of bookkeeping" and often had to stand in line, grumbling, to pay his bills in person because he waited too long to post them by mail — Ellis did not like to bother himself with thinking about cash flow; he was much too busy at the museum. Besides, he had a system that seemed to work just fine.

Ellis dutifully wrote his monthly checks for the minimum amount on each bill, and when a card was declined, he would take it home and give it a well-deserved rest, stowing it in a tin Band-Aid box in the drawer of the telephone stand. (Ellis liked to imagine it recharging like a battery in the dark.) He would go about life, paying the minimum amount on the hibernating card and, after a year had passed, return it to his wallet, resuscitated and ready for swiping. Of course, sometimes it was necessary to apply for an additional card, but Ellis was always surprised at the number of banks offering their products through the mail. It was as simple as picking out a pair of socks at Sears.

"How's devil woman?" Logan asked him. She pulled out the second chair and sat down. Ellis sighed and shook his head.

"She still giving you trouble?"

"I think I know what is wrong," Ellis finally said.

"What?"

"I will tell you what. I think she feels threatened by me."

"Oh, Ellis."

"Yes, ma'am, I most certainly do. I should never have shared that folder with her."

Ellis had left on Judith Ziegler's desk a manila folder chronicling his brushes with fame as a docent at the Thomas Alva Edison Winter Estate. Ellis's picture had been in the AAA Florida guidebook, his hand gesturing toward the Japanese bamboo. There was also a snapshot that ran in *The News-Press* of him bidding good morning to America with Willard Scott, back when Willard was the weatherman on NBC's *Today* show. A story from *Condé Nast Traveler* mentioned the "odd, fastidious little guide who, if he were squatty and shorter and dressed in an ill-fitting black suit, might even pass for the old inventor himself."

"What makes you think she's threatened by you?"

"Because I know many people," he answered. "I have connections . . . like Larry Livengood . . . and Willard Scott."

They sat quietly for a few minutes, watching the people walk into and out of the small restaurant, each scene separated by the comforting clanking of the small cowbell that hung from the horizontal aluminum handle of the door that Ellis always pushed open with his forearms so he would not contract any of the cold or flu germs left behind by fellow diners. When he was confronted with a door that pulled open, he would either use his yellow Edison Winter Estate ballpoint pen as a lever or, if traffic was brisk, simply wait for someone to leave, then catch the door with his elbow. As a last resort Ellis would pull a moist, citrus-smelling towelette from the wallet-size packet of antibacterial Wet Ones he always carried in his back pocket. In Ellis's mind, the only drawback of living in a temperate tourist destination was that sniffling, sneezing visitors from Rockford and Munich and Syracuse and Liverpool all brought their influenza germs with them, and this made day-to-day living potentially hazardous for an eighty-year-old man whose subtropical immune system would likely be caught surprised and thus defenseless against an invasion of such foreign cold-clime germs. Ellis had never missed a day of work. He did not intend to sully that record.

"I need to talk to you about something, Ellis," Logan said.

She reached across the small square table and took his hands in hers.

"What is wrong, Logan? You look very worried."

"Oh, Ellis . . . I don't know how to tell you this."

"Tell me what?"

"You are just the cutest, sweetest, oddest man I've ever known. I didn't know God made men as sweet as you."

"Why are you crying, Logan?"

"Ellis . . . Brendon and me . . . we're moving back to Erie."

Ellis raised his eyebrows. "To Pennsylvania?"

"Yes."

"But why? I thought you liked Fort Myers."

"Oh, Ellis, sweet Ellis . . . because I've lived down here for five years, and I'm still a waitress. There are no good jobs here, Ellis. I need a good union job. I've got to make me some money."

"But you are an excellent waitress," he said. "You are the finest waitress I have ever had the pleasure of knowing."

Logan smiled and wiped the tears from her cheek.

"I need more for Brendon," she said. "I've got family in Erie. I can make more money there."

Ellis sighed and stared blankly at the tabletop. "Is there something I could say that would change your mind? Perhaps I could get you a job at the museum."

Logan shook her head. "No. This is what I need to do. I've thought a lot about this, Ellis. I should have never come down here. It's just been a big mistake. I mean, like, school, for example. Brendon's cousin,

Mark? He's learning algebra in the fourth grade. The schools are better up north, Ellis. They're just so, so much better . . . and . . ."

Ellis nodded politely as she spoke her case, but in his mind he had quickly crouched down in the wobbly dinghy that was his life, lest he lose balance and fall overboard. He would stay low, regain stability, all the while studying the ballast that lay about him. What could he rearrange or throw away or add so that he could stand again in this little boat that had served him so faithfully for so long?

So much had changed in so very little time: his new boss; the tearing up of his entire street so that the city could lay new sewer pipes (the dust in his house had been unbearable! He would wake up some mornings and actually feel a fine but nonetheless gritty coating on his teeth); the loss of his young friend, and, he realized now for the first time, his safety net for the upcoming, uncertain years of his life. Of course, he was in excellent physical condition for a man his age, but no one knew what tomorrow would bring.

Ellis's throat tightened and he swallowed. "You will miss Fort Myers," he finally said.

"No," Logan answered. "But I will miss you, Ellis." She noticed Ellis's chin tremble slightly before he started speaking again.

"You know, Thomas Edison called it 'The Eden of Florida.' He said, 'Fort Myers is the only true sanitarium in the occidental hemisphere, equaling if not surpassing the bay of Naples in grandeur of view and health-giving properties.' "

"Oh, Ellis. We'll come visit you."

"You will miss Fort Myers very, very much. . . . Mr. Edison said, 'There's only one Fort Myers, and 90 million people are going to discover it.' That is what Edison said."

"Oh, Ellis."

Chapter Seven

Geena knew early on that her boy was different from the mold of Pangborn men, neither boyish nor feminine, but a sensitive, inventive child who appreciated beautiful things.

Nathan hated getting his hands and feet dirty, especially the sensation of dried mud on his skin, and anytime he came inside after running about the neighborhood in his bare feet, he immediately scrubbed at the soles with a wet washrag until they were pink again. He did not like horses because of their smell. And in toddler playgroups he showed such an undying fascination with dolls that his mother finally bought him one of his own.

"He's intrigued by them," she told her husband. "There's nothing wrong with dolls, Barry."

"There is if a boy's playing with one. That's just not right, Geena. I don't like it."

86

So the small doll, whom Nathan named Toody, went underground, hiding in the hard-cardboard tube of rarely used Lincoln Logs during the day and sneaking beneath the race car–theme sheets at night, after Barry came in to say good night. Alone, when he played, Nathan would use his father's old baseball mitt as a bassinet.

Nathan and his mother evolved, growing smarter and sneakier. And by the time he entered junior high, Nathan had perfected an ability to please and manipulate his father and simultaneously satisfy his own feminine side. His mother thought him nothing short of brilliant. When Nathan chose the flute as his instrument for junior high band, he also developed a sudden, inexplicable love for father-and-son hunting trips. Nathan was quite good at football, a starting defensive end his sophomore year for the Sublette Badgers, and though he didn't want to reenlist his junior year, he did so because he knew it would be a strong counterbalance to trying out for that year's spring musical, *Grease*.

Nathan subscribed to and devoured each issue of *GQ*, but at the same time left unread copies of gun magazines and *Sports Illustrated* lying around the house in spots his father frequented.

When Nathan went out to drag Leonard Street with friends on Friday night, he would wear his cowboy boots to soften the impact of a microfiber Hugo Boss purple shirt. "The chicks can't keep their hands off this, Dad," he said.

As Geena watched Nathan grow up, she thought: No wonder the boy sleeps all the time — he's maintaining and developing dual personalities. I'd be tired, too.

Geena drove south on U.S. 41. On the far horizon she saw the skyline of Atlanta, tiny from this far out, reflected in the mid-afternoon sun, and she immediately thought of the little clusters of white, plastic high-rise buildings on the game of Life she and Nathan used to play when they watched movies. How many times had they played it over the years, constantly changing the rules, and it would drive Barry crazy the few times he joined them.

Contrary to the directions, players didn't have to get married once they passed the red space on the board that demanded as much. And if you spun a six, you could divorce your spouse if he or she was proving to be too expensive or bothersome, and then you could remarry if you spun another six.

In Nathan's game of life, the artists could make more than the doctors if they spun a seven twice in a row. ("The odds of spinning two sevens in a row are slim; so is getting 'discovered,' but we need to make it a possibility.")

At one point Nathan showed great frustration with the little, plastic, pink and blue, cribbage-like pin people that you pushed into the holes of the cars, and he took Magic Markers and colored some of them brown and some of them black so they could have some interracial marriages. *This* was life, he said. Real life.

With the beginning of his sophomore year came the first real rumblings of discontent and overt challenge to his father. The Pangborn family was a large donor to Colorado State University (the laboratory wing of the new veterinary school was being named in their honor), and all the Pangborn men had graduated from CSU with one degree or another. At the beginning of his senior year in high school, however, Nathan announced his intention to attend the more liberal University of Colorado in Boulder. "It's like granola," his grandfather liked to say, "filled with fruits and nuts," and Geena would roll her eyes at the cliché that he thought so original.

The news was enough to prompt a hurried meeting among Barry, his parents, and Geena in the main office downtown.

"What's got into that boy's head?" Brit asked.

"He's just different, Brit," Geena answered. "He's always been different."

"He's different because you've let him be different," Dot added, and then, turning to her son, barked, "I warned you that you weren't spending enough time with him. This would not be a problem if you were home more often and not . . ."

"Not what, Momma?" Barry interrupted. "Not out making money for this family? I've cleared 18 million so far this year. That's two more than anyone else. Even Ronnie."

Geena had always noted the lack of praise Pangborn sons received from their parents. She wondered more than once if it was simply stoic Swedish behavior or a clandestine plan of Brit and Dot's to create in their sons a drive to prove themselves worthy. Barry's desire for his parents' praise was strong; Geena could tell by the way he looked at them expectantly when sharing the good news of a seven-figure closing, and the way he would sometimes lower his head and close his eyes when he realized that he would have to walk away, empty-hearted, once again.

Geena was largely silent at the meeting, having long ago been convicted for not raising a proper Pangborn man. Barry sat next to her, looking at the floor as his father shared the details of the upcoming family convoy to Fort Collins he was planning for the Golden Ram alumni banquet. The coded message was clear: *That goddamn son of yours will be going to CSU.* And, like the good son, Geena knew Barry would somehow comply. His parents exerted a perpetual and omnipotent force on their family, like the pull of the earth's gravity that holds — imprisons? — the moon in a predictable, well-behaved repeating pattern.

Geena now looked over at Safe-T-Man sitting in the seat next to her. The steady stream of air from the AC vent was blowing the black marabou boa she'd found at a yard sale somewhere in northern Mississippi. It appeared to be tickling his tanned neck, and Geena reached over to move it to the outside of his collar.

"Is that better, sweetheart?" she asked.

Was it Barry or was it men in general? Did they all turn into assholes after you married them? You're not like that, though, are you Safe-T-Man?

Suddenly Geena heard a loud bang from somewhere ahead, quickly followed by a succession of crashlike sounds that came with the rhythm and speed of a piece of paper being crumpled into a ball. Pairs of red taillights popped on, and Geena, too, quickly braked to blend into the slowing traffic.

A white envelope smacked against the windshield and stuck there. It was a subscription renewal for *Entertainment Weekly*, bound for Tampa.

And then another envelope . . . and ten or twenty more. In an instant the air was filled with various sizes of rectangular mail fluttering about in the sunlight like magnified confetti.

Traffic came to a stop. Geena smelled diesel fuel. Intuitively she knew something was wrong. Her pulse picked up speed, her throat grew tense and dry. After a few minutes she pulled onto the shoulder of the road, got out and locked her doors, then walked ahead sixty yards to find the problem.

An eighteen-wheeler had drifted off the road at an unfortunate moment, colliding head-on with two pillars that supported Georgia State Road 46. The bridge had collapsed atop the trailer, the weight of that mass causing the contents of the truck — all of the next day's North American southbound mail for millions of Floridians — to jettison out the back doors.

Other people left their cars and joined Geena on the scene, though none were brave enough to approach the cab and driver, fearing that the ruptured fuel tanks could blow at any second. The cab seemed to be as compressed as a Coke can crushed by a cinder block, with no sign of doors or windows. The driver had obviously fallen asleep at the wheel. Geena wondered if he had had a seizure. Had he been taking drugs and needed to stay awake? Had he made love to his wife into the wee hours of the morning, knowing he'd be gone, on the road, for two weeks?

Geena looked at the wreck with cautious, sideways glances, squinting as if she were looking toward a bright light because she wanted to shield herself from any straight-on, unfiltered sightings of death . . . because whoever was in there was most certainly dead.

I hope he was sleeping when he hit. . . . You poor, stupid man. . . . How many mothers lose their boys to avoidable acts of violence?

It was an odd, frozen moment. There was no one to save. The troopers would not arrive for another eight minutes. Onlookers unconsciously were too shaken to get back into their cars and tear down the freeway again.

It was then that Geena noticed the thick, brown canvas bags of mail scattered about the grassy ditch. Though some had been ripped open and appeared to be spilling blood of white paper, others had escaped harm, with drawstrings intact. She wandered about them as if looking at flowers in an unfamiliar garden. Geena nudged a full one. They were heavy, maybe fifty pounds or more.

And then she came to a curious sight. One bag had been cleanly sheared in two, the remaining half sitting on its end with the contents inside, a surreal and strangely peaceful-looking detail born from such a violent, deadly occurrence. It reminded Geena of a barrel of apples at a roadside stand . . . so inviting . . . cute . . . so ripe for potential.

She walked over and scooped out a handful of the mail and started looking at the addresses, an exotic mixture of fruits and Spanish: Coconut Drive. Maravilla Street. Avocado Drive. Ricardo Avenue.

All were streets in Fort Myers.

Geena tossed the mail back into the open sack and stood there, looking down at it. She could not make herself turn and leave. There was something so endearingly vulnerable about this little bag of mail, and she felt some inexplicable attraction to it, a maternal attraction, responsible, the same way one feels when coming upon a warm, unhatched bird's egg that has fallen from a nest into the grass. It was a feeling she had not experienced for several months.

I can't take this with me. Why do I want to take this little bag of mail? What would happen if I didn't?

Geena knelt down and caressed the smooth envelopes on top of the heap. She stood to leave and, then, hesitating, knelt down again.

What are you doing?

Geena looked over her left shoulder to see if anyone was watching, but there was no one. She wedged her fingers between the canvas and the earth and lifted the bag into her arms, carried it to the car, and set it on the floor of the front seat. Back on the highway, she surveyed the wide grassy median that dipped between the north- and southbound lanes, and when she spotted a break in the pines she engaged the front-wheel drive of her SUV, cut across, and joined the flow of cars heading the way from which she had come. Geena got off at the next exit, then headed south on U.S. 41, otherwise known as the Dixie Highway.

For some reason, ever since leaving Sublette, Atlanta had been Geena's final, planned destination. It was relatively warm, far enough away, and sprawling and crowded. She was certain she could hide there. She'd already lied to three people along the way, claiming it was her home, so wouldn't these lies carry twice the weight and guilt if she did not indeed drop anchor in the Peachtree City?

But nothing she saw there connected with Geena enough to draw her off the freeway, and before she knew it she had passed downtown and its gold-domed Capitol. The airport, too, was soon in her rearview mirror. Geena had considered stopping at a Delta Crown Room for some free hors d'oeuvres and a beer, but she didn't when she realized she'd probably leave a digital trail when checking in.

So southward she traveled until hunger stopped her at an interchange in north Macon. Geena pulled off onto Arkwright Road and began considering her options as she passed a buffet of restaurants.

Arturo's Authentic Mexican . . . They might serve free chips and salsa if I ordered a beer. . . . God, those wings at Hooters would be so good right now — but at least ten bucks. . . . Ooh, ooh, Dragon Palace! Wonton soup and shrimp with snow peas! . . . I refuse to eat another tube of gas-station peanuts or McDonald's cheeseburger.

Geena stopped in the parking lot of a Kmart. For the fourth time since leaving Sublette six days ago, she riffled unsuccessfully through the glove compartment for stray dollars or loose change. Geena had long ago given up on excavating anything small from beneath the front seats. She broke two nails trying to work her way past all the mechanical seat-altering hardware crammed beneath. Why had carmakers done away with one of the most sensible, easy-access storage spots ever created? She used to be able to cram anything and everything beneath a car seat, and now it was nothing but a black hole for anything smaller than a McNugget.

Gas had consumed all but thirty-four dollars and sixteen cents of Geena's money, and she realized now how stupid she'd been to spend so much — or anything, really — on the multiple garage sales along the way.

Coin by coin, dollar by dollar, Geena again counted what remained, laying it on one of Barry's old button-down shirts she had spread across Safe-T-Man's lap like an afghan.

This is it. This is everything. I am totally screwed. I have no choice but to go back.

She reached for her purse, pulled out her wallet, then her credit cards, and flipped through them as if reminiscing over a stack of photographs. With an unlimited credit line on her American Express Delta Skymiles card and a fifty-thousand cap on a Continental OnePass Visa, she could walk into any store in this whole state or anywhere and buy anything she wanted — even a car.

Yeah, right, if I were still alive. And I'm not. Remember?

Geena looked at Safe-T-Man. "All I want is one nice meal!" she said. "I just want to eat until I'm full. Is that asking too much?"

She breathed in the smell of the nearby restaurants' collective fan exhaust, detecting French fries and garlic and some variety of grilled meat. Her mouth watered, her stomach gurgled in hunger.

"Okay, enough is enough. I lose. You win."

She pushed open the door of her Excursion, climbed down, and headed for the restaurant, planning the menu in her mind: egg-drop soup, wonton soup, maybe three egg rolls, and one or two expensive seafood entrées. And then she would check into the nicest hotel that Macon, Georgia, had to offer. Afterward, she would call Barry and grovel.

I can't believe I'm going to let a little discomfort ruin this whole thing — but how long could I go on like this? How far? I'm running out of gas. I'm running out of continent. I can't believe how stupid I've been to think this would work.

Geena tried the door of the restaurant, but it was locked. A sign in the window said it opened at 6:00, and it was just short of 5:15.

She returned to the car to wait. Seated, Geena looked over at Safe-T-Man. His plastic skin had softened in the warm sun, and he seemed to have lost some air. Instead of looking forward, through the windshield, Safe-T-Man's chin had fallen ten degrees. Geena followed his gaze and noticed he was now looking at the bag of mail at his feet. She reached down and scooped out a handful of the envelopes.

There were bank statements from Charlotte, Visa statements from Delaware and Nevada. There were private letters and cards, most of them from Midwestern cities and towns like Cleveland and Toledo and Terre Haute and Lansing, and though she was tempted to open these items of personal correspondence she did not.

Geena started looking at the first names on envelopes and wondered if she would have picked them over Nathan. A psychology major in college (she had dropped out after her freshman year to marry Barry), she'd always believed that people grew into their names, that a Bob would inexorably transform into an anonymous blob. A Hillary was destined for L.L.Bean and prep school. An Addison most likely would wear a bow tie and not be afraid of cocktails that sported paper umbrellas. Barry wanted a Michael, Geena wanted a Cole. Nathan was their compromise.

A computer-generated letter with no return address suddenly caught Geena's eye.

"Ellis Norton," she said. "Ellis!"

Though it was a name Barry had vetoed in the first round, Geena liked names that ended with an "s" sound, intriguing to the ear because though they sounded plural

100

they were singular. Ellis also sounded both male and female, and the bearer of the name was surely destined to understand the psyches of both genders. Ellis. It simultaneously sounded Old World and Southern California. Truly, it would have been the perfect name for a boy who could change the world.

Geena turned the envelope over, but there was no return address on the back, either. What was Ellis getting here? Who was cowardly or deceptive enough to withhold his identity? For being so thin, it was a heavy envelope, and the weight was lopsided.

Geena tore off the end of the envelope, blew inside to puff it up, and pulled out a shiny new SunBank MasterCard for Ellis R. Norton of 2459 Wilna Street.

"Well, hello there," Geena said.

Chapter Eight

In the life of a tour guide there are "off" days and "on" days, and the kind of day you have is determined by a host of controllable and uncontrollable variables, both visible and invisible: Did the guide have breakfast that morning and a good night's sleep? Is he bothered by postnasal drip or a hangnail or a haunting, negative encounter with a salesclerk from the day before? Are there any tense global or national situations du jour that might create an aura of anxiousness in the group? Is the barometric pressure rising? How high is the pollen count?

Add to this the wildly diverse dispositions of an entire group of strangers: Are they naturally curious or intellectually lazy? Did *they* get a good night's sleep? Is one of them depressed from a bad marriage or an impending bankruptcy and therefore overly contrary? What are their education levels? Do they even care about things like the mechanics of the motion picture camera? Do some of them feel fat that day? How close is it to lunchtime — and does anyone have a blood-sugar problem? Is it overcast and unseasonably cool, and are they peeved because they spent two thousand dollars to come down for a week from Pittsburgh only to have to go to Wal-Mart and buy a sweater they didn't need?

Ellis was experiencing — or rather, shepherding — what felt to be an ideal tour, a ninety-minute chunk of sparkling perfection that seemed as rare as the passing of a particular comet. Jasmine blossoms perfumed the air on this October morning. A warm breeze blew through the bamboo, causing the papery leaves to rustle and the pipelike stalks to sway and creak. The late-morning sun warmed the dark green shells of the turtles in the fountain and caused the rippling surface of the Caloosahatchee to glitter. Everywhere on the Edison estate, Yankee heads tilted backward, letting faces bask in the sunny warmth.

This ten o'clock group was largely comprised of a charter bus filled with retired engineers and their spouses from upstate New York. And, much to Ellis's delight, they were absolutely insatiable, lobbing po-

lite question after polite question after polite question. At one point Ellis noticed
that Martin Storey's group was en-
croaching upon them, and he made an executive decision to let them pass on by.
This was his only tour scheduled this
morning, so he did not have to rush.

"I do not want to take too much of your
time, ladies and gentlemen," he said.

"This is why we're here," answered one
man. "You could take all day if you want."

Ellis leaned to the right to find the voice
in the group. It was a balding man with a
plain, green T-shirt tucked into khaki
shorts, and new tennis shoes with white
socks. He wore a yellow baseball cap with
the red Kodak logo.

"But the beach beckons, I am sure," Ellis
answered.

"This is why we came to Fort Myers."

"Specifically to see the Edison home?"

"Yes, sir, that's correct."

Ellis brightened. "Well, then . . . do I
have some wonderful stories for you!"

Judith Ziegler had mandated that certain
key facts about the inventor be conveyed in
each tour, and this cut down on the
amount of time Ellis had for sharing his
more colorful anecdotes. But on this exquisite morning, an opportunity!

In the shade, on the boardwalk constructed around the immense banyan tree outside the laboratory, Ellis began spinning story after story. He told of how the nearly deaf inventor, when courting both his wives, taught them Morse code so they could tap out sweet nothings on the palm of his hand instead of yelling them out for all to hear.

He talked of how Edison lived inside his head and was oftentimes barely aware of his earthly existence . . . and of how he was standing in line one time to pay his taxes (which were late), and when it came time for him to make his transaction he could not remember his name. Ellis loved to playact this scene for his visitors, and he would step back and forth between two spots on the sidewalk, switching from character to character as he portrayed both Edison and the tax collector.

"Can I help you, sir? . . . Sir? . . . Sir!"

"Yes? Oh, yes!"

"What is your name?"

"Pardon me?"

"Your name."

"I don't know, sir."

"Then I cannot help you."

Ellis continued, "And the great inventor, one of the most fabulous thinkers in the history of mankind, had to go through that line until he found someone who knew him and told him his name."

Polite, muffled laughter floated upward from the group.

"I am very serious. That is a true story."

Pleased, but not wanting his guests to leave without a lingering taste of rock-solid respect for the great inventor, Ellis quickly changed moods. His smile melted into solemnity. For effect, he took off his white straw hat and held it in his hands.

"And now, I would like to leave you all with something to ponder."

Ellis cleared his throat and swallowed. He raised his chin, looking slightly upward, creating a profile seen in patriotic wartime posters.

"Now and then someone comes along whose footstep makes a very great, a very deep imprint in the roadway that is humanity. Such a man was Thomas Alva Edison. And when he died in 1931, to show respect for this esteemed individual, the entire city of New York plunged itself into darkness for twenty-four hours. That was the kind of man he was. Because without Mr. Edison, you, my friends, could not have watched television this morning or used an electric razor. I could not have toasted my bread. We owe our lives and, indeed, our very survival as a species to this gentleman who called Fort Myers home.

"And as you go about your day and are troubled by obstacles that seem absolutely insurmountable, remember the words of this man, whose ferocious tenacity brings to mind Helen Keller, who also was deaf: 'I never failed once. It just happened to be a two-thousand-step process. If we did all the things we are capable of doing, we would literally astonish ourselves.' "

Of course, one anecdote that Ellis had especially dropped from all his tours was the Edison's-last-breath story. He had not told it since bringing home the stolen test tube from Larry's house. The paraffin-sealed tube had alternately caused anxiety and delight, and he'd been moving it to a new hiding place every few nights, as if it were a high-profile, sought-after hostage.

In the evenings, with all the shades drawn, Ellis would bring it out to its special display spot, which he had devised out of a base for an electric toothbrush and one of his mother's old black velvet blouses. He surrounded the former with the latter, like a skirt around a Christmas tree, so that it appeared as though the test tube were bobbing vertically in a miniature, wavy sea of crude oil. On the opposite side of the room he attached a small flashlight to a windowsill with duct tape, pointing it at what he now called "The Final Breath Display."

Ellis often spent his evenings rearranging the Edison Room, which was comprised of a series of tables he'd accumulated at neighborhood garage sales. To help make the fifties and sixties furniture appear historic, Ellis set out crocheted doilies of various sizes, and on these sat his collection, which had grown significantly since he had bought a computer and discovered eBay.

Ellis had more than two hundred items, including a seven-inch-tall bust of the inventor cast in some dubious material called Bronzite . . . a Thomas Edison Smurf doll (Ellis thought it slightly vulgar but cute enough to include) . . . an unsealed porcelain Jim Beam whiskey decanter of the diminutive inventor with a cork top that was made to look like a lightbulb . . . a Thomas Edison phonograph with the original horn and five cylinder tunes, including "I May Be Crazy But I'm No Fool."

On the east wall hung a gilt-framed reproduction of a portrait of the inventor in his fifties. Ellis had always thought him a handsome man. Yes, his head was rather large for his body — in fact, Edison's father had remarked on this minutes after the boy was born — but the man's eyes . . . oh, those eyes! Even after all these years, Ellis could not make up his mind. Were they young John Wayne's or middle-aged Paul Newman's? Ellis had once overheard a female tourist in the gift shop say the inventor's lips reminded her of Kevin Costner's, but Ellis bristled at the very suggestion. Mr. Costner was not a classic! Mr. Newman, however, a classic, indeed. Ellis had written an e-mail to Francis Ford Coppola, suggesting that he film a biography of the great man and cast Newman in the role.

Ellis and many of the retiree docents often lingered around the Edison home after their duties ended for the day. But while most of them chatted in the employee lounge, Ellis busied himself with responsibilities he had assumed over the years and could not relinquish, small but significant acts of civility that the younger people took for granted.

Ellis made certain, for example, that the pencils in the blue Lee Memorial Hospital coffee mug were always turned points down so that no one would poke themselves when reaching for one. He also helped the ladies keep an eye on the merchandise in the gift shop and would let them know when a particular item needed restocking. Ellis kept a folding lawn chair in the janitor's broom closet, and on busy days he would sit himself in the pathway to the parking lot and dispense driving directions and restaurant suggestions to tourists who were leaving.

But on this day Ellis had other plans that would prevent him from completing these tasks. Logan was taking him out for dinner to say goodbye. She and Brendon were leaving for Pennsylvania tomorrow.

Ellis opened his locker and reached for his cardigan but stopped short.

"And what is this?"

Someone had punctured a Ziploc bag over one of the J-shaped hooks. Ellis peered through the plastic. There was a small book inside.

Ellis immediately looked over his shoulder. Tom and Walt were talking at the table, their hands encircling Styrofoam cups of coffee, but they were as oblivious to Ellis as they always were. Tom Waitman and Ellis had not spoken ever since Ellis had told him he was talking too fast on his tours, and the guests could not understand him.

Ellis unhooked the plastic bag and opened it and took out the brown-leather book. It smelled musty, as if it had been stored in a Florida garage. The cover was plain with no writing. He opened it and found page after page of someone's lovely handwriting in what he thought was black ink from a fountain pen. It looked unhurried and ornamental — people did not write like this anymore.

A fuchsia Post-it note was sticking out of the middle like a bookmark. Someone had written a message, and Ellis raised his chin so he could read it through the bottom half of his gold-frame bifocals. It said, "Protect this from J. Ziegler. She'll send it to the Edison museum in New Jersey and it belongs here in Fort Myers. God bless you."

But what was it? Ellis turned to a random page and began to read.

17 February 1886. I took corn muffins to Dearie and the boys in the laboratory. He was quite unpleasant with me again. He was most curt. I realize his work with the goldenrod is of utmost importance, but why is he so dis-

missive of me? Have I upset him in some way? Can he possibly have already lost the love in his heart for me?

"My dear God," Ellis whispered. He looked over his shoulder at the two men again, then opened to a different spot and read some more.

2 April 1888. He is angry again, indeed pouting like Theodore, Charles or any other small boy, because he caught nothing but two catfish on the pier today. Some days I think his gray moods will deliver me two steps shy of insanity.

Mina Edison was a prodigious letter and journal writer, and much of her thoughts and life milestones were thus well detailed for posterity. But there was a two-year period of darkness, during the earlier years in her marriage to Thomas. Historians have few letters and no journals from this time. What they do have is Thomas's letters, and they portray a dry season in the marriage, a period of self-doubt and insecurity and depression. He wrote, "If you knew how much I love you, darling, you would never fear or worry for an instant about such things (flirtations) or ever be jealous. Don't you know that the fixed law of the organic world requires one man for one woman and that all normal well-balanced men never have the least desire to contravene that law, it's only the ill-balanced degenerate and conceited egotist that does such things."

This small brown book had to be the missing link of correspondence! It had to be Mina's. Who else called the great inventor "Dearie"? But where on earth did it come from? Larry! Of course, it was Larry, it had to be. But why hadn't he given it to him on that night weeks ago?

Then again, this was a Ziploc, and Ellis doubted that Larry would buy Ziplocs because he was such a spendthrift. Ellis, on the other hand, loved Ziplocs and stocked them in four different sizes. He liked the silky feel of the thick, smooth plastic and how items, once stowed in a Ziploc, were safely segregated from the elements, even air and water. He enjoyed the very act of sealing a bag, zipping the raised ridges together, then running them through his forefinger and thumb until a tiny satisfying click indicated that the seal had been made and all within was safe and well. Whenever Ellis borrowed anything from anyone, it was always returned in a fresh Ziploc, their name inscribed on it with a black Sharpie marker.

Ellis looked at the book in his hands. Where had this been hiding? How long had someone known of its existence? What secrets of the heart lay within these pages?

"Hey, Ellis," Tom Waitman said. "Come on over here, I wanna ask you something."

Ellis wrapped the journal in his cardigan and joined the two men at the table. "Yes, Tom. Are you still angry with me?"

"No, hell no, I'm over that. . . . I've got a question. I heard a rumor that the new director is gonna get rid of Holidazzle. Do you know anything about that?"

"No, I do not, but if she did it would be a very good thing."

"What . . . don't you like Holidazzle?"

"Not particularly," Ellis answered. "It is an embarrassment. The Europeans on my tours are aghast every year at the gawdy decorations. They find them very disrespectful to Mr. Edison, as do I."

"Well all I know is she's gonna have one helluva battle on her hands if she tries to stop Holidazzle. Everyone loves Holidazzle."

What the three men did not know was that Judith was standing on the other side of the partly opened oak door as they spoke. She was on her way to retrieve the second half of a Dairy Queen strawberry milkshake when she heard their voices through the crack in the door and stopped short to listen, undetected.

"Ellis?" Logan said. "Are you okay?"

She had taken him to his favorite restaurant, the Bob Evans across the river in North Fort Myers. Since he couldn't walk to it, his visits there were rare, making it seem even more special.

Before him sat a plate filled with all his Bob Evans favorites — country-fried steak, cottage cheese, pumpkin bread, and truncated green beans cooked with small chunks of ham — but indeed he had barely touched his meal. All Ellis could do was stew over the journal, worrying that he had not hidden it well enough. Perhaps he should not have stowed it in the microwave oven with the test tube of Edison's breath, but it was his favorite hiding place. Perfect, really. Would burglarizing hooligans ever think of checking the microwave for drugs or money or jewels? Certainly not. But what if they were hungry and decided to help themselves to some of the Paul Newman Gourmet Popping Corn? (In fact, when Ellis's house was burglarized two years earlier, the thieves did break into a box of Ho Ho's on the kitchen counter.) What if they simply put the popcorn on top of the journal, as if it were a plate, and zapped it for the two minutes and thirty seconds? The cover was leather, and leather was an animal product, and animal products were cooked all the time, so maybe no harm would be done. But he couldn't be sure what would happen. Oh, the oppressive weight of these fabulous possessions!

Ellis smiled at Logan and asked her about the apartment she had found up north, but her answer washed over him as water runs over rocks. Ellis's mind had already wandered back into the increasingly tortuous obstacle course that had become his life, and he wondered now, as he nibbled on his pumpkin bread, if he would be able to find a safe on eBay.

Chapter Nine

"You really get paid to do that?"

"I sure do," Geena answered.

"I've never heard of such a job. You'd think Oprah would have that on her show or something."

"Oh, no, they'd never agree to that. Delta doesn't want anyone to know about it. You can understand why."

Geena Pangborn sat in an aqua vinyl chair in Nails by Sandee on Pierce Avenue in Savannah. At her feet was the owner, Sandee Cass, who'd been spending more time than usual on this set of toenails because the day had been slow, and the details of Geena's job fascinated her.

Over the past twenty minutes, Geena had been sharing with Sandee her transient life as a quality control scout for Delta Airlines. Her division was small, she said, but important, just herself and three others, and it was their job to fly full-time, both in coach and first-class, and be the most demanding customers possible: May I have a pillow? May I have a blanket? May I have *another* pillow? I don't care for my chicken Kiev. Why don't you have *Marie Claire* magazine? Why do you have so many men's magazines? Why can't you give me an aspirin? I can't believe this is first-class and you won't give me real cutlery — I can't cut with this plastic thing.

"And when they crack and let me have it, then I write 'em up," Geena said.

"Isn't that bein' ugly?" Sandee asked.

Geena nodded. "But if we didn't do it, you wouldn't get good service. People need to know they're being watched . . . babysat. We're all just grown-up kids. Don't you think we act better if we're afraid of getting in trouble?"

Geena then wondered if she would have left Sublette and Barry if her mother had been alive, judging her and writing her up from somewhere in the wings. Would she be cheering her on or verbally slapping her across the bottom and telling her to get back home and stop whining? Would she say something like, "Get over it, Geena. At least your husband didn't run away and leave you with a two-year-old to raise by yourself."

Sandee shook her head and continued brushing on the first coat of Tahitian Orchid polish. "Oh, Miss Ellis," she said. "That job would make me feel horrible."

"I'm surprised I haven't been murdered yet," Geena said. "But I constantly dye my hair. I own fifteen pairs of glasses. I try to change my appearance just in case someone figures out who I am. Of course, it helps that most businessmen on the road are assholes. I just blend in with all the rest of them. . . ."

"Ohmigawd," Geena interrupted herself. "I forgot to ask. You do take credit cards, don't you? I just assumed you took credit cards. I don't have a cent on me."

"Yes, ma'am," Sandee answered. "Visa, MasterCard, and Discover."

Setting all this up had been surprisingly, alarmingly easy. In the same mailbag as Ellis's credit card Geena had found an Ellis-bound form from UniCen Health Insurance in Cincinnati, and it was a good thing because Geena hadn't known she would need his Social Security number in order to activate the credit card.

"I'm sorry," the MasterCard representative had said. "But the phone number you are calling from does not match the record of the number we have on file."

119

"But I'm on the road . . . on business," Geena said. "I had my mail sent to me in a FedEx bundle. Don't you make exceptions?"

"Can you give me your Social Security number?"

"Oh hell, excuse me, it's my door. Someone's at my door. Can you hold on a second? . . . Ma'am?"

"Yes."

"Please. Just a second."

Geena set the receiver on top of the phone booth in the 7-Eleven parking lot, dashed back to her car, and returned with the health document. After telling her imaginary visitor to make himself comfortable — "I'll be right with you, I'm almost done. Help yourself to that wine." — she recited the number to the woman.

"Thank you," she replied. "And your mother's maiden name?"

Mother's maiden name! God, what else will she want? . . . Mother's maiden name . . . Mother's maiden name . . .

Geena assumed that Ellis was a good Southern boy, and didn't all Southern mommas give their maiden names to their sons as first names? Florida wasn't truly Southern, but Ellis did sound like a last name.

Gina's forearm twitched in an impulse to hang up. Yet she had to say something! It was like being stumped on a TV game show during the final round. When they watched *Jeopardy* together, Nathan would always say that silence laughed in the face of statistics because if a contestant said anything, no matter how far off base, she increased her chances of winning . . . by the tiniest fraction, of course, considering how many millions of possible answers she could pull from the ether. But still, a chance. There was always a chance.

"Ellis," Geena said.

"Thank you," answered the woman.

Sweet holy God. Doin' the happy dance here. Doin' the happy dance heeeeeere.

Geena suddenly remembered the time she and Barry went to Mexico and their American Express card was refused at an art gallery in Zihuatanejo. They called on the cell phone to ask why, and the representative told them the purchase and location didn't match their spending profile, and that was what had triggered the response. Next time, the rep said, if they planned on traveling to an unusual location (unusual for them, anyway), they should call and warn the credit card company ahead of time so they'd know it was them using the card and not someone else.

"I need to let you know that I'm going to be on the road for quite some time," Geena said. "Can you mark that in my profile?"

"Certainly, Mrs. Norton. Where do you plan on traveling?"

"Pretty much throughout the South. Georgia . . . and Florida. And it's my only card, so I'll be using it a lot."

Chapter Ten

The sleeping arrangements of Thomas and Mina Edison had mystified Ellis for decades.

In a peculiar architectural and marital configuration, the two-storied parental sleeping quarters of Seminole Lodge were separated from the main house, the upstairs bedroom (Thomas's so-called doghouse) being connected by a catwalk and the downstairs bedroom (Mina's) by a covered veranda. It was said that the inventor, a chronic insomniac, also used a freestanding staircase that led from his room into the garden, so he could come and go to the laboratory all night long and never bother his slumbering wife. Truly, it seemed as if the two bedrooms had been designed as separate apartments.

Ellis often pondered the negotiations of this couple's conjugal visits. Was there a secret knock or specific night of the week?

Was there a sign the inventor gave at the dinner table . . . say, a lamb chop bone standing on end in the uneaten mound of mashed potatoes? Would Mina herself plant the seed of passion in hopes it might flower sometime later that night beneath the tropical moon? Would she look at him in that coy, chin-down, eyes-upward way that Doris Day did with Rock Hudson in the second half of *Pillow Talk*?

Over the years, Ellis had spent several weeks collectively in Thomas's doghouse, which was as spartan as a Hemingway-novel hospital room, with white walls and nothing but a bed, a nightstand, and a desk. Thinking it too plain, years ago Ellis had hung on the wall over the bed a framed botanical print of a pink-orange plumeria blossom he'd found at a yard sale on Avocado Drive. Within days of her arrival, Judith Ziegler took it down because it was not of the right period.

It was well past midnight, and Ellis found himself sitting in new territory . . . at the wicker secretary in Mina's bedroom, the very spot from which she had penned thousands of letters . . . and perhaps even the entries of the candid journal he'd been reading.

He'd always considered Mina's room too

fussy. The walls were covered in flowered wallpaper, and it had white wooden and wicker furniture with accents of pink splashed about with abandon. There were chairs upholstered in floral-print fabric, and a white wicker recamier sat before the fireplace.

Ellis surveyed the desk. The 1945 desktop calendar from Lee County State Bank and Trust Company. The yellowed Funk & Wagnalls Concise Standard Dictionary. The letter to two gentlemen named Edward and Bob that Mina had started but never finished. Who *were* these two men? Ellis had hoped he'd find mention of them in the journal, but he had yet to discover any new clue in this mystery.

Ellis's favorite item on the desk, however, was something that looked like a tiny set of matchbook-size encyclopedias that fit snugly into a pressed-cardboard holder. Each had a different colored binding with a gold-embossed word or two — the red one read PHOTO WAFERS, the green one THUMB TACKS, the yellow KEY TAGS — and you could pull each one out individually, open the cover, and retrieve the needed objects from the hollowed-out book. Ellis wondered what he would store in such a thing if he had one at home.

Postage stamps? Maybe his medicines and vitamins? Vitamin E somewhat matched the yellow box. Warfarin, his blood-thinner medication, obviously belonged in red.

A passing truck suddenly backfired on McGregor Boulevard, and Ellis looked up and out the window. From this spot he could see Rachel at the Well, the Grecian-style fountain of a curvaceous young woman pouring water from a vessel that graced the entrance to Edison Park, Fort Myers's oldest subdivision. When the builder first unveiled the statue, it was naked, and Mina Edison raised such a stink that the sculptor had to return and add on some plaster folds of drapes to conceal her breasts. Ellis's mother had always thought Mina's outrage a vulgar display of abusing her role as a celebrity wife, but as he sat here now, for the first time Ellis realized that indeed it would have been quite distracting to look across the street at such nakedness, and Lord only knew the number of traffic accidents it might have caused over the years.

Bathed in light from the streetlamp overhead, Rachel's skin took on a ghostly chalky-white appearance. The mature, voluminous vine of bougainvillea that hovered over her head had started creeping

126

downward again, and Rachel's forehead had disappeared as if enshrouded in a green fog. Ellis made a mental note to call the City of Fort Myers the next morning and tell them it needed trimming.

Ellis reached for his beige canvas bag on the floor and pulled out the Ziploc that held the journal, which he had renamed "diary" because it lent a more secretive, deeply personal air to the book. He got up from the secretary, walked across the room, and lay down on the recamier. Ellis hated the fact that he had to shuffle around in the dark like some vandal, but in these post-Larry days, he did not dare enjoy the estate during daylight. Of course, he had not told Judith Ziegler about his cache of keys, because a woman such as she would seize them and probably write another scolding letter for his personnel file.

With the help of his buttercup yellow, pen-size Edison Winter Estate flashlight, Ellis opened the diary and began to gently turn the pages. There were plenty of entries about Mina's plants, and on sightings of specific species of birds at Seminole Lodge, and on her dealings with Queenie, their cook. She had included details of her dealings for another cow so she could meet the demands of her husband's growing obsession with milk. In his later years he was quaffing a pint every two to three hours. (Ellis had read in the archives that the inventor once held a glass of milk up to the light and said, "The Almighty is still the greatest chemist.")

And, over the span of three months, Mina had recorded her successful efforts to strong-arm the state of Florida into letting her and her garden club dig up and sell the pine saplings that were being displaced by construction of the Tamiami Trail, the highway that would one day connect Tampa to the bigger city on the tip of the peninsula.

But what Ellis enjoyed most were the passages that dealt with her husband. They were the most candid correspondence he'd ever seen, much more so than the letters to her mother and sister Grace that he'd read over the years in the archive room. Indeed, there appeared to be very good reason why this journal had never been seen.

I have been asking Thomas to join me for lunch in town for days now, and finally, today, it came to pass. As we ate, he told me of the progress of his rubber trees, and that the Brazilian coffee plants appear to have developed some sort of blight. (I, too, have noticed the black spots; in fact, it was I who told him about the problem.)

I realize now I should not have pushed him into leaving his work to have luncheon with me. We sat in Dillon's, Dearie chewing his food into paste as he always does, looking at the wall, and thinking about everything but me. Sometimes I feel as if I live with a man who is not twenty years my senior but one hundred and twenty, and his mind has left him for the remainder of the time he has in this body. My Thomas is not of this Earth. I feel as if I am living with a spirit who cannot find peace. He floats from laboratory to bed and back again, then perhaps out to his beloved pier for fishing. He sleeps wherever and whenever he wants. He is more cat than man, but at least a cat grooms himself.

What a luxury it must be to live with a man who goes to bed at the same hour and remains there to watch early in the morning, when his fierceness finally wanes and the soft child within returns to his profile. He has reached out for you sometime in the night, and his arm rests, innocent but reassuring, across your hips. I have tried to sneak upon Dearie as he sleeps, but more than once have alarmed him so have stopped.

How ironic it is that I am married to this great man who is famous for forcing mental connections that produce monumental devices which transform humanity, yet he cannot connect with me. My dear Thomas, where are you? I am starting to think that I will never have you again. What is it about me that you do not need? That you do not want?

The first few times Ellis read this passage, he rolled his eyes at what he thought was nothing short of melodrama. Yet this evening, in the darkness of her bedroom, he unconsciously recited the last two sentences out loud to himself: "My dear Thomas, what is it about me that you do not need? That you do not want?"

And again: "My dear Thomas, what is it about me that you do not need? That you do . . . not . . . want?"

Uppity and spoiled, perhaps, but Ellis had to admit she was eloquent. Mina obviously shared Ellis's distaste for contractions of words. Perhaps she, too, considered them lazy and vulgar and a symbolic step toward the compression and eventual crushing of civilized language.

Outside again, on McGregor Boulevard, Ellis walked home beneath the towering royal palms that lined both sides of the street. With their thick, straight, lichen-spotted trunks, they looked like gray pillars supporting a bridge, and indeed many a Midwestern tourist thought the trees had been caked in a smooth layer of concrete to protect them from errant cars. When the breeze blew, as it did now, the treetops looked like the sparklers children twirl on Fourth of July, sticks topped with heads of blooming, fluid chaos.

Ellis never tired of this walk; the royals connected him to the inventor. It was Edison who thought of the idea to line McGregor with the royal palms, and he himself donated and planted the first seven hundred of them, including these, which Ellis would occasionally stop and pat as though they were lazy, old dogs.

Ellis came to a rise in the sidewalk where an ambitious root from a jacaranda tree had long ago pushed up one side of the concrete square a good three inches. He stopped and looked down, and his mind wandered back to a day some seventy years ago.

His entire life, Ellis had never been comfortable with velocity. It was why he didn't drive. It was why he hated playing baseball. When his father forced him to participate in neighborhood games, Ellis would stand in left field, praying the ball did not come his way, and when it did he simply watched it fall to the ground, then retrieved it and rolled it into a baseman, underhanded, as if he were bowling. Ellis hated the idea of something falling on him, something he did not ask for.

One day when he was nine, Ellis's father Harry was standing with a friend in the front yard, drinking beers and watching a pack of boys ride back and forth on their bikes. It had been a prosperous year in Fort Myers — the soldiers who had trained at the airfield east of town fell in love with the climate and were returning in droves after the war to start their families — and Santa brought bikes for nearly every boy that Christmas. Ellis got one as well, though it had since leaned on a wall in the garage, untouched and shiny.

"When's Ellis gonna learn to ride that thing?" asked the friend.

Harry Norton drained the last of his Old Milwaukee, then threw the bottle into the grass. "Right now," he answered.

He stormed inside the house and burst unannounced into Ellis's room, where he found his son gluing glitter onto a fence he'd cut from brown construction paper. He needed it for the small china Dalmatian he'd gotten in his Christmas stocking.

As Irene Norton was working in her dress shop downtown, Ellis was dragged from the house, sobbing and pleading with his father. (Later that night, deep blue bruises would blossom on his heels from the deadweight thumping they took going down the front steps of the porch.)

Harry commanded Ellis to get up on the bike. Ellis crumpled to the ground like a pair of empty coveralls. With one hand his father held up the bike, with the other he lifted his thin, pale son by the arm, into the air, and plopped him onto the seat.

"Grab the handlebars, Ellis!"

"Father . . ."

"I said, 'Grab the handlebars, Ellis!' "

His vision clouded by tears, Ellis anemically took hold. He felt the bumps of turf as his father pushed him across the yard, and when he finally opened his eyes he looked down and saw that he and his bicycle were consuming yards of sidewalk at a frightening pace. Familiar images rushed past him like water released from a dam. He could hear his father huffing behind him as he ran, holding on to the back of the seat.

"You're doin' it, Ellis."

"Do not let go, Father!" he yelled. "Oh, Lord, please do not let go!"

"Don't be such a baby."

"Please do not let go! . . . Please!"

"Just ride, Ellis! . . . Go! . . . Jesus, your mother's ruined you."

Ellis then noticed that the smell of beer and tangy man-sweat had suddenly disappeared. He turned to look back and saw his father hunched over and panting on the sidewalk. Harry looked up and waved him on: "Go, Ellis! Go!"

Afraid that he might fall if he stopped, Ellis kept pedaling, all the while looking back at his father, who was growing smaller by the second.

And then, just before the intersection of McGregor and Cordova Street, the front wheel of Ellis's bike collided with the rupture in the sidewalk, catapulting him over the handlebars and headfirst into one of the royal palms.

Later that afternoon, as Ellis lay in bed

with twelve stitches in the crown of his head, he heard his mother and father fighting in their bedroom. The content was no different from all the other arguments, but this time there was a different timbre to their voices, as if the last, fraying threads of some kind of restraint — a leash, perhaps — had been severed.

"You've turned that boy into the biggest pansy in the world."

"You just can't get over the fact that I'm more successful than you."

"I could care less about your stupid dress shop."

"You're half a man, Harry. You're just half a man."

But then came a series of sounds Ellis had never heard, the back of a man's hand colliding with flesh and bone, a collapse to the floor, a man quickly groveling for forgiveness, a strong mother absolutely silent. . . . Silent!

Not really certain what he'd heard, Ellis finally drifted off to sleep. His father left the house. And when two of his drunken friends carried him back home four hours later and put him to bed, Irene Norton went to work.

In the garage, she pulled from his truck a folded piece of heavy canvas that Harry used as a drop cloth in his plastering job. She took it inside, spread it out on the bed beside her snoring, passed-out husband, and then, pulling him by the arm, rolled his body from stomach to back onto the canvas. She then folded the second half of the canvas over her husband and, with her upholsterer's needle and thread, proceeded to sew shut the three sides as if he were sausage in a ravioli.

After that, Irene Norton, daughter of the Teamster's chief in Camden, New Jersey, proceeded to whack at her defenseless husband with Ellis's Louisville Slugger as if she were trying to bust up a piece of ice, being careful to avoid the head so he would have faculties enough to leave and survive on his own after she had finished with him.

The next morning, Ellis awoke and discovered that one of the three chrome-and-vinyl chairs around the kitchen table was missing. His mother stood at the stove, stirring oatmeal.

"Your father is gone," she said. "He is not coming back."

Chapter Eleven

Being married to a man who never read novels or watched movies, and having lived seventeen years in one-screen Sublette, Colorado (the Hi Plains Theater), Geena's list of missed new releases was long indeed. So when it came time to choose hotels, she had one prerequisite, that it have video-on-command. Certainly an ocean view was a plus, as she'd had at the Sea Turtle Inn in Atlantic Beach, but it was movies, the stories of other peoples' lives, that now filled her as nothing else could.

In the past two weeks Geena had watched so many films from hotel room beds, they'd begun to blend together in her mind like the ingredients in an oscillating food processor. (Was it Kate Hudson or Ashley Judd or Sarah Michelle Gellar in that movie about a blind date and a cute guy and a lost shoe . . . lost dog? . . . lost love?)

Geena was halfway through *Simply Irre-sistible* when she heard the knock of room service at the door. This was her third night at the Marriott on Daytona Beach and her second of filet mignon with baked potato and roasted asparagus and carrots.

The waiter was in his early twenties with a small sculpted square of black beard centered just below his lower lip and a variety of different-sized silver rings that pierced the cartilage edges of his ears.

"Where do you want this, ma'am?"

"You can put it on the bed."

"How about over there on the table? You can sit in the chair and watch TV."

"Okay," Geena answered. "Thanks."

He set the tray down on the table and looked about the room as Geena signed the check. She added on a six-dollar tip, then totaled the bill.

"I'm into Asian stuff, too," he said. "Very cool. Buddha's like my idol. He's so mellow."

Geena looked up and saw him staring at the blue statue of Buddha flanked by two lit, red candles on top of the television set. The previous day she'd spent two hours and nearly three hundred dollars at Karma by Karmen, a New Age store squeezed between a T.J. Maxx and Dollar General on

North Beach Road. Besides the lapis Buddha, Geena bought six Carlos Nakai CDs, a pyramid-shaped incense burner carved out of malachite, and a hardcover book entitled *Harmony to Go: Feng Shui for Your Car.* She hadn't intended to buy so much, but walking the aisles of the store provoked memories of her husband . . . like the time Barry came in one day from work, smelled lemongrass-scented incense perfuming the family room, and said, "Jesus, Geena, what is that? It smells like a French whorehouse in here" . . . and when she tried to convince her husband to abandon the stuffed pheasant mounted over the fireplace in the den because it created an imbalance in the yang energy . . . and the time she caught absolute hell for having the upstairs doors reconfigured because they would bang into each other when opened into the hallway.

" 'Arguing' doors cause quarrels and fighting within the family, Barry," she explained. "You'd know that already if you would have come to my presentation at Rotary."

Geena had worked at a New Age shop her first year in college, and when she dropped out to get married and move to Sublette, she convinced her boss to let her take some merchandise and try to sell it on commission. Barry had told her his father didn't like his sons' wives working in the business, and she was afraid she'd be bored in such a small town.

Shortly after returning from their honeymoon on Maui and her first-ever trip by plane, Geena went to work peddling her tools of enlightenment, speaking to any civic group that would have her. She coaxed Max Rollins, owner of Sublette Merit Drug, into letting her display some crystals for sale in the glass case beside the cash register, between the perfumes and Timex watches. For sales leads, she read the News of Record column in every week's edition of the *Sublette Herald*, which included details of hospitalizations of local residents. The day Faye Reimer came home from the hospital in Denver after getting radiation for pancreatic cancer, Geena sold her some colored glass bottles and a book on chromatherapy. To the newly divorced Lisa Jacobson she sold a drum onto which she could transfer her anger and help reset her internal biorhythms. ("Imagine each beat being a footstep that takes you farther and farther away from the past and into a new future.")

Quickly, the Pangborn clan's reaction evolved from chuckling to eye-rolling to disgust.

"You're stalking people," Barry told her.

"I'm helping people in need, Barry."

"I won't have it, Geena. We own a business in this town. I don't want people avoiding me because they're afraid my wife is gonna try to pawn off some of her New Age voodoo on them. You need to find something else to do. Why can't you just be happy spending money like Devin's and Ronnie's wives?"

"How different is this than your dropping by some widow's house to see if she wants to sell her ranch?"

"Please, honey. My mom's having a cow over this."

Before they married, Barry would lay with her on the floor of his apartment, side by side, the two of them holding hands and listening to a Dick Sutphen past-life regression tape in hopes of finding clues as to why they'd been drawn together in this incarnation. He would accompany her to the occasional crystal shows held at the Holiday Inn out on I-25, even when they coincided with a Rams home football game. Always, Geena could bury her nose in his neck and expect to smell the sandalwood-ginger blend of oils she'd mixed to match his personality.

Then they got married, and this man she fell in love with ceased being the man she fell in love with, and Geena wondered how she could have been so blind. All his older brothers had mixed and baked their adult lives with the same recipe: BS and a wife at CSU, then back home to momma's nest, where they would do anything, say anything, feign any emotion to stay on track.

I will never forgive him for pretending to be something he's not.

Though Geena had signed the check and sat down on the couch before her food, the young waiter loitered near the television.

"Do you want the tray back?" she asked.

"Oh, no. I'll pick that up later when you're done."

Still, he did not move to leave. He unconsciously started to shift his weight from foot to foot. What Geena did not realize was that this twenty-two-year-old junior at Ormond Beach Community College, Zachary Kuhn, had nearly convinced himself that this woman who had ordered medium-rare beef the past two nights was indeed some red-haired celebrity whose identity escaped him just now, and he wanted to pin a name on her before leaving. Celebrity sightings, after all, were infrequent but not unlikely at the Daytona Beach Marriott. Just a week earlier the diva rock star Fuchsia had stopped in for an overnight stay between concerts in Miami and Atlanta. Zachary had to drive to four supermarkets before finding her special request of strawberry Fanta, and she reordered her medium-rare cheeseburger three times before finally eating a third of it, then throwing the rest out the window, littering a bed of azalea bushes and split-leaf philodendrons below.

Was she Bruce Willis's wife? Kim Something? Jessica? He wasn't sure, but Geena had to be an actress . . . a singer . . . or at least from California. Good-looking women in Daytona didn't bother with Buddha.

"Is something wrong?" Geena asked.

"Are you who I think you are?"

Geena felt a sudden flaring of panic in her chest, which she quickly extinguished with reason. Ensconced in business hotels for days now, she'd been monitoring the TV and Internet news and, other than a small update on her disappearance in the *Denver Post* — still, no comment from the family — interest in Geena Marie Pangborn's disappearance had not seeped beyond the boundaries of Kit Carson

County, Colorado. It was as if the Pangborns, hoping to protect the integrity of
their name and empire, had sandbagged
the perimeter of the region so that news
would not leak out. No, she convinced herself. There was no way this young man
could know who she was.

"Who do you think I am?" she asked.

"I'm not really sure. But I've seen you in
movies."

"You have?"

Zachary Kuhn smiled. "Haven't I?"

"Did you see *Legally Blonde*?"

"No. Was that you?"

"At least you could lie and say you saw
it."

"But I didn't."

"Did you see the Golden Globes?"

"Movies aren't my thing. Sorry, but
that's the truth."

"Then what is your thing?"

*Geena! God! You've been watching too
many trashy movies!*

The young man was tanned and thin and
long-waisted like Nathan, with curly dark
brown hair that brushed against the top of
his shoulders. A surfer? He wore his black,
clunky diver's wristwatch like a loose
bracelet as it slipped about on his wrist.

Many times in her southbound odyssey

Geena had felt uneasy around men, even men as young as this, and as she looked at Zachary Kuhn, she recalled a study she had learned in her intro-to-psychology class her freshman year, about a pod of captive dolphins and how they reacted to humans. Researchers asked a variety of people to jump into the water at the same time, and in nearly every case the dolphins first approached young children, preferably females. With the children removed, their next choice was women and, lastly, men. Evidently there was an unconscious aggressiveness in male body language — unconscious to humans, anyway — that kept the dolphins at bay. While men moved as if they owned the space around them, women moved as if they were simply borrowing it. Out of apparent fear, the marine mammals avoided men even if they were their only choice. The truth was — and Geena recalled this now with a smile — dolphins chose loneliness over the company of men.

Yet this man — boy? . . . what was he . . . twenty-one? — before her moved about his world in a willowy manner with an economy of physical energy seen even in the way he languidly blinked his eyes. His arms, hanging loosely at his sides, were more adornments than tools. Even the bobbing of his Adam's apple appeared to occur with the exaggerated slowness of the manatees Geena had seen on Florida Public Television.

"My thing?" he asked.

"What do you like to do?"

He shrugged his shoulders. "Hang out, I guess. There's a coffeehouse over on Hartman. I just hang out there. I've got some friends I write poetry with."

"What kind of poetry?"

He looked at her, hesitating, then said, "Mostly political poetry. Social commentary stuff."

Oh God, say something else that starts with P. What gorgeous lips. They belong on a woman.

"Political?" Geena asked.

"When you live down here with all these shrivs, you tend to rebel against anything conservative. They're all Republican."

"Shrivs?"

He smiled, as if caught in a lie. "Shriveled people," he said. "Retirees."

Geena laughed. "That's awful."

"You try living down here."

"Old people aren't that bad."

"Not all old people are shrivs. . . . Shriv's an attitude."

"Oh?"

Geena fell back onto the striped, navy-and-tan upholstered chair in the corner of her room. She had already drunk both minibottles of chardonnay from the wet bar, something she considered an extravagance because Barry had always refused to pay such inflated prices.

"Yeah. My friends and me, we've got this all figured out. People who retire to Florida are a certain type of people. They can emotionally cut themselves off from their children and grandchildren and move south just because they don't like being cold. It takes a different kind of person to do that. They're like incredibly self-absorbed. It's why they drive like shit, why they're always having wrecks. They can't see anybody but themselves. It's all me, me, me, me."

Geena listened from the chair, nodding. *God, he sounds like Nathan.*

"Shrivs are brain-dead," he said. "I mean, there's a reason we don't have any serious art down here. The intellectual seniors stay at home in Ohio and New York or wherever because they want things like lectures and foreign movies. . . . I've got this poem called 'Einstein Has Left the Building.'"

"Can I hear it?"

He shook his head, wrinkled up his nose. "Nah."

"Oh, come on."

"It's free verse. I mean, it's probably not your thing."

"So try me. How long is it?"

"Long."

Geena shifted her weight, then pulled her feet up, one by one, onto the chair and placed them in a lotus position. "So give me the first couple of lines."

"You really want to hear them?"

"Yes."

"I'd feel stupid."

"How do you think I feel when I have to take my clothes off for hundreds of millions of people in several countries?"

Zachary quickly looked away, his neck flushing. "But that's the movies," he said. "That's not real. You're not there."

Zachary put his hands into the pockets of his baggy blue jeans. Geena wondered if she'd live long enough to see the demise of this unfortunate fad of young men hiding their best assets under multiple folds of denim. So much of the seventies had been resurrected, but why not the tight jeans on men? She thought of Nathan, whose corduroy pants had billowed over his flat rear end. The boy had had no butt; apparently this had been a trait of her father's as well.

"Why aren't you wearing uniform pants?" Geena asked.

"I spilled cream of broccoli on them. I had to change into my jeans. . . . I need to go."

"Oh, come on. Read me some poetry. Let me turn down the TV. Do you want to sit down?"

"No, that's okay. But I probably should go."

"Come on . . . what's your name?"

Stop stalking this boy!

"Zachary."

"Come on, Zachary. I'm lonely. I'm tired of TV. I like poetry."

"You do?"

"Yes. I was a poetry major at Princeton."

Princeton!

"Well, it's not really finished. It's kind of a work in progress."

"So read what you have."

"I've got it memorized . . . what's done, anyway."

"Okay."

"Right here? You just want me to recite it right here?"

"Yes."

Zachary shrugged his shoulders. Clearing his throat, he then stood up

149

straight, locked his hands behind his back, and focused on the far corner of the ceiling. His smile faded away.

Too cute! He looks like those kids in the spelling bees on TV.

"They migrate south, like wildebeests following the rains, monarchs chasing the sun, because all they want is their skin to be warm, and the free dinner rolls at four o'clock. They feast on Grisham and Bush and Limbaugh and art that matches their pastel-colored sofas. They never seek the cause of the wound but simply want it fixed. . . . Ozone? Isn't that a cologne?"

Zachary paused and looked at Geena expectantly.

"Keep going," she said.

"Florida is their mistress, used for pleasures of the flesh, but their hearts and allegiance and money lie back in Schenectady, where the frozen ground awaits their return, and they will rage against this final passage until the very last second . . . because they fear what they do not know, and they know nothing because they have never asked why.

"That's all I've got," he said.

Geena stood up. "It's really great."

No. Sweet.

He raised his eyebrows in surprise. "Yeah?"

He . . . is . . . so . . . cute! . . . No more wine!

"Yes. Very cool."

"Which part did you like the most?"

"Definitely the dinner rolls. And the anti-Bush stuff."

Indeed, Geena had grown weary of the Grand Old Party. The 2004 presidential election was in full swing when she left home, and Barry's brother Gary had just taken the reins of the Kit Carson County Republican Committee because State Farm Insurance had transferred the current chairman, Kevin Schlosser, to Wichita. Gary was the third Pangborn, after Brit and Barry, to serve in the post.

The problem, however, was that Gary's wife Sue had left him that fall, and it was the duty of the chairman to host the annual fund-raiser, the Lincoln Day Banquet.

"We can have it at our house," Barry said.

"I've already done this twice," Geena answered. "Once for you, once for your parents. It's a lot of work, Barry."

"Please."

Whenever someone in the Pangborn family needed anything that called for creativity, they looked to Geena and her stapler and glue gun. For Halloween one year, with just two hours' notice, she transformed her nieces into lovebirds for the Girl Scout costume contest, which they won. With Nathan at her side, either in a backpack or a crib or, in later years, sitting on the floor with a game, she would build Dot's Easter Sunday hats, using flowers and ribbon found at Hobby Lobby and Michael's, and Dot would pass them off as one-of-a-kind creations from a milliner in Telluride.

Geena had grown up spending her days after school in the back of Castle Rock Floral Shoppe in south Denver, watching her mother create arrangements for the city's social elite with whatever materials satisfied her whim. One Easter she sent Geena to the trash Dumpster outside to fetch brown paper bags from King Soopers, which she crumpled and used to replicate cold spring ground, from which rose half-opened crocuses and daffodils to symbolize the Resurrection.

When Michael Jackson came through town on his *Thriller* tour in the eighties, he was greeted in his suite at the Brown Palace Hotel with an arrangement that featured not flowers but a bouquet of wire whisks and whips of various sizes, spray-painted the colors of the rainbow to simultaneously satisfy the man's love for childlike fantasy and darkness, with a nod, of course, to the lyrics of the album's hit song, "Beat It." The entertainer was so pleased, he called the floral shop personally to thank them. Geena's mother, though, thought it was a prank until the day she died.

It was from her mother that Geena learned the basic, most-often-overlooked mantra of decorating: Figure out how much in materials you think you'll need . . . and then buy quadruple that amount, no matter what your intuition or pocketbook tell you. Otherwise, the job will look meager and hungry and wanting. It was human nature, in fact, survival instinct, to crave abundance, and Geena learned how to create the land-o-plenty look from a master.

It had been an unusually moist spring in northeastern Colorado when Barry asked her to plan the Lincoln Day banquet again. The normally beige buffalo grass that blanketed most of Geena and Barry's ranchette had taken on a subtle, pastel-like green-blue hue. Geena decided to have Gary's Lincoln Day Banquet outdoors, behind the house. She bought three hundred white Chinese lanterns and replaced the lightbulbs so they alternated between red, white, and blue. The floral centerpieces on the table included a profusion of daisies that Geena had set overnight in red- and blue-tinted water so the petals would change color. She painted and cut out from wood one of those vacation-spot, comical photo-op setups you stand behind and poke your face through. This one showed the couple from Grant Wood's *American Gothic*, but the famously somber farmer and wife were smiling and wearing reelect-Roy-Evans-for-Governor buttons, and instead of holding a pitchfork the man was giving a thumbs-up sign. The woman's cameo brooch had been replaced by a pin of a smiling elephant head.

Just minutes before the first guests arrived, Geena, the family's lone registered Democrat, remembered to pull her KERRY 2004 sign from the front yard.

"Mr. Kerry's sleeping in the garage tonight," she told Barry.

"I was hopin' he would."

"Why didn't you ask me to take it down?"

"It's not for me to ask, Geena. Those are your beliefs. . . . Now . . . that said . . . you know Mom would have pulled it out herself."

The day after the banquet, Geena slept until almost noon, and when she went out to get the newspaper she discovered the reason her husband had gotten up so early that morning. A new Kerry sign, this one a third bigger and printed on both sides, was standing where the old one had been.

Geena leaned against the lit fountain in front of the Marriott and looked again at her watch. Zachary had told her he got off at ten, and it was already six after. She imagined him hiding with his friends behind some window, watching and laughing at the horny old movie star who'd asked him to go clubbing.

What the hell are you doing here, Geena?

"Hey!"

Geena turned and saw him jogging across the parking lot. Zachary had replaced his white shirt and burgundy bow tie with a yellow-and-orange tie-dye, swashbuckler-looking top that laced from the neck down to his sternum and had long sleeves that gathered at the wrists in elastic. When he got to her, he was out of breath and his cheeks were flushed. She had not noticed earlier how white and straight his teeth were, how pink and fresh

155

his gums. She wondered how long he'd been out of braces, and then tried to remember how many years Nathan had worn them.

"You ready to go?" Geena asked.

"Yeah, except for one problem. I'm like almost out of gas."

"I can drive."

When they got to the Excursion, Zachary started to open the front door and saw that Safe-T-Man occupied the passenger side. Saying nothing, he shut the door and moved to get into the backseat. Geena laughed.

"You can move him to the back," she said. "You won't hurt his feelings."

"Okay."

"Fasten his seat belt."

"Of course."

Zachary scaled his way onto the passenger side of the SUV's front seat. Geena could tell he wasn't used to getting into such a tall car. After he buckled his seat belt, he surveyed the parking lot with a look of tethered bewilderment and satisfaction, as when a child crawls onto a lifeguard stand and sees the world from a new, adult perspective he's never even imagined.

"What do you drive?" she asked.

"Honda Civic. It's my mom's old car. . . . That one." As they drove across the parking lot, he pointed northward to a metallic gold car covered in crude, hand-painted sentences. Like a stream of water, they rambled on and on until they ran out of surface and then, undaunted and frantic, curved or sharply turned in another direction and continued on their way. A few days earlier, as if she were working a maze in a children's magazine, Geena had visually followed the line of words all the way to the end on the right side of the front bumper.

"I wondered whose that was," she said.

"Yeah, it's mine."

"What does it say?"

"It's *The Waste Land*. . . . T. S. Eliot? . . . My friend and I got crazy one night and painted it."

"Why are some of the words orange?"

"We ran out of paint. It's a long poem."

She had meant for them to go dancing, but that was before Zachary brought out his rubber, Gumby-green, First National Bank of Flagler County coin purse and produced a marijuana cigarette.

"Do you get high?" he asked.

"I've been known to," she said. (Indeed, she had not smoked pot since college, before meeting Barry.) "But you're too young."

He's not that much older than Nathan. . . . Could Nathan have grown facial hair like that?

"Yeah, right."

"No, really. I shouldn't do it."

"Yeah, right."

They parked in the crowded lot of Cypress Estates Golf and Country Club, amidst full-size Buicks and Mercurys and Oldsmobiles, many of which were adorned with some version of the American flag on the rear windows or on the bumpers next to a decal from Triple-A. Zachary liked this spot because the police ignored it. "People who join Triple-A aren't risk-takers," he said. "Cops know that. They don't hassle them."

On this night, the Mel Langely Orchestra was playing for a dance, and as Geena and Zachary passed the cigarette back and forth, they watched smiling retiree couples drift from their cars toward the clubhouse. Geena noted lots of gold lamé and lacy shawls and white belts and white shoes and men's jackets the colors of summer squash and watermelon and creamy mint. A warm breeze was blowing, and occasionally she caught a whiff of men's aftershave and floral perfume. They

158

all seemed so far away, so absolutely un-connected to her, as if they were another species and she were watching them on a *National Geographic* television special.

"Look how they hold hands," Geena said. "That is so sweet. My God, they've been married forever."

Under the effect of the pot, simple ob-servations seemed to morph into weightier truths that deserved more scrutiny: They've . . . been . . . married . . . for-ever. . . . Married . . . forever.

Zachary slumped in his seat, his bare, tanned, size-twelve feet planted on the cushioned dashboard. He had tuned the radio to a classic blues station; Billie Hol-iday was singing "How Deep Is the Ocean."

"Does this feel excellent or what?" he said.

His arm lazily rolled into her line of vi-sion, and Geena accepted the cigarette, now just a third of an inch in length. Zachary had put it in a bobby pin so they wouldn't burn their fingers.

"It's all yours, man," he said. "I'm . . . so . . . . gone." His hand fumbled for the controls on the side of his seat, and at the word "gone" he began to sink backward to a lying position. "I'm like at the dentist's, man. Here I go. Oh, man, I am so cool."

Though she had coughed after the first few draws, Geena had quickly grown accustomed to feeling the prickly smoke in her lungs — the result of living all those years with a chain-smoking mother — and she had been sucking at this cigarette with a hunger that prompted Zachary to chastise her . . . but he said this was all hers now . . . and all of this is mine . . . so all this belongs to me. . . .

She looked over at Zachary. "He is lying down," she now thought . . . or said out loud? . . . "He . . . is . . . lying . . . down . . . lying . . . lying . . . He. Is. Lying. . . ."

So languid everything was . . . so warm. As if measuring up a new, foreign foe, Geena looked at the smoldering cigarette for a moment, and she suddenly was overcome with an inexplicable consuming desire to see this dying roach vaporize into nothingness . . . so she set to task . . . a long draw . . . another . . . and then, finally, in midbreath, a brief burning sensation on her lips, nothing painful really, more like cold ice on a delicate part of the body. She licked the fragments of thin paper from her lips and brought them into her mouth, where she could feel them swell and soften with saliva.

Geena held her breath for as long as she could, trapping the smoke within her, and when she finally opened her eyes and saw the empty bobby pin, she began to cry, saddened now at what she had done. Indeed, something could change form and disappear forever. Here was the proof. Here . . . was . . . the . . . proof.

"Nathan," she said. "Oh, my son . . ."

By the time Geena looked over at Zachary, he was sitting up and staring at her. She dropped her chin so that her red hair fell over her face like a stage curtain pulled early to shield erring actors from any further embarrassment. Geena lay back down on her reclined seat and turned on her side, away from him, facing the door.

"Are you okay?" Zachary asked. He hesitated, then gently laid his hand on her shoulder. "Hey . . . are you okay?"

He waited a few moments, then clumsily crawled over the console between them. There was not much room on the seat, but he lowered himself beside her, squeezing his legs past the steering wheel, until they lay there, like stacked spoons. Zachary put his arm around her. He buried his nose in her hair and whispered into her ear, "It's okay. . . . It's gonna be okay."

Go away . . . this isn't right.

Yet she did not move. It had been months since anyone had touched her like this . . . weeks since she'd even heard her true name spoken. Two nights ago, just before falling asleep, she whispered it again and again after realizing how foreign it had become. She had felt so vaporous and invisible for so long now, more spirit than corporeal being.

Not one person in this world knows where I am.

Zachary pressed himself tighter against Geena, and she became aware of the warmth of his body, felt his heart beating against her ribs, the moistness of his breath on her neck. She quickly flipped to her other side so she could look in his eyes and connect. Zachary appeared puzzled and worried, and she immediately wanted to comfort him. He breathed in to speak, but before words could come Geena leaned into his face and kissed him lightly on the lips, then retreated, and again, then retreated, as if repeatedly testing the temperature of the water with a toe.

As they fell into a long kiss, they rolled as one until Zachary was lying on top of her. Geena slipped her hands beneath his shirt and ran them across the smooth skin of his back.

"Oh!" she exclaimed. "God!"

He reared back so that he could read her face. "What?"

"What is that?"

"What?"

"You've got a pierced tongue."

"Yeah, big deal."

"Uhn!"

It was a sound of surprise and disgust. "Why didn't I notice it before? I am so stupid."

"What's up? I thought you were cool."

She pushed at his shoulders, and he took the cue and rolled off onto the console between the seats. Geena sat up and began to rub her forehead as if it ached. She used a deep sigh to separate herself from the moment and clear her head so she could move onward and away from this situation.

"I'm sorry," she said. "This is stupid. I'm married, for God's sake. I'm a mother."

"Oh . . . like Hollywood's a paragon of morality?"

"I'm not an actress."

He paused. "Then what are you?"

Geena looked outside the window at three seagulls noisily fighting over a French fry in the parking lot. It was a large fry, the width of an adult's pinky finger, and had proven too heavy to carry away and hoard by oneself, so the most aggressive of the three birds was hopping about, stabbing at the air with his beak and squawking, doing his best to exude dominance so the others would give up and go away and he could peck it into more manageable pieces. . . . Or was it a she? How could you tell? How could anyone? That changed everything, didn't it? Suddenly a moment of male avarice was transformed into an act of female survival.

That is all I'm doing: surviving. They owe me this. They owe me more than this.

Every time Geena used Ellis Norton's MasterCard, along with the fleeting wave of guilt came a strange, more lasting and comforting connectedness to the rightful bearer of the card, faceless, yes, but human nonetheless. She would stop all this, she had to, she knew that. . . . sometime soon; but with no demands from anyone and no appointments to keep or goals or to-do lists to handle in this transitional life, there had been a blending of hours and days and weeks and, soon, months.

"What are you?" Zachary asked again.

Geena looked away from the gulls, but instead of looking into his eyes, she stared at the lonely, glowing, round red light of the radio. "I don't know," she answered.

She drove him back to the Marriott and, after watching Zachary's car disappear down Roland Boulevard, crawled into the backseat. As she lay in the crook of Safe-T-Man's arm, Geena thought of Nathan, and she remembered the day he'd come home from a wrestling tournament in Denver, looking sheepish as if he had a secret, then finally breaking into a full-face smile and revealing for his mother the pea-size silver-pearl stud in the center of his pink tongue.

Chapter Twelve

Ellis's dinners at the Banana Leaf Café had not been the same since Logan moved back to Erie, yet that did not keep him from breaking his routine. His reserved table and the fact that there were few restaurants within walking distance of his home on Wilna Street still beckoned him to dine there six nights a week. It used to be five, but he no longer had Logan to drive him to a movie and dinner on Saturdays. For variety's sake, Ellis once tried the sweet-and-sour shrimp at the new Chinese take-out place between Denture Depot and Pascal's Caribbean Grocery on U.S. 41, but suffered a long night of diarrhea and vowed never to return.

When Judith Ziegler invited Ellis to dinner, he asked that they eat at the Banana Leaf. Tom Poenbrook, the owner, took quick notice that the old man was not alone.

"Ellis!" he said. "Aren't you going to introduce me to your girlfriend?"

"This is not my girlfriend, Tom. This is Judith Ziegler."

She offered her hand to Tom. "I work with Ellis at the museum." Ellis noted that Judith said she worked *with* him and did not say she was his boss.

At the table, Judith noticed the ELLIS SITS HERE! sign on the wall but said nothing. "I like this place," she said. "Great local charm."

"Yes. It is a very good restaurant. The service has not been the same since Logan left, but the kitchen is very clean. I have seen the kitchen. One time I even helped Tom wash dishes when someone called in sick."

Ellis ordered his usual grilled tuna salad sandwich with cheddar, tomatoes, and yellow mustard. Judith had the special of beef tips over rice with steamed broccoli and butter. They did not talk much about work, but over the course of the meal each of them cautiously tossed out a few personal details. Judith was surprised at Ellis's computer literacy and that he owned a digital camera. Ellis learned she was a single mother of a ten-year-old daughter, and it bothered him that this very personal detail

167

of his new boss had escaped his radar. Was there a photograph of the child on her desk at work? How could he have missed such a thing?

"Where does she go to school?" he asked.

"Edison Park."

"That is where I went to school!"

"Really?"

"Yes!"

"It's a charming old building. I'm surprised it hasn't been knocked down."

"There is a kapok tree in front. My class planted it when I was in the first grade."

Ellis briefly entertained the thought of showing her the scar on the inside of his left forearm, from the time Billy Vaughan had smashed and rubbed him against the hard, thorny trunk in the eighth grade.

"So you grew up in the neighborhood?" Judith asked.

"I have lived in this neighborhood since I was two. I remember McGregor Boulevard when it was paved with crushed shells. They used to drive cattle down McGregor. That did not please Mina Edison in the least. She thought us all very uncivilized. That is what mother always told me."

"Irene — right?"

Ellis unconsciously raised his eyebrows

and paused. "Yes," he said. "She lived to be a hundred and one."

"And your father?"

"Oh, I do not know when my father died, but I am sure he has because he did not have a healthy lifestyle. My father left us when I was nine. He tried to come back one time and say that mother had kicked him out, but he was only lying."

Judith pushed her fork into a piece of coconut–Key lime cream pie, the Banana Leaf's signature dessert. As always, Ellis declined on the final course. It was his secret to keeping so trim, and he wondered whether he should share this advice with Judith, who, he noticed, was usually snacking on something sweet at work.

"Then we have something in common," she said.

"Oh?"

"I was raised by a single mother. It's a very formative experience, isn't it, Ellis? Do you think there's a reason we're drawn to these august, historical male figures?"

Ellis nodded but did not know what to say. He truly had never given it much thought.

"Do you ever see your father?" he asked.

"Never," she answered. "He has no desire to see me."

She paused and stared blankly at something on the far wall behind Ellis, and, as if she were a daytime soap opera actor reading cue cards offstage, she began to speak again before reconnecting with his inquiring gaze. "He left because my mother refused to get an abortion. They were both actors on Broadway."

"Broadway!" Ellis said.

"They met on the set of *The King and I*."

"How romantic!"

Ellis suddenly realized he had let his guard down and quickly distanced himself again from Judith. She was, after all, the woman who had unnecessarily written him up four times in the past five months, and he wondered again now exactly why she had invited him to dinner.

The knowledge that he possessed the contraband test tube and journal added to Ellis's uneasiness, a stagnant guilt that had puddled in the basement of his subconscious and refused to evaporate. It felt a lot like the time when he was thirty-six and he broke one of his mother's cherished china saucers, then snuck out in the middle of the night to bury the pieces beneath the house. What was it about hiding things — bad things — beneath the house? He'd seen a story on the news about a serial burglar on Pine Island who'd hid his cache — a collection of televisions, iPods, gold jewelry, and thirteen cases of Cakebread chardonnay — beneath his house. And didn't that young man in Milwaukee, the one who mutilated all those teenage boys . . . didn't he bury their body parts beneath the porch? How many secrets were hidden beneath the floors of peoples' homes? What was buried in the dirt beneath Seminole Lodge? Had anyone looked? Is this where Mina's journal had been found — and who had found it, anyway?

Ellis had read just under one-fourth of the journal. It had been written day by day, entry by entry, and that was exactly how he thought it should be experienced. He remembered devouring *The Diary of a Young Girl* by Anne Frank in one night and feeling abandoned for quite some time after that, and he did not want this to happen again. Besides, it made for a more realistic experience to read Mina's thoughts at the pace at which they were written. It was so cinematic! Her inner thoughts slowly unfolded like the plot of one of his favorite, older classic movies that did not pander to impatient, modern-day sensitivities.

"How do you know my mother's name?" he asked.

"You can't have my job, Ellis, and not have heard of your mother. She started Holidazzle."

"That is correct."

"That's what I want to talk to you about. . . . You don't like it much, do you?"

Ellis's back straightened, his jaw tightened.

"Don't worry, neither do I. It's tacky and not suitable for a national historic treasure, at least not in the way they do it. And it's hell on the house."

Ellis remained silent, afraid to say anything. What did she want? What trap had she placed before him? This awful woman! He should never have come to dinner with her in the first place.

"Did you know they pound holes in the walls to hang their little wreaths or whatever it is they hang? Holes in the walls, Ellis . . . in one of Florida's most significant historic homes. And then they fill them with Crest!"

Judith stared silently at Ellis for a few moments. She then leaned across the table and looked in both directions to see if anyone might overhear what she was about to say.

"I want to put the kibosh on Holidazzle."

Ellis shook his head matter-of-factly. "Oh, I am afraid you cannot do that," he said. "It is tradition. The board would never stand for it."

"The board fired Larry and hired me," she said. "The board has changed, Ellis. They're under pressure from *The News-Press* to be a better guardian of this estate. Come on! Are you saying you like Holidazzle? Do you like those ignominious plywood snowmen propped up on the great inventor's porch?"

His plate removed by the waitress, Ellis set his hands on the table, one on top of the other, the upper patting the lower as if to comfort it.

"I think it is vulgar," he finally answered.

"Then help me get it stopped."

"That is not possible."

"You're the monarch that rules over Edisonia, Ellis. People respect you in these matters."

Ellis, who had been examining his cuticles in order to avoid eye contact, looked up at Judith in surprise. He felt the back of his neck and his forehead and cheeks warm with blood.

"Your opinion carries a lot of weight on

these things, Ellis. And what I need from you is to go with me to the city council and try to convince them to let me unplug Holidazzle."

Before Ellis's mother died, she had appointed a successor to lead and organize Holidazzle, Mary Jayne Hartupee, wife of Gene Hartupee, founder and owner of Gene Hartupee Appliance, with eleven locations on Florida's Gulf Coast, stretching from Bradenton in the north to Marco Island in the south. Their son Bruce had been crowned king of Edisonia in 1976. Their daughter Rhonda was named queen two years later.

There was a seemingly arbitrary but respected hierarchy to the decorating of the Edison estate for Holidazzle, and Mary Jayne decided who decorated what; Irene Norton herself had left her in charge before dying. It was said that as many as five hundred women, many belonging to the Lee County Women's Club, worked each year on the project, and each knew where she belonged in the pecking order according to what she was assigned to decorate.

Newcomers began by stringing garland and ribbon on the white picket fence along McGregor Boulevard. From there, if a young woman had toiled on unpopular, demanding committees during the rest of the year, or if someone had died or simply grown too old to decorate a more coveted spot, she would move inward . . . *upward* . . . closer to the heart of the house. Over the years she progressed from fence to yard, from yard to swimming pool. If Mary Jayne liked her, and she was, say, a young bride who'd just moved back home to reintegrate with her old, established Fort Myers family, then she might be able to skip the pool altogether and move right into the kitchen of the guesthouse. Mary Jayne decorated the dining room, the summit of Holidazzle, and she would do so until she died.

Judith had arrived too late to stop this year's Holidazzle, but she did try to minimize further damage to the estate. First, she demanded that the women wear sterile, surgical-blue booties over their feet when inside the house. Second, despite this year's theme being "Christmas in the Caribbean," the women were by no means allowed to sprinkle sand on the historic Persian rugs, as they'd intended.

"I really should not get involved with such matters," Ellis said.

"But you must. You love the home, Ellis.

You love Mr. Edison. If anything's been crystal clear to me, it's that."

Ellis nodded but did not know what to say. What he wanted to do was share some of the details from his secret, nightly walks through the forest of Mina's emotions. Oh, the things that woman would do to try to keep her man happy, and to no avail! She opened all his mail. She special-ordered his Hoffman cigars from Cuba and made certain their New York tailor kept him in suits, lightweight blue or gray in winter and white in summer.

As she watched her husband grow increasingly frustrated by the lack of fish in the river, she had workers extend the dock again and again, fifty feet at a time. ("It is now 1,140 feet long, and I don't suppose it's stopped growing yet," she wrote.) Finally, in desperation, Mina convinced the game-and-fish officials in Washington to restock the Caloosahatchee because her husband was always cheerier after tussling with and landing a substantial tarpon.

In another entry, one that Ellis had re-read time and again, Mina talked of how she spent an afternoon wandering among the shops downtown — his mother was mentioned by name! — searching for a new perfume that might peel her husband from his workbench and into her bed . . . or at least onto the veranda for tea.

On his way to the laboratory, he will take a different path each time, stopping to smell a fragrant gardenia or plumeria. But what of his flower inside, here at this desk?

Ellis knew very well that Thomas Edison was the man entrusted with a weighty task indeed: cracking nature's elusive codes for humanity's progress and, thus, long-term survival on this planet. It made perfect sense that he would focus so intently on his work. But was this reason enough to be so blind to the feelings of his wife? How could he not notice the loneliness and anguish of the mother of his children?

Ellis wished he could have been the inventor's personal assistant. He would have alerted him to her sadness, to her fears that her husband had strayed and found another lover. He would have tried to reassure her. He would have bought a monogrammed, embroidered handkerchief, wrapped it in pink tissue paper with a sprig of orange blossoms tied into the bow, and set it on her secretary while she was gardening outside. Other little surprises would follow — a bluebird's feather, perhaps, or the season's first kapok blossom — all left without a note so that she could fool herself into thinking they were gifts from her husband. Mr. Edison would deny it, of course, in his usual blustery manner, but she would think he was fooling, and it would have emboldened her enough to punch her way into his hazy, private atmosphere and connect with him in some way, a hand on the arm, or, even better, a lip to lip. Ellis knew from the movies that estranged lovers did not reach out if they feared rejection. (The most recent example he could remember was that handsome young man in love with Reese Witherspoon in *Sweet Home Alabama*.) It was safer to stand alone with dignity intact. If a woman didn't test the waters, she could always fool herself into thinking that things were all right, that her man still loved her even if he did not.

After dinner and a quick visit to Eckerd's to pick up Ellis's blood-pressure medicine and some new Dr. Scholl's Odor Destroyer pads for his work sneakers, Judith dropped him off at home. It was a lovely evening with no humidity and a slight breeze sweeping off the river, causing the palm fronds to rustle and sway. A flock of wild green parrots, off feeding on mangoes all day long, squawked overhead as they returned to their nests in the live oaks on Shadow Lane.

In the past Ellis had always used this time after dinner to futz around in the Edison Room, dusting and rearranging his memorabilia. Lately, however, he'd reserved this time for Mina. He went inside to retrieve the journal from its current hiding place in an empty box of Tide on the shelf over the washing machine, then came outside to sit on the metal glider on the porch.

Ellis hoped all afternoon that today's entry would include more of Mina's musings on Thomas Edison's first wife, Mary, and their publicly problematic marriage.

It was Mary Stilwell who brought the inventor to Florida for the first time. Shortly after marrying Thomas she became a sickly woman, diagnosed with rheumatism and dyspepsia. Doctors suggested that she, Thomas, and their two children spend their winters outside of Jacksonville. Mary was thrilled with the idea; perhaps now, with Thomas away from his laboratory in Menlo Park, they could finally spend some time together and she could get well.

Yet he would leave them in Florida time and again, drawn to his unfinished work in New Jersey, and at the age of twenty-nine Mary died. It was always unclear to Mina just what it was that killed her. Could someone actually succumb to minor digestive problems and sore muscles? Or was it something more systemic than that . . . a breakdown of spirit hastened by loneliness and a constant feeling of doubting one's worth to one's husband?

Perhaps it is unfair to doubt his love, but he did, after all, need a new mother for his children, and quickly. Who better to marry than the daughter of a fellow inventor, someone who understands an inventor's restless nature and is tolerant of his prolonged emotional and physical absence?

Did he seek me out as he would seek a chemical or plant for one of his experiments? Was I a convenient ingredient?

How common it is for women to marry men who do not suit them! How often we fall in love and marry simply because a man has made us feel beautiful and desirable.

Sitting on his porch, Ellis read the

journal entry for that day, a disappointing explanation of a problem Mina was having with Queenie, the cook, who was using too much salt on Thomas's lamb. Ellis was surprised at how Mina could obsess over the most insignificant matters. Did the peeling paint on the arbor entrance to the Edisons' pier truly deserve a half page of consternation?

From inside the front cover of the journal, Ellis pulled a photograph of Mina he'd downloaded from the Internet. It had taken him an entire evening to find an image of her from the era in which these thoughts were written. Her hair was pulled up in a chignon, as it was in nearly every picture at every age. Ellis wondered what it would look like down around her shoulders. He concentrated on her lips and tried to imagine her speaking.

More than once, Larry Livengood had said that the real occupant of Edison's "doghouse" bedroom should have been Mina. Larry considered her strident in an unladylike way and less than beautiful, with the overly bushy eyebrows of a Mediterranean farm woman, a slight overbite, and a figure beyond Rubenesque.

Perhaps that was too critical a review, Ellis thought now. Admittedly, Mina was no Claudette Colbert or Elizabeth Taylor, but she did have large, expressive eyes — were they brown? — like those of a heroine in one of the newer Disney movies. All she needed was to lose a few pounds.

Suddenly Ellis's attention was drawn by a growing sound from down the street, the amplified mosquito whine of one of the motorized, wheeled toys that belonged to those awful boys in the new house down on the river.

All over Fort Myers, new-money families from the North were buying the quaint but expensive riverfront homes, razing them, and building immense, faux-Mediterranean polymer-stucco palaces with electric gates that cut off the river views from all who lived on the street.

Yet the worst part of this reality was that most of these homes seemed to house overindulged children who, if older, tore down the street in their behemoth chrome-detailed trucks or, if younger, rode on motorized scooters that were a menace to all. The new boys at the end of Wilna, ten and eleven years old, both blond-haired and overweight, had flattened the plumbago around Ellis's mailbox. They had run over the Thompsons' cat and left him twitching in pain on the asphalt. Three neighbors, including Ellis, never received their new Sprint Yellow Pages because they'd been piled on Ellis's sidewalk, soaked with lighter fluid, and set afire.

Ellis had spoken with the mother, who had long red fingernails and rarely drove her black Hummer without talking on the cell phone at the same time. She said boys will be boys and that he should mind his own business.

He set the journal on the glider, walked out to the sidewalk, and stood there, watching the boys and their scooters grow larger and louder. As they approached his house, Ellis, internally grimacing at the noise, held up his hand in the manner of a crosswalk guard. The boys, not accustomed to authoritative obstruction, stopped and looked at each other in surprise. The older one laughed.

"Yeah?" he asked. "What do you want, old man?"

Ellis set his hands on his hips. "You boys are going to hurt someone with those scooters," he said. "Did you know they are actually against the law? I called city hall to ask."

"My dad says we can ride them."

"Well, your father is wrong. I will need to speak with him."

"We got a right to ride these scooters."

"You do not have a right to terrorize the neighborhood, and that is what you are doing. Look at mother's plumbago. You have ruined it."

"You're an asshole," said the other boy.

Ellis, who had bent down to better hear them, straightened up.

"And you need to learn how to speak with respect to adults, young man. If you do not stop riding those scooters and those other four-wheeled contraptions on this street, I will be forced to call the police."

"You call the police and we'll get you, you old faggot."

"Young man!"

"Yeah, you old fag."

The older boy started up his scooter, the younger followed his lead.

"You boys come back here!" Ellis yelled over the whining of the engines. Without looking back, the older boy thrust his arm in the air, flipping Ellis the bird.

Disgusted, Ellis swatted at the white-blue cloud of exhaust left in their wake. His hands shook and his jaw trembled. Why did he let these boys upset him so? Regina Shawn, his neighbor, who was a psychology professor at Edison Community College, had told him that if he simply

184

ignored them they would let him be. "You've seemed irritable lately, Ellis," she'd said. "Is something bothering you?"

"Oh, no, I am fine," he had answered.

Yet Regina had been watching him lately from the kitchen window, and as he went about his simple life, pulling the mail from his box at the curb or sweeping off the driveway beneath the carport, the old man appeared to be increasingly preoccupied — distressed, even — about something. He wore a new veil of resigned sadness over him, as if he knew he was losing something or someone very dear, and there was nothing he could do to save it.

Chapter Thirteen

Sublette, Colorado, straddled U.S. Interstate 70, a midcontinent concrete river running east to west through the desertlike landscape, providing a twenty-four-hour flow of restless North American humanity through town. Occasionally there floated by a carcinogenic, desperate personality who would come ashore and take advantage of his anonymity and the locals' rural, trusting nature and commit some awful act to make a fast buck or satisfy a desire. Kidnapping was unlikely but possible.

For example, just after the Sublette-Holyoke football game, a thin, mustachioed man driving a red Camaro with Illinois tags tried to coax, then pull, one of the Zimbelman girls into his car outside of Arby's, and if it weren't for the can of Mace her father had bought and made her carry in her purse, townspeople said, she very well might have shared the same fate as Geena Pangborn.

As if scripted by Geena herself, this incident occurred just one week after her mysterious disappearance, which quashed most of the more sordid rumors buzzing through town, such as one that said the grieving, wealthy mother had been found dead in her SUV on a gravel road south of town near the feedlot, a gun in her hand, a bullet in her brain, and a suicide note lying on the passenger seat. (A different version included a single red rose accompanying the suicide note.) It was rumored that the Pangborn family, related by marriage to the Kit Carson County sheriff, covered it up to avoid implication in her death.

Another rumor posited that Dot Pangborn, who made no secret of her disenchantment with her daughter-in-law from the day she married her son, paid Geena *fill-in-the-blank-with-a-figure-higher-than-one-million dollars* to leave Sublette and never return.

Yet a third story had Geena withdrawing most of the family's fortune from the First National Bank of Sublette, leaving them nearly destitute. This one surfaced shortly after one of the Pangborn granddaughter's debit cards was mistakenly rejected at Pizza Hut and duly noted by her two surprised friends.

Then came Britany Zimbelman's near-abduction, and the rumors vanished as quickly as Geena had. Gossip once laden with judgment took on a tone of paranoia. Parents suddenly forbade their teenagers to walk from the high school, across the wheat field, to get lunch at McDonald's. The Sublette Police Department quickly organized a Good Stranger/Bad Stranger seminar for the kids at Sublette Elementary School and gave them all red plastic whistles on key chains to attach to their backpacks.

It was rumored that Geena was last seen ordering a Beef 'n Cheddar sandwich and Diet Coke at the Arby's drive-through, and townspeople unconsciously began to avoid the restaurant, forcing the Eichert family to lay off three of their part-time high school employees.

Most people left Barry Pangborn alone because they weren't sure what to say to him. Silence meant you didn't care. Expressing condolences was akin to saying you had no hope, that you took his wife for dead. Most people opted for a vague statement of sympathy, using words like "misfortune" and "this trying time," sounding as if Barry had just lost his job or one of his brothers had been arrested for domestic violence.

The week after Geena left, Lorraine Stahlecker, the head receptionist in the Sublette office of Centennial Realty, came forward and told Barry about the phone conversation she'd overheard between Dot and Geena, the one in which she'd cautioned her daughter-in-law about getting a new dog because it might die in her care, as did her son.

Upon hearing the news, Barry bolted from the office and climbed into his copper-colored Dodge Ram truck. City crews had just seal-coated the street the day before, spraying down a layer of steaming asphalt followed with a heavy dusting of gravel and sand, to be smooshed down into the black goo and strengthened by passing tires so that it might not crack and grow into potholes quite so quickly during the spring thaws. It was always easy to tell when the city was seal-coating streets by the number of skinned knees on kids who had wiped out on their bicycles in the gravel-and-sand mixture. Barry, who still had a scar on his left elbow from a particularly bad wreck when he was twelve, spun out in the gravel in his Ram, shooting pebbles a good twenty feet in his wake.

They rained upon the windshield of his brother Gary's Durango, making clicking sounds upon impact, bouncing off, arcing downward, and falling back to the ground.

He found his mother at the Methodist church. She was helping to decorate it for a good friend's fortieth wedding anniversary. Two months earlier Dot had volunteered, expecting to send Geena and her creative flair.

"Mom!"

Barry saw light emanating from the stairway to the basement and made his way across the sanctuary, the burgundy carpet in the aisles muffling the sound of his black Nocona boots.

"Mom!"

"We're down here," said a voice that was not his mother's.

In the community room, Dot was doing her best to salvage a crumpled gold-colored bow she'd tried to fashion around the back of a folding chair.

"I need to talk to you."

"Can't it wait, Barry? I'm very busy."

"No. It can't wait."

Dot looked up at her son with surprise that soon melted into curiosity. This man, her normally unexcitable son, was rapidly running his tongue, back and forth, across the surface of his two front teeth. And his hands! His fingers were fluttering nervously like the little vinyl tassels the kids used to have on the ends of their bicycle handlebars.

The second-youngest of the five Pangborn boys, Barry had always been the physically strongest but also the most reticent, the most patient and nonconfrontational. This was the only son who did as he was told and rarely asked why. This was the son who, though he could carry his biggest brother in a bear-hug hold from the barn to the back door (a good twenty-five yards), also got his plastic eggs stolen every Easter by his brothers after the hunt in the back meadow. If Dot needed something done, she went to Barry. Barry always said yes.

"I'll be right back, Louise," she said.

He took her into the cloakroom, shut the door, and flipped on the fluorescent lights. A buzz filled the quiet, confined space. In a corner lay a pile of artificial Christmas wreaths, piled up like car tires, and a cardboard box of angels' halos made from bent wire hangers covered in silver garland.

"Why in the hell did you tell my wife that she would kill a puppy dog?"

191

"Barry! Please! Watch your tone with me."

"Well, did you?"

Silent, Dot looked away from her son, toward the front of the small room. What was that piece of paper taped onto the back of the door? A schedule of some sort? Whose names could she read from this far away? Snyder . . . Walkinshaw . . .

"Jesus, Mom! I don't know too many people who would knock down a grieving mother like that. What the hell were you thinking?"

"I will not have you talk like that in a church, Barry Allen Pangborn."

"Oh, and a helluva lot of good Jesus has done me this past year." He impulsively stomped his foot on the brown carpeting. "Shit!"

The heavy grief accumulating inside him like sand for the past two weeks had been blown away, or, at the very least, rearranged by winds of anger, and it was a welcome distraction. Barry stepped away from his mother and ran a hand through his thick black hair.

"Barry! Get ahold of yourself! You're acting like a child. What would your father say?"

"So you're denying it."

"Of course I'm denying it. Who would accuse me of doing such a thing?"

"So you're lying."

"I am not! What has gotten into you?"

Barry left his mother and slowly ascended the stairs back into the sanctuary, which was dark except for the sunshine pushing its way through the stained-glass windows. He had not been to church since Nathan's funeral nine months ago, but as he walked back to the entrance, he unconsciously found his favored spot and dropped into the smooth, wooden pew. He gave a labored sigh then let his chin drop to his chest and closed his eyes.

I hate her. . . . I wish it was she who had run away.

He still held on to the slim but significant hope that his wife might be alive and mad as hell and hiding somewhere to teach them all a lesson. It was just like Geena to overreact, especially when it came to dealing with his parents. God, how they locked horns, and had from the very beginning. It was Brit and Dot who thought their middle son should marry Adrienne Plautz, and Barry knew why. Like all his siblings' wives, she was meek, a pleaser, as acquiescent and airy as a piece of wadded-up pink tissue paper, and blond to boot.

And then came Geena, a blonde, yes, but she dyed her hair at least twice a year, everything from platinum to flame red to jet black. And though Dot was a past president of the Kit Carson County Garden Club, Geena refused to water her yard in the summer because she said it was a waste of increasingly precious aquifer water, and she had planted native desert cacti instead of thirsty perennials.

Barry recalled the Christmas — How old was Nathan? Twelve? Eleven? — when Brit ignored Geena's explicit wish not to buy her son a gun. And when Nathan pulled the green wrapping paper from his new Remington 16-gauge "Youth version" shotgun with gold-plated trigger, Geena, sitting on the floor in a lotus position, calmly unfolded her legs, stood up, and disappeared into the kitchen. As she listened to the men in the room admiring the grain of the rifle's walnut stock, she reached high on a shelf in the pantry and pulled down a Rubbermaid container of spray paints. Geena scanned them over — "Ah, yes, perfect choice!" — returned to the family room with the can in her hand, grabbed the shotgun from her husband, held it at arm's length, and, straining from the weight of it, proceeded to spray the entire gun the same glossy hot pink she'd last used for Noreen Montoya's baby shower centerpiece.

"Jesus, Geena!" Brit yelled. "What the hell are you doing?"

Grunting, he stood up to stop her, but Geena retreated, walking backward, toward the safety of the kitchen, all the while keeping her finger depressed on the nozzle as she turned the barrel in her hands so as not to miss a spot.

"You're ruining that gun, Geena!"

The Pangborn grandchildren looked at each other with wide eyes. The sisters-in-law shook their heads. Of course Geena was painting the gun, of course she was.

Suddenly the snakelike hissing of the spraying stopped. The room was silent.

"There!" Geena said. She set the paint can on a coffee table that she'd fashioned from a circle of beveled glass atop an antique wagon wheel they'd unearthed down by the dry creek. "It's lovely. Now . . . which of you manly men would like to go hunting? You'll look fabulous."

Sitting in the church pew in the dim sanctuary, Barry realized now that this very stubbornness and independence that had sparked so many fires in his marriage over the years were also the very traits that drew him to her in the first place. Perhaps he unconsciously had allied himself with a woman who relished battle and would help defend, even enhance, the parts of his personality that he liked and seemed to have lost.

Chapter Fourteen

The trip across Alligator Alley took longer than Geena expected. Distractions were many. She had never been to south Florida — Arizona was the Pangborn family's winter vacation venue of choice — and this landscape intrigued her like no other had: misty table-flat swampland filled with tall grasses of different hues of green and yellow, and random clumps of sabal palms that looked like the truffula trees from Dr. Seuss's *The Lorax.*

"It's a great story," she explained to Safe-T-Man, her hands on the steering wheel of the Excursion. "Nathan loved it. It goes like this: 'I am the Lorax, I speak for the trees, which you seem to be chopping as fast as you please.' "

It had been a cold night in the Everglades, and around noon the alligators emerged by the thousands from their underwater burrows. After surfacing like small submarines, they crawled up on the muddy banks of the man-made drainage ditches along the interstate and lay there, en masse, their thick skins absorbing the warmth of the sun.

Geena, who had stopped to look three times in forty-some miles, was glad she'd bought a pair of high-power Nikon field glasses at a shop in Coral Gables. It was the details of these creatures that most interested her. Though menacing, the line of their mouths actually turned upward at the very last inch, hinting of a subtle, *Mona Lisa* smile. She admired their brown-green skin, the color of algae, which produced perfect camouflage for carnivorous life in an inland body of water. Their backs of pointed bumps reminded Geena of the tiny mountain ranges on a topographic map in a classroom.

At the western end of Alligator Alley, some distance before the road turned northward, at Naples, and became the less exotic-sounding I-75 once again, Geena saw an exit for Everglades City. Intrigued by the name, she turned off and headed toward the old fishing village.

She pulled into the crushed-shell parking lot of the Everglades City Rod & Gun Club and went inside and took a seat at the immense, antique wooden bar, which was devoid of customers. On the walls were old, framed black-and-white photos of past patrons, including Mamie and Ike Eisenhower, Teddy Roosevelt, Ernest Hemingway, Thomas Edison. The bartender was an overly tanned, middle-aged man, shaved bald with sun spots freckling his scalp and a small gold hoop earring in his left ear. Even with his belly, he reminded Geena of Mr. Clean without the smile.

"What kind of fish is that?" Geena asked, pointing to a mounted monster that was as long as her Excursion was wide.

"Tarpon," he answered.

"God, it's huge."

"Game fish. Good fightin'. We've got the best tarpon fishin' in the world here. Especially up in Boca Grande Pass."

Geena shook her head.

"Up past Fort Myers."

"How far am I from Fort Myers?" she asked.

"Forty-five miles. Fifty, maybe."

"What's it like?"

He gave her a quizzical look. "What do you mean?"

"Fort Myers. . . . I've never been to Fort Myers."

Before heading west across the swampy peninsula, Geena had had trouble filling her days, having grown bored with massages and pedicures and matinee movies and walks on the beach. She loved to shop, but there was no one to praise and validate a fabulous find, and she missed buying surprises for the people in her life — even Barry.

She began to purchase items of fashion for Safe-T-Man: a bottle of Contradictions cologne by Calvin Klein, which she dabbed on the collar of his two new shirts, one of them a long-sleeve, minifloral-pattern Dolce & Gabbana that would have looked fabulous on Nathan, though Barry would have never let him out of the house with it on. At a yard sale somewhere in suburban Miami she'd bought a 1970s, brown yarn-and-suede zipper jacket with a patch-covered hole. The patch featured snowcapped brown mountains, blue sky, and the words LIONS CLUB — BUTTE, MONTANA. Thinking his baseball cap too conventional — his personality had evolved since Tulsa, and he was more boy-friend now than protector — Geena bought him a leather Greek fisherman's cap.

And he no longer spent his evenings in

the car. Geena now brought Safe-T-Man into the hotel rooms with her. She enjoyed seeing what each maid would do with him when she left for the day.

Some preferred to set Safe-T-Man on the chair, and one even took off his shoes, crossed his legs, and set the TV clicker in his hand. Another laid him on the bed and, as if he were sleeping, tented his face with Geena's *Better Homes and Gardens*. At the Biltmore in Coral Gables, he was plopped on the toilet with his pants down around his ankles. This latter position actually bothered Geena at first. She felt as if she'd been violated, the victim of a crime. That was when she noticed that someone along the way had stolen the new Calvin Klein briefs she'd bought for him at the outlet mall outside Brunswick, Georgia.

Geena had intended to stay longer in Miami. She loved the Cuban culture, especially the little cups of thick, corn-syrup-sweet *café Cubano* and the tropical-colored, Spandex clothing and the buildings the hues of the chalky mints found at restaurant cash registers. Yet two days before her trip across Alligator Alley she decided to run a Google search on Ellis, and this changed her plans. She found but one item, a photograph from *Travel + Leisure* of Ellis Norton pointing to a stand of bamboo at the Thomas Edison Winter Estate. It said he had been a tour guide there for fifty-three years! If there were just one Ellis Norton in Fort Myers, Florida, he was a thin, old man with excellent posture. He tended to pull his pants up a little too high in that manner that old men do, as if afraid their trousers will follow their tired skin in its irreversible, glacier-slow drift south. He was wearing what she thought was a uniform, a sky blue polo shirt with the museum's insignia, and long khaki, elastic-waist shorts with immaculate white tennis shoes and black support hose pulled up all the way to the knees like a Catholic schoolgirl.

And then, noting the tired-looking beige, straw hat, she wondered why he did not buy a new one . . . unless . . . unless . . . and suddenly this thought dropped into her consciousness like a ripe apple falling from a tree and into an empty metal pail . . . unless he could not afford a new hat.

Oh . . . my . . . God!

It occurred to Geena now for the first time that she might have taken this poor man's only credit card, and she pictured him walking out to his mailbox every day and opening the little metal door in hopes that it had finally arrived. She imagined him surviving on eighty-nine-cent boxes of Kraft macaroni and cheese as she'd done in college.

He's so thin!

If no wife, did he have children to look after him? Wouldn't they have popped up on Google when she typed in *Norton* and *Fort Myers?* Who was the Norton behind Norton's Suncoast Dry Cleaning? Who was Lacey Norton, CPA, on Six-Mile Cypress Parkway? Surely this man wasn't alone in this world. How many people were unequivocally, irreversibly alone?

Seeing Ellis had had the effect of a strong pinch on a sleepwalker's arm: Though the physical body notes the pain and it reacts by flinching and turning in a new direction, the pinch is not enough to fully waken the person, pulling her from that leaden, fuzzy world and back into clarity and concreteness.

"Where are you from?" asked the bartender. "I can't place your accent."

"San Antonio," Geena answered.

"Doesn't sound like Texas to me."

"Then you must not know south Texas very well."

From a former patron's abandoned glass

near her on the bar, Geena fished out two half-melted ice cubes and held them on the lids of her closed eyes. The bartender looked at her curiously and continued slicing lemons. "So you're on your way to Fort Myers," he said.

"Yes."

"Vacation?"

"No," she answered, ice cubes intact. "Business."

Geena had no definitive plans for Fort Myers and Ellis Norton, yet for days now her destination had seemed inevitable. Reason had been elusive these past few months — Why would God let such a gifted young man die the way he did? — so she had let go and allowed the simpler laws of physics to take over.

Down, down, she'd drifted. It made such perfect sense to be here right now, at the bottom of the continent, an object that has finally rolled to a stop with no place else to go.

"I'm very tired," Geena said. "I'm very hungry. Please feed me something."

Chapter Fifteen

The Asplundh Tree Expert Company truck pulled into the empty parking lot of the Edison estate just as the morning sun was creeping high enough to infuse the warm, misty air with a hint of pastel pink. Having heard the rumbling of the large diesel engine, Judith Ziegler left her desk and was outside to meet the orange truck as it crept to a stop, its brakes squeaking.

Wearing a red silk Dana Buchman suit with mandarin collar, Judith walked over to the passenger-side door and swatted it twice — *bang, bang* — as if it were an errant elephant she wanted to get moving on its way. After a moment, the door tentatively swung open. Judith bent down to take off her black sandals, then reached up, grabbed the parenthesis-shaped steel handle along the door frame with one hand, and, much to the surprise of the young driver and his companion, pulled herself into the cab and slammed the immense door a little harder than was necessary.

"Good morning, gentlemen," she said, and then, noting that the driver was Hispanic, "Buenos dias. Let me show you what we need to do." She set her sandals in her lap and pointed toward an opening between a eucalyptus tree and the caretaker's cottage. "That way. *Mucho trabajo.* Much work. *Rápido, por favor.*"

Judith had a short window of opportunity here. A Fort Myers city ordinance prohibited any engine-driven lawn-taming device from being fired up before 7:00 a.m., but the first of her docents would start arriving at 7:45.

The truck moved slowly through the densely landscaped grounds, the branches of banyan and poinciana and mango trees scraping along its sides.

The Edisons' white, two-story Seminole Lodge, with a roof of red-cedar shingles and a wraparound veranda populated by wicker furniture, hid in the middle of fourteen acres that Thomas Edison liked to call "my jungle," and it was not an overstatement. Like most newcomer snowbirds to Florida, the inventor found himself buying and planting a variety of tropical flora simply because he was so excited that something as lovely as a hibiscus blossom could thrive in his new home and not succumb to frost.

By the time he bought the land in 1885, the man was rich, and he spared no expense in creating a botanical garden unparalleled in Florida. He sent five men around the world to collect flowers and trees and shrubs that would thrive here. There was a twenty-foot-square bed of banana trees; one thousand pineapple plants from Key Largo; pecan trees from Jacksonville; royal palms from Cuba; Indian rubber trees, pomegranates, lychees, and coconuts and tamarind and sugarcane, and more than eighteen hundred varieties of flowers. He and Mina designed grassy alleys, created by planting twin lines of mango trees and royal palms and Australian pines, some of which ran the entire length of the property and were broken up only by lovely stone fountains.

Yet over time, while the grounds did not fall into disarray, they certainly had strayed from their roots. Under Larry Livengood's tutelage, any friend who had a plant on the lanai that outgrew its pot could take it to the Edison estate and transplant it somewhere on the grounds. Cub Scout troops donated and planted orange and grapefruit trees. Mother-in-law tongue plants had freely spread until they looked like waist-high walls of green fire. Women's clubs noted the lack of roses and quickly filled the void, though, because there really wasn't enough direct sunlight, they always appeared leggy, with few flowers.

Judith had found the original landscape blueprints rolled up and standing in the dust behind a filing cabinet. Armed with grants from the Sierra Club and the Nature Conservancy, she set about restoring the grounds to their original condition. This meant, unfortunately, that the very-popular, so-called sausage tree must go.

"That's the one," Judith said. "Come on. We've got to hurry."

Within five minutes one of the men was ascending in the cherry-picker. Accompanied by the strained whine of a chain saw, limb after limb of the tree began to fall to the grass below as if they were corpulent geese being shot down from the sky.

Native to Kenya, *Kigelia pinnata* is indeed a remarkable tree. Africans used it to treat psoriasis and eczema, syphilis and skin cancer. It was used to cure ringworm, tapeworm, and pneumonia. Not surprisingly, perhaps due to the suggestive shape of the fruit, it was also considered an aph-rodisiac.

But Judith knew that the reason her do-cents so adored the tree was that it always amused the tourists, who would giggle and ooh at the brown-gray fruits hanging from the limbs like new, uncut rolls of bologna, some of them nearly a full meter long. Even the dullest of docents could use this tree to squeeze a smile from the most jaded visitor. Marvin Reinhold, a four-year docent from Poughkeepsie, New York, would say, "Now, this tree was planted by a man who was Thomas Edison's good friend . . . his name was Oscar . . . [pause of three seconds] . . . Oscar Mayer."

But according to the horticulture blue-prints, it was an impostor, a latecomer, a party-crasher, and though it provided comic relief aplenty, the sausage tree had no historical significance whatsoever. It had to go.

Frank McComer, Marvin Reinhold, and Joe Dessem were the first docents on the scene, and though Judith had told them what happened and why and then returned to her office, they could not stop watching the Asplundh crew of three. One ran the stump-grinder, and as the circular blade noisily whittled away at the obstinate round hunk of wood in the ground, the other two men, in protective goggles, using a rake and broom, set about cleaning up the sawdust that blanketed the grass like beige snow.

"Can you believe she did that?" Marvin said. "How does she get away with these things?"

"I heard she's sleeping with the mayor," said Joe.

"Nah," added Frank. "Who'd take *her* to bed? Would you?"

"That's what I heard. I'm just telling you what I heard."

"I can't believe she'd cut down that sausage tree. Everyone loved that sausage tree."

"Good morning, gentlemen."

It was Ellis, who had come from behind. The men turned to meet him. And though all three had noted his increasingly bristly nature these past few weeks and tried to avoid him, this morning's happenings caused them to reach out in solidarity.

"Ellis!" Marvin said. "Look at this mess." He gestured to the now-sunny spot before them. "Can you believe this?"

Just weeks ago Ellis would have thrown himself into their camp . . . would have burst unannounced into Judith Ziegler's

office and demanded an explanation . . .
would have probably called the mayor's office and his friend, Stefanie Maddox, at
Eyewitness NewsCenter 4. Yet that sausage tree did not belong there — Ellis
knew that now.

In addition to the lovely, heartbreaking
divulgements of loneliness and longing in
Mina's journal, she had also included details of another love, the plants of Seminole
Lodge. Mina appeared to know not only
the location of every shrub, tree, and
flower on the grounds but also their Latin
names and countries of origin. Ellis was intrigued at how much ink and verbiage she
could devote to describing one of her beloved orchids or bromeliads. It reminded
him of Katharine Hepburn's character in
The Glass Menagerie and her unnatural
obsession and love for her collection of
delicate hand-blown animals.

It is my opinion that the true beauty
of orchids comes not in their exquisite
petals, but in their implied expressions, and it is most often an expression of sadness or, at the very best,
melancholy. While some say their centers are reminiscent of female
anatomy, I see them more as open

211

mouths with somewhat pouting lips. Each sings a song that falls somewhere between mild discomfort and debilitating anguish.

The Green Swan orchid (Cycnoches chlorichilon) on the McGregor-side porch has the most tragic expression of any orchid I have seen. It is nothing short of a grieving mother as she wails out loud at the scene of a sudden, unexpected death of her only child. So sad is this orchid that I cannot help but feel uplifted because even in my darkest hour I have not felt such grief.

So intrigued was Ellis with these humanlike details of plants that he began researching them in the new community archive room that Judith Ziegler had set up in an old bungalow adjacent to Seminole Lodge.

Reading from a handful of books on tropical flora, Ellis quickly learned that most orchids did, in fact, appear to be moping. He wasn't so sure about the crying-mouth bit, but most orchids, though cheery in color, did have lines that subtly drooped downward, reminding him of a sad clown's face.

He also soon realized he'd been giving

short shrift to the important horticultural assets of the Edison estate. Up to this point, the only detail of plant life that Ellis had routinely shared in his tours involved the banyan tree outside the museum. And even this information, he realized now, was inaccurate, just as Judith had tried to tell him.

The tree had been given to Edison by his good friend Harvey Firestone, who brought it with him from India as a host gift. In Ellis's tours, he said it was the largest banyan tree in the entire world.

"Can you prove it's the largest, Ellis?" Judith had asked.

"Can you prove otherwise?" he countered.

That afternoon, Judith found Ellis as he was drinking his water on the bench outside the ticket booth.

"It's in India," she said. "Calcutta . . . here." Judith handed him a color photograph she'd downloaded and printed in her office. "Look," she said. "It's the size of Manhattan."

Ellis looked at the picture and scrunched his eyebrows in doubt.

"Is this from the Internet?" he asked. "You cannot believe everything you see on the Internet, you know."

They were fascinating, these trees! Why had he never taken the time to understand them before? Ellis knew the banyan was called the "walking tree" because it grew so fast, but he did not understand how. He did not realize that, if left untrimmed, a banyan can advance across the landscape, consuming city block after city block after city block, like the blob in the old science fiction movie that starred Steve McQueen. New strands of roots sprout from the outer, far-reaching limbs, then dangle and grow downward like loose ropes until they reach the ground and root themselves, where they wait patiently to be absorbed in the ever-expanding trunk.

To win doubtful docents' loyalty as she removed intruding shrubs in her quest for historical accuracy, Judith had posted the yellowed landscape blueprints on the bulletin board in the employee lounge. Ellis studied these and then would search out specific trees and bushes on his walks around the grounds. Of course, most of Mina's treasured orchids were long gone, but whenever Ellis came upon one in an elbow or cranny of a tree, he took a picture of it with his digital camera and surfed the Web that night until he identified it. If it was a variety mentioned in the secret journal, he took great joy in knowing that it might be the very plant that had comforted this lonely inventor's wife in those years long since gone.

One day Ellis walked into Judith's office and handed her an envelope.

"This is for you, madame."

She looked at him, perplexed, and realized he would not be smiling if this were a letter of resignation. Judith tore open the envelope and unfolded a color photograph of a purple-and-white-spotted orchid.

"You have missed something," Ellis said.

"What do you mean, Ellis?" she asked.

"This is a photograph of *Odontioda Star Trek 'Harlequin.'*" He said it slowly, as if he were repeating a phrase from a foreign language phrase book.

"That's the plant's name?"

"Yes. I found it on a bough of one of the oaks. Near the pool. In your zeal to eradicate everything that is not historic, you missed this one."

"You've lost me, Ellis."

"It is a modern-day hybrid. Its name is Star Trek. *Star Trek* did not air until the 1960s. So you see, this plant did not exist when Mina was alive."

With this newfound knowledge of the landscaping of Seminole Lodge, Ellis could not get upset by the butchering of the sausage tree when confronted by his fellow docents that morning.

"The Edisons did not plant this tree," Ellis told the trio of men. "Larry did. He brought it back from Africa when he went on safari."

"Doesn't matter," Marvin said. "It was a great tree."

"She's just too much of a bitch," Joe said. "We've gotta get her out of here . . . somehow."

"I hate those new damned time cards," said Frank. "It's like I never left General Electric. I didn't retire to punch a clock again."

Ellis did not like the time clock, either, and in a quiet rebellion he had been printing each day's entry in the exact same spot on the card, creating a small, navy blue blur of superimposed and therefore indecipherable numbers. Curiously, no one had said anything about it.

Chapter Sixteen

"Please, please, everyone, come into the shade of this benevolent gumbo-limbo. I want to show you something."

Ellis's group of fourteen visitors looked at each other with curiosity but obeyed and followed him off the sidewalk and into the grass — the new signs clearly stated PLEASE REMAIN ON SIDEWALK — whispering and giggling like schoolchildren on a field trip who have just been granted permission to break the rules.

"I promised you a surprise at the very beginning of the tour, and I always deliver on my promises."

He looked upward and pointed to something high in the canopy of the tree. "Up there, where that large limb on the left runs out over the porch. Do you see those small yellow flowers in the elbow? There are four of them, almost the color of daffodils."

Several of the tourists brought their hands to their foreheads as visors, squinting as they looked upward, but most of them soon began to frown and shake their heads. Indeed, the small orchids were a good twenty feet up in the tree. If it were not for Ellis's new pair of field glasses, he would have missed them himself just four days earlier.

From his back pocket Ellis pulled a photograph of the yellow *cattleya,* taken by Mike Rathbun, the landscape maintenance man. Ellis had coaxed him into taking his camera up in the cherry-picker with the promise of giving him four of his employee passes to the museum. (Judith Ziegler had cut in half the number of free passes allotted to employees, and Mike's brother and his family of six were coming from Iowa for vacation.)

"I have a photograph here, which I will pass around, and as you absorb the beauty of this very special specimen, I will share an enlightening piece of history with you."

Ellis handed the picture to a young woman in the group, then cleared his throat and brought his hands behind his back. "I will quote Mina Edison in her precise words: 'The orchid is a contrary plant who is not content to be on the ground among the dirt and hubbub of life. I so greatly admire her ability to sit aloft, her roots dangling freely in the air like the legs of carefree children swinging from the edge of the pier. She needs air and air alone. She requires no one. Only something so beautiful and self-sufficient can dare to be so aloof.' "

Ellis brought his hands together in a single, gentle clap. "Is that not lovely?" he said.

Yet missing from the journal, unfortunately, was advice on the care and propagation of orchids. Ellis had begun to collect orchids on his own, and he was having trouble.

Larry Livengood, who continued to insist that it was not he who had planted the journal in Ellis's locker, drove Ellis to Home Depot and helped him pick out a sampling of epiphytes, all of them suspended from the greenhouse ceiling in slatted wooden baskets that reminded Ellis of miniature orange crates.

He bought eight, each laden with surreal, oversized blooms, for a total of $202.67 and brought them home to his backyard on Wilna Street. Ellis hung them from the rain gutter — an easy reach because the wire hangers on the baskets were nearly two feet long — arranging them in an equidistant manner like mile markers on a highway until they ran the entire length of the house. When the breeze off the river caused them to sway, they reminded Ellis of the earrings Elizabeth Taylor wore in *Cleopatra*.

Yet within days they began to languish. The thick, green, cardboardlike leaves turned yellow, then brown around the edges, then finally dropped to the ground. Ellis had never owned a pet in his life, and he was greatly bothered by the nagging feeling created by having something under his care that was unhealthy and unhappy and was, in fact, slowly dying.

He called Home Depot and asked them what to do. A man in outside-garden suggested he throw some manure or compost onto them. Ellis bought a bag at Tropical Hardware, a short walk from his house, but it was all for naught.

When they were nothing more than baskets of contorted brown sticks, Ellis threw them all out and started anew. This second time around, he spent nearly three hundred dollars. The lady at the checkout counter told him his Visa card had been rejected, and he had to pull out a second, his last one, from his wallet. Ellis wondered when his new card would arrive from MasterCard. How much time had passed since he'd applied? Two months? Three?

Ellis escorted his group back across McGregor Boulevard, to the museum and library, where he liked to end his tours with a question-and-answer session beneath the banyan tree. He relished this moment of the tour and always hoped for a fresh, provocative question. It reminded him of that weekly, combative question-and-answer session in Britain that he sometimes watched on C-SPAN, when Parliament members were allowed to fire candid, unrehearsed, and pointed queries at the prime minister, and he had to hop out of his seat each time, rush up to a podium, and answer them as best as he could. Ellis loved the drama of it — Would he know the answer every time? — and wondered why the president of the United States was not subjected to such scrutiny.

A mother who had been pushing a sleeping baby in an umbrella stroller raised her hand. "Is it true Mr. Edison had a photographic memory?" she asked.

"I am glad you asked that, madame. I need a volunteer to help me with that answer. Who would like to volunteer?

Anyone? . . . Now, do not be shy."

A thin arm with well-manicured pink nails impulsively popped up near the rear. Ellis was surprised to find that it belonged to the young, attractive woman who'd seemed to be skulking toward the back of the group for much of the tour. She had been hiding behind mirrored sunglasses, and her lips were coated in a daring red lipstick. A green floral-print scarf had been draped over her head and tied beneath the chin as if to hide her hair. She reminded Ellis of Greta Garbo in her reclusive, latter-life years, a woman who had given up the limelight but not fashion.

"Yes, young lady," he said. "What is your name?"

She hesitated for a moment. "Irene."

"Irene! Why, that was my mother's name! You are awfully young to be an Irene."

She smiled, saying nothing.

"Irene, please go into the museum office and tell Gloria at the ticket counter that Mr. Norton would like to borrow her Fort Myers telephone book. The white pages, please."

She returned with the Sprint Lee County phone book and handed it to Ellis.

"Thank you, but I am not finished with

222

you, young lady. Come stand here beside me, please. . . . Now . . . I have opened this phone book to page 573. I want you to look at it for a moment . . . just a few seconds, that is good . . . and now I will close it."

The woman looked at him quizzically.

"Now," he said. "Please tell me who had the phone number 523-6114."

The woman smiled, the group laughed.

"That's impossible," she said.

Ellis shook his finger at her. "Not impossible, madame."

"There are hundreds of numbers on that page."

"Impossible for you and me, perhaps, but not for the great inventor."

Ellis turned toward the group at large. "Ladies and gentlemen, this is what Mr. Edison would do to entertain his children. Oh, they would do their best to stump their father, but this ingenious man could correctly match a number to a person every single time."

Just as his mother used to do, Ellis lowered his chin and looked at his people from over the top of his bifocals, as if his glasses were a bothersome filter that diluted the power of his stare and point.

"Every. Single. Time!" he said. "Each

blink of Mr. Edison's eyes was like a shutter click on a camera. The great inventor could read an entire book in fifteen minutes. . . . It is nothing short of amazing!"

Ellis always ended this anecdote with the same line, and the last word, perhaps precipitated by the buzzing of the "z", would fill him with something that felt like electric current. Goose bumps would inevitably cover his arms and then slowly melt back into his skin as everyone shook his hand and patted his back and said their goodbyes, thanking him for a lovely tour.

Yet it didn't happen this time. Nor did it on Tuesday . . . or the previous Friday. Ellis felt as if something had been sucking the energy from his tours. He tried to counter this by infusing them with his exciting new research about the estate's flora, and his visitors did indeed seem interested in some of the more exotic tales, such as how *dieffenbachia,* also called dumb cane, got its nickname from being fed to slaves in Jamaica to swell their larynxes so they couldn't speak and thus plot revolt.

But it was hard to ignore the truth completely: The stage lights had been irrevocably altered. The scene was dimmer now, and bluer. What appeared to be eccentricities for so long had begun to blossom into acts of selfishness. Why did Thomas Edison refuse to eat what other hosts served and instead sup on the sardines and crackers and spinach he'd brought with him? Why did he steadfastly refuse to dance with his own wife because he considered the act nothing more than a lingering expression of the barbarian in the human race? Why did this man, whose first job was as a telegrapher, give his first two children the embarrassing nicknames of "Dot" and "Dash"? And why would he sometimes tease them to the point of tears, just as Ellis's own father had done with him?

Recently, Ellis also revisited his own brush with the famous man, one he had shut away years ago in some mental corner cabinet.

Ellis was six and attending one of Mina's well-known teas in the yard of Seminole Lodge. Needing to go to the bathroom but afraid to interrupt his mother's conversation, Ellis wandered into the house himself, and when he pushed open the bathroom door off the parlor he found himself confronted with Thomas Edison himself, sitting on the toilet with his pants around his ankles and reading a copy of

The Fort Myers Tropical News. Edison scrunched his untamed white eyebrows and frowned. "Go back outside, little boy," he commanded. "Shoo!" And he rattled his opened newspaper at Ellis, as if scaring a cat off the kitchen table.

Ellis fled the house, back to his mother, and did not realize until he reached her that he had peed his pants.

As Ellis shared the yellow *cattleya* with his visitors, Judith Ziegler was standing just twenty feet away, hidden by a dense wall of Japanese bamboo as she talked with the architect she'd hired to restore the caretaker's cottage.

"Please," she said to the architect. "Just a minute. I need to hear this." She walked over to the bamboo, leaned into it, and cupped her hand behind her ear, listening to Ellis recite Mina's ode to orchids.

Judith immediately assumed that it was made up — *Ellis! Will you ever learn?* — because she did not recognize the passage. She'd read sixteen biographies of the inventor and most of the documents not only in her own museum's cache but also those in West Orange, New Jersey, and at the Chautauqua Institution in western New York, which, having been founded in part by Mina's father, harbored much of her lifetime's correspondence.

But the phrasing of this passage . . . it sounded so much like Mina . . . fussy and opinionated with no contractions in the syntax, bordering on hyperbole . . . much like Ellis, she realized now. Was it authentic? Why had she not come across it? There was no way he could have made this up. It was pitch-perfect.

Judith knew that Ellis had been spending his extra time in the new resource library, but this passage was nowhere in it; she knew this for certain. And why would this man, whom she had privately likened to a jealous mistress of the inventor's, taken a sudden interest in the Unworthy Wife he had scorned for so long?

Judith turned again to the architect. "I'm sorry," she said. "Now where were we?"

And as he told her of his concern about the distance between joists in the first-floor ceiling, Judith scratched out a note to herself on the cover of her blue spiral notebook: *Google-search Mina and orchids.*

From the driver's seat of her Excursion, Geena watched Ellis eat a hot dog at a picnic table in the shade of a poinciana tree at Bright Ideas, the Edison home's outdoor café, which was famous for its lemon-yellow slushee known as Genius Juice. She noted how he sat up straight with his knees and ankles touching as if they were tied together, and how he chewed each bite of food into extinction before swallowing.

He has got to be the cutest old man I've ever seen. This is Ellis. Ellis is right there. This is Ellis R. Norton.

Geena could not peel her eyes from him the entire tour, and when he had asked for a volunteer at the end, she popped up her hand without thought, despite her new wariness about being recognized.

When Geena arrived in Fort Myers the day before, she checked into the Holiday Inn Select, drawn by the upscale retail mix at the Bell Tower Shops across the street.

After Banana Republic, after Mole Hole, after Anna's Morocco and a surf shop that Nathan would have loved, she stopped into a cyber coffeeshop to have a latte and Google her name. Geena found one article, a two-paragraph update in the *Denver Post*.

SUBLETTE — Police still have no

leads on the whereabouts of a woman from a prominent real estate family who disappeared two months ago.

Geena Marie Pangborn, 38, of Sublette, was reported missing Oct. 22 after shopping at a downtown Sublette drugstore. She is blond and of medium height and was last seen driving a bronze Ford Excursion. Anyone with leads as to the whereabouts of Pangborn is urged to call the Kit Carson County Sheriff's Office at 354-5555.

Geena wondered if this was the result of a diligent, self-disciplined reporter who was good at follow-up, or if Barry had called the newspaper and asked them to run another story.

She tried to picture him now, at home. What was he wearing? What was he eating for dinner every night? Whoppers and fries? Leftover beef stew or spaghetti sauce from the freezer? Did he think of her when he ate it? In bed, alone, at night, did he cry? Did he watch their Good Sex videos and masturbate? She thought of Barry's broad back and the constellation of moles that was just one brown dot away from being a perfect version of Taurus, his birth sign. This branding was one of the traits that convinced her it was okay to marry him. She reasoned: How could a man who carried on his back the sign of the zodiac that represented resourcefulness and business savvy be anything but a great provider? For the longest time Barry didn't believe her, but then once while on vacation in Puerto Vallarta she outlined the bull in lipstick to prove her point.

Walking back to the hotel, Geena was admiring the new striped espadrilles she'd bought at Chico's when she suddenly looked up and saw a Florida Highway Patrol trooper just fifty-some feet ahead of her.

Geena gasped. He was standing directly behind her Excursion, looking at the license plate. Scowling, he was writing something on a small clipboard.

Shit! God! . . . "She is blond and of medium height" . . . Okay, good, mine's still red.

Not missing a step, Geena took off her watch and stashed it in her large kilim-rug purse.

"Excuse me, officer," she said.

He looked up.

"Do you have the time?"

The trooper looked at her, then at the

Ironman watch on his wrist. "Two forty-two," he answered.

"Thanks."

Geena started to walk away, then stopped. "Excuse me again."

"Yes, ma'am?"

"Are you ticketing that car?"

"Ma'am?"

She stepped closer, trying to catch a glimpse of what he'd written. "I mean, I'm parked over there for the movies, but maybe I should move my car if there's a time limit or something. Is there a time limit?"

"No, ma'am. I'm not ticketing this car."

"Oh . . . okay, then. Well, thank you."

"Yes, ma'am."

Geena stood there, not sure what to do next.

"Is there anything else?" he asked.

"Oh, no," she said. "I just . . . well . . ."

"Yes?"

Quick! . . . What? . . . What?

"I've just . . . got a thing for men in uniform I guess. You're very handsome. Have a nice day."

Geena walked across the parking lot, toward the cineplex, wondering the whole way if he was watching her. She went inside and watched from the door, and when he left, Geena hurried back to the Excursion and drove to a Michael's crafts store she'd passed on the way into town.

Twenty minutes later Geena emerged with fourteen rolls of adhesive contact paper and an X-Acto knife. Then, in the parking lot of an apartment complex off Summerlin Road, she spent the next three hours transforming the appearance of her car, from tasteful metallic bronze to a random, crazy-quilt of blues and pinks, reds and tangerines, zebra stripes, faux-wood paneling, tiny stoplights and frogs and black-and-white checkerboard and polka dots. It was surprisingly easy to do, the knife following the lines of the car with ease, and the result was precise with clean edges.

Thanks, Zachary.

She'd seen enough of Florida by now to learn that the young man's car adorned in the words of *The Waste Land* was not that unusual, and she would fit right in. Over the past several days Geena had passed a battered mustard yellow pickup with a line of Virgin Mary statues glued across the roof and an old Ford Pinto covered in leftist-leaning bumper stickers. She had also seen more outrageous, sprawling tattoos on both men and women in the past week than in the first thirty-six years of her life combined.

232

Florida seemed to be filled with fragile people, loners who had broken off from the stronger collective core of humanity and tumbled down to the bottom of the barrel where they knew no one, were held to no standards, could do as they pleased without reaction. Geena, who had grown tired of living in the fishbowl of Sublette, realized that it would take a lot to get noticed here, something very extreme, like getting eaten by an alligator or, as she'd read in the paper that morning, throwing a newborn baby out of a car window on a bridge and letting it fall to its death in the river below, all because palm trees were agents of the devil and they had commanded you in the constant whispering of their fronds to kill your own child. This is what a would-be mother, whose name was Champagne, told police.

Geena also needed new tags for her car, and she'd determined that Ohio would provide the perfect cover in this town. Everywhere she looked she saw retirees from the Buckeye State with their red-blue-and-white OHIO: BIRTHPLACE OF AVIATION tags. In the same condo parking lot in which she disguised her Excursion, Geena found beneath the long carport a tarp-covered silver Buick Park Avenue with

Cuyahoga County plates. It seemed a safe choice because of the dried green grass clippings, whipped up weekly by a leaf blower, that had accumulated upon the form-fitting tarp like several dustings of snow. For whatever reason, the owners had not made it south this winter. Geena wondered if one of them had had a stroke or a heart attack. Or maybe their son died in a car crash and left them in charge of their grandchildren.

I will never be a grandmother.

From her newly disguised car, Geena watched Ellis finish his hot dog, then wipe off the entire white plastic table with his napkin. As he disappeared into the administration building, Geena recounted the tour in her mind and shook her head in disbelief. What were the chances of her pulling Ellis's own real mother's name out of the ether like that?

What were the chances of any of this happening? . . . Nathan's death . . . the serendipitous wreck of the mail truck . . . the inexplicable sixth sense that had helped her activate Ellis's credit card? Who could explain such things?

Cosmic forces at work here. This was meant to be. I am here to be with him.

Chapter Seventeen

Judith Ziegler slammed down the already cracked receiver of the phone and unconsciously reached for her glass decanter of peanut M&M's, only to find it empty. She then pulled open the thin top drawer of her desk and began rifling through its mess of contents, half of which she'd inherited from Larry Livengood. Somewhere in here . . . among a commemorative Statue of Liberty Coin . . . a business card for Randy Masella, licensed chiropractor on Boy Scout Drive . . . somewhere in here . . . a small crystal, pyramid-shaped paperweight with the etched-in inscription PERFECT ATTENDANCE, 1962, FORT MYERS KIWANIS CLUB . . . somewhere in here was a round aluminum tin of tangerine-flavored Altoids . . . somewhere. Or had she taken it with her yesterday to Naples, where she spoke to a group of retired Bausch & Lomb executives at the Pelican Bay Country Club?

Judith stood up and walked out to the desk of her volunteer assistant, Betty Graves, whose candy jar appeared to refill itself with the ease and regularity of a spring bubbling up from the ground, and always with the irresistible hard candies of Judith's childhood: sweet-sour orbs the colors of the rainbow, disks of artificial but nonetheless silky butterscotch, cylinders of pastel Smarties. The small squares of clear cellophane appeared to procreate in Judith's purse, in her pockets, on the floor of her car, and at times she seemed to shed them as a bird molts feathers. Such sweets, she told herself, were the ideal lubricant for life when it seemed rusty and reluctant to move in the desired direction.

Judith had just spoken with Susan Freeland, the councilwoman who'd pushed hardest to hire her. She called Judith to tell her that the five board members of the Lee County Women's Club had shown up at the Monday council meeting to express their outrage at the Edison home's new leadership. Two new policies in particular — bans on using the estate for family pictures, and as a venue for weddings and anniversaries — had caused more ire than expected among the families of old Fort Myers.

"Did you have to piss off Marjorie Dorth in your first month here?" Susan said. "I can't express enough how upset she was."

"Her daughter can get married in a church or on the beach like everyone else," Judith answered.

"Her father's one of the biggest investors in the downtown renewal effort."

"She made me very well aware of that."

"Think creatively here, Judith. Listen . . . I'm with you on getting rid of that abomination called Holidazzle, and I'll support you on the record. But can't you compromise on this wedding stuff at all? Maybe let them use the grounds but not go near the house?"

"Susan . . . You want this place on the National Register by next July. Please tell me how I can do that when the local ladies insist on treating it like their private country club and dollhouse."

Judith leaned back in her Herman Miller chair and looked at the framed print on the wall, *Sinjerli Variation IV* by Frank Stella, a circle comprised of various colored, crisp, curved, white-edged interlocking lines that repeatedly crossed each other like Los Angeles freeways. This was one of Judith's favorite works of art; she thought it was testament to the idea that all forces must interact and cooperate but not blend into one another so as to dilute their focus and missions. She loved Stella's work for the same reason she despised Mark Rothko's. His large, fuzzy squares floated peacefully in the middle of a rectangular sea of color, but these squares also had blurred edges, as if they were ice cubes melting in the sun, and in her mind this made them anemic. Left alone, they would grow smaller and less significant, diluted and devoured by the majority surrounding them, their voices lost forever.

"I'm making changes, Susan," Judith said. "I don't expect to be popular. We're making progress here, we really are. The interpretive center's going to open by Easter."

"I do have some good news," Susan said. "I'm no longer getting those phone calls from that old docent."

"Who?"

"The one who sounds like an old schoolteacher."

"Ellis? Ellis calls you?"

"My assistant calls him Mr. Fussy. He calls all the council members. Or at least he used to."

"What would he say?"

"We know everything you're doing down there, Judith. He's like the little tattletale everyone hated in grammar school."

Judith smiled to herself, imagining Ellis's warped, incensed version of her improvements to the estate. Certainly her most elder docent was a pain in the ass, but at least he had passion, and so few people had passion anymore. The masses always seemed to float about in an opium haze, lazily grazing in the field of pop culture, raising their heads in search of something new as they chewed on the old. There was nothing lazy about Ellis, nothing lukewarm. He had a fire raging within, kindled by Lord only knew what, and Judith hoped that she, too, would be burning so fiercely when she was eighty years old. Ellis still left her notes with ideas and comments on her decisions, but they'd become less vitriolic since their agreement at the Banana Leaf Café that Holidazzle must be quashed in the best interests of the estate.

"Can I make a suggestion?" Susan said.

"Of course."

"Get out there and shake some hands. Too many people don't know you. You're too much of a mystery. . . . You are going to the coronation ball, aren't you?"

"I wasn't planning on it."

"Go."

"Oh, Susan, must I?"

239

"It would be political suicide not to."

For most of the half million residents of Lee County, the annual Edison Pageant of Light celebration meant nothing more than a televised nighttime parade that included hundreds of illuminated floats; Midwestern high school marching bands here to escape the gray, cold winter; and a grand marshal who was usually either a University of Florida athlete or retired NBC weatherman Willard Scott, who had a house on nearby Captiva Island, or an actor from some canceled sitcom like *Gilligan's Island* or *The Love Boat*. But for the old, multigenerational families of Fort Myers — the Cadillac and Buick dealers, the furniture and jewelry store owners, and the like — the keystone event of the pageant was the coronation of the king and queen of Edisonia. To Judith, it appeared to be their version of a debutante ball, but with unwitting Monty Pythonesque details.

Each year, a board nominated twelve college-age men and women to join the Royal Court of Edisonia. These dukes and duchesses of this mythical kingdom were introduced at a coronation ball, as though they had traveled from some other faraway kingdom: "From the House of Johnson, Miss Heather Johnson, daughter of Mr.

and Mrs. Bruce Allen Johnson."

Dressed in formal gowns and white-tie and tails, each would solemnly enter and either curtsy or bow to the audience, and after the announcement of each young woman and man, there followed the sound of recorded trumpet fanfare, dubbed by two teenagers in court jester outfits who pretended to blow into skinny brass horns the length of broomsticks. Above the crowd, hanging from the ceiling, were the homemade crests of every Fort Myers family officially recognized by the Kingdom of Edisonia.

One was crowned king, another queen, and with their scepters and faux-fur-and-purple-velvet capes trailing behind them, they would take their places up on the thrones, flanked by gilded palm trees upon a dais. Judith had inferred that even though official ballots were sent out to all the families who were members of the Kingdom of Edisonia, one still had to pass the scrutiny of a secret committee in order to compete for the throne. She knew that royalty had to be childless — How unfortunate for the family that learned this too late one year — and it helped to have grown up on the pricier "river side" of McGregor Boulevard.

"I'm assuming it's all very political," Judith said to Ellis, whom she'd called into her office one day to explain it all.

"Oh, yes . . . very much so," Ellis replied.

"And you were a duke. I saw it in the newspaper clippings."

"Yes, but I was not king. My mother warned me that I could not be king."

"Why not?"

"My father had already left us. You see, it would have been shameful to have a king with no father."

Ellis's face suddenly brightened. "But I was the only young man who knew how to dance properly. Mother taught me. I got several compliments that night on my dancing, including one from Mina Edison herself."

Judith ruminated on the councilwoman's thoughts as she retrieved a lime-flavored sourball from Betty's candy jar, unwrapped it, popped it in her mouth, and, not having any pockets, unconsciously pushed the cellophane into the elastic waist of her flowing, beige silk pants. She knew that Susan was right about the upcoming ball, that she must go and be the most gracious woman there. But she needed an invite in order to join a table, and she knew that not just any table would do.

Just as the number on a signed lithograph displays the value of the piece of art, the number of a person's table at the pageant ball broadcast to everyone his level of seniority among old Fort Myers. Bertie Nusbaum, ninety-six years old and a close friend of Mina Edison, had table number 1. The Rayner family, owner of orange groves and donator of the swampland that had been filled in for the new university, had table number 2. Any table lower than 50 was significant, and anything beyond 200 laughable. Table number 1 sat directly beside the throne, and as the table numbers increased, so did their distance from the throne until somewhere around 120 the tables spilled out the doors at the back of the Fort Myers Exhibition Hall and onto the concrete outside, where decorators had cordoned off an area with potted areca palms so the high-number people wouldn't be reminded every second that they were sitting in a parking lot.

No bank president or newspaper editor new to town could bump ahead in line. They, too, had to sign up for a number and, through the decades, baby-step their way closer to the throne. And some years they might be frustrated to find a new, younger group sitting two or three tables ahead of them because, although one generation could not pass their enviable low numbers on to the next, a good mother and father would have registered a number for their children on the day they were born, so that when they finally reached black-tie age they could altogether avoid the ignominious label of "sweaters," the pejorative used to describe those relegated to their high-number tables outside the air-conditioned banquet hall.

"I need to find Ellis," Judith said to Betty. "Do you know where he is?"

Betty reached for her glasses hanging from a chain around her neck and pushed them onto her face. She inched her nail down the weekly docent schedule on her desk, then looked at her watch.

"He had a ten o'clock, but that should be over by now."

Judith had given up her search for Ellis by the time she stopped at water's edge to check on the restoration of the mortar-and-limestone seawall. From the bank, she put her hands on her hips and looked outward, into the Caloosahatchee glittering in the midday sun.

Her eyes followed the long pier, which

stretched out into the river nearly four hundred feet and was capped on the end by an open, tin-roof cabana. Judith recalled the anecdote of how Mina frequently lengthened the pier to improve her husband's fishing, and she now pondered both the sweetness and sadness of this indulgence, an obsessive inventor's wife, alone and desperate for her man's adoration and attention, reaching out to him in a language he might notice. Judith wondered why Mina had tried so hard, and whether she would have left Thomas had she been born two generations later. What was that line in a marriage that separated personal need from obligation to fulfill an agreement? How much of herself must a woman abandon to survive in a marriage? What was fair? And how much was unkind?

What Judith had most loved in all her research of the Edisons was sorting through the black-and-white photographs. In doing so she'd detected what she thought was an evolution in Mina. In earlier photos with her husband, in the pier-extending days, she seemed tender and vulnerable, subtly curling inward like the leaves of a languishing plant as it begins to dry out from lack of water . . . and beside her, the greatest inventor of the century, a diminutive man but with a cocky posture and electrified stare that made all in his presence subservient.

She liked to contrast this with a photo taken decades later, only a few years before Thomas's death. Mina is standing behind him, chest out, a confident and peaceful smile upon her face, her hands resting on her husband's shoulders as if to say, "All this . . . all this belongs to me" as he slouches in a wheelchair, scowling at the camera.

Judith thought of her ex-husband, John, and how in the last weeks of their marriage she had finally squeezed from him the true source of his discontent: You don't need me, he said. You're too strong. I want to be needed.

She'd married him because she liked him. She was lonely and she wanted a child. John was great company with a good, active brain and lovely cheekbones. They liked the same things, bicycling trips and cooking Asian food, reading magazines on Sundays and driving out to farflung rural towns to partake of their quirky, crop-based rituals. (The Mecklenburg, West Virginia, Onion Relish Festival had been a favorite find.)

Their turning-point conversation sounded

like the dialogue in Dr. Seuss's *Green Eggs and Ham*, artfully, painfully succinct:

You want to be needed?

Yes, he answered.

But for you to be needed, then I must be needy. And I am not.

That's right. You're not.

I cannot.

I know.

So good-bye?

I guess so. Yes. Good-bye.

Though the sun was bright, making it difficult to stare directly out at the water, Judith suddenly thought she saw something move on the end of the pier beneath the cabana, something behind one of the pilings. Was it a pelican? A cormorant? The pier was speckled with their white droppings that not even the pounding tropical afternoon rains could wash away.

And then . . . then . . . yes . . . damn him! . . . yes . . . she noted the brim of a white hat poking out from one side of a piling. Though he had not been out on the pier for more than four decades, and though it was supposed to be closed to human traffic because the pilings had decayed, Ellis had decided to visit it after reading Mina's account of watching the crabs scuttle about in the sandy bottom of the river beneath the pier. (In a journal entry, she told of how she passed the time when sitting with her husband as he was lost in thought holding a fishing pole.)

Judith walked to the seawall end of the pier.

"Ellis!" she yelled, waving at him as if summoning a boater. "Ellis!"

He stood up from the bench and turned and looked landward. Unperturbed, he waved and slowly began to walk back. All the while, Judith coached herself back to calmness, sounding like some self-help stress-buster tape. *You need something from him. Don't blow this. He's okay. You can't kill Holidazzle next year without his help, and you need his table number. Keep this all in perspective. Don't over-react.*

Finally Ellis was back on shore with her beneath the shade of the Australian pines.

"There's a reason that pier's closed, Ellis. It's very dangerous. You could have fallen in."

"The pier is fine," he said. "And what a lovely view can be had from that bench on the end."

"Please don't do that again. Not until we get it fixed."

Ellis said nothing.

"Promise me," she said. "Ellis, promise me."

"Very well."

They turned and began walking back toward McGregor and the museum office. "I wanted to talk to you about something," she said. "About the pageant."

"The pageant?"

"Yes. I'm assuming you go."

"Of course."

"What's your number?"

"I am number 17. But I do not get a table."

"What do you mean?"

"You must reserve the table on Table Day at the Hall of Fifty States on the first Tuesday of every January. And I choose not to reserve a table."

"What do you do then?"

"I go and visit beforehand. When it is time for the pageant, I leave. I do not much like the pageant itself anymore. The boys and girls of today are not fit for royalty. They do not even walk with their backs straight. And the dresses these girls wear are not proper."

"Would you get a table if I said I wanted to go?"

Ellis stopped and looked at Judith, surprised.

"To the pageant?"

"Yes."

"But why?"

"I'd like to see it."

Ellis scrunched his eyebrows, looking inward.

"But the table has eight seats. You and I make two. I do not know who else I could ask."

"We can invite employees of the estate. I would pay your fees. I'm guessing there are fees to pay."

"Oh, yes! Two hundred and fifty dollars per table."

"I would pay that. And you can introduce me to everyone in town. I'm assuming you know most of the people associated with the pageant."

"Of course I do."

Judith returned to her office and found one of Betty's pink WHILE YOU WERE GONE slips on her desk. Mike Turlock of the Lee County Sheriff's Department had finally returned her call.

"Okay, Mike," she said out loud to herself. "Let's bust some chops."

Chapter Eighteen

"Mr. Norton?"

Ellis did not hear the woman at first. He was engrossed in the task of rearranging the books in the museum gift shop to his liking, moving to eye level the biographies of Thomas Edison that included the most details of Mina Miller Edison and banishing to the bottom shelf those that mentioned her only in passing, as if she were a college degree or childhood anecdote.

"Excuse me . . . Mr. Norton?"

Ellis turned around and immediately recognized the woman from his 2:30 tour the previous day.

"Well, hello," he said, brightening. "Did you misplace something on the tour?"

She took off her dark glasses and put them in her purse. Such a strange purse! He had noticed it before. It was a Mary Poppins purse, large and hanging from her shoulder on long, dark brown leather straps. What was it made of? A rug?

She pulled from the purse a palm-size spiral notebook with a pen clipped to the red cover. "My name's Irene Wolff — w, o, l, f, f — I'm a reporter with the *Cleveland Tribune* newspaper. I'm here to do a story on Fort Myers. Actually on Fort Myers and Naples, but Naples bored me. I thought it was too nouveau riche and antiseptic. I wanted to capture the real Florida."

Oh, Geena, you do sound so smart and Ellis-like!

"A reporter!"

"Yes."

"I was raised in Fort Myers, young lady. Only six blocks away, on Wilna Street. I can tell you many things. What would you like to know?"

"Actually, what I'd like is to write a profile on you."

"Me!"

"If that's okay."

"But why?"

"I'm a travel writer. I always try to feature a place through the people who live there. I took your tour the other day. . . ."

"Yes, I know. You volunteered for the phone book demonstration yesterday."

"Yes."

"And you were here on Sunday. You had on a yellow dress with very small white squares."

"I didn't mean to scare you. I mean, I hope you didn't think I was a stalker or something."

"Not in the least."

"I love your tours."

"Thank you," he said, subtly bowing his head.

"So would you be interested in the story?"

Ellis brushed at a gray spot on the sleeve of his white cardigan sweater; biographies of the great inventor tended to gather dust on the shelf.

"You know," he said. "I was featured in *Travel + Leisure* magazine. And on Eyewitness NewsCenter 4."

Geena knew exactly where to go; she'd driven past Ellis's house six times since coming to town. It was a gray-and-white stucco bungalow-style with a sweet porch swing and interesting collection of dying orchids that swayed from the east rain gutter in their wire-and-wood baskets.

As she pulled into the driveway, Ellis backed out of his darkened house and locked the door. When he got to the car, he put his hands on his hips and smiled and shook his head. "My goodness. I do not believe I have ever seen such a car as this."

"I'm a frustrated artist," Geena said. "Here. Let me help you in . . . Where would you like to eat?"

"Do you know of the Banana Leaf Café?" he asked.

"Do they take credit cards?"

"No, they do not."

"I've got to keep all my business expenses on a company MasterCard. Do you know The Prawnbroker?"

"Oh, yes! But that is expensive."

"It doesn't matter. I'm not paying for it."

I will pay him back. I will pay him back every cent.

As they headed south on McGregor, Ellis kept turning and looking over his left shoulder as if he were being followed.

"Why is there a mannequin in your backseat?" he finally asked.

"Isn't he great?" Geena answered. "He's my companion. That's the only man I need in my life."

Ellis looked at her quizzically, then again at Safe-T-Man, then at her again, then he finally let it go and subtly shrugged his shoulders and relaxed his tightened forehead, finding peace with the idea.

"He is very handsome," he said.

"Isn't he?"

"Where did he come from?"

"At my bachelorette party before I got married. Have you ever been married?"

"Oh, no."

"Have you lived in Fort Myers all your life?"

"My mother and father moved here when I was two. I am a New Jersey native, but it is not my home. This is my home."

There was a thirty-minute wait at The Prawnbroker, which opened its doors each day at four with early-bird specials that included rectangular fillets of fish accompanied by baked potato or heaping amounts of rice pilaf. Ellis and Geena sat in the bar. She ordered a glass of chardonnay, he drank water and, prompted by her many questions, comfortably fell into a recitation of his daily life, peppered with vignettes of his past.

"Are you not going to write any of this down?" he asked at one point.

Geena took out her notebook and scribbled phrases that caught her fancy, and each time she did this Ellis looked down and tried, while talking, to read what she considered worthy of being recorded.

Geena loved his openness, his way of re-counting details without a filter. It re-minded her of Nathan and how he could drive Barry and the other nonverbal Pangborn men from the room when he got lost in recounting a movie or conversation. Nathan used a range of tones and voices, and he could twist and stretch his facial muscles as if they were Silly Putty. He owned every Jim Carrey movie in existence.

Suddenly their conversation was inter-rupted by electronic music coming from somewhere close to the floor. It took Geena a few seconds to recognize the theme from *Pee-Wee's Playhouse* that Nathan had downloaded and programmed into her cell phone. It had been weeks since she'd heard it. She'd turned the phone off when she left Sublette, in fear of being detected or traced in some way, and realized now that she must have mistakenly pressed the power button when fumbling for the pen and notebook.

Geena reached down, pulled the phone from her purse, and looked at the readout: Barry.

Oh, my God — he's looking for me. He's still looking for me!

Her fingers twitched as she consciously fought the instinct to flip open the phone and answer. Instead, she simply held it in her palm, looking at it and silently counting the rings, which she knew were four to each chorus of the song.

"Are you not going to answer that?" Ellis asked.

"No," she replied.

A few moments later Ellis said, "You may answer it if you wish. I will not consider it rude."

Finally it stopped, and Geena pushed the call-history button. She discovered six full screens of the same number. He had tried to call two or three times each day, sometimes at three or four in the morning.

What does that mean? . . . What if something's happened? . . . But what emergency could there possibly be? . . . Leave me alone, Barry. I'm sure you don't expect to find me. You're just going through the motions. Go back to your momma now.

Immersed in thought, Geena sat, stone-faced, looking straight ahead. Ellis tried to follow her gaze across the room. What was she staring at? That overweight man in the Hawaiian-print polo shirt? The framed watercolor of the roseate spoonbills wading in the surf?

Realizing she might not return to him

for several minutes, Ellis tried to lure Geena back into the present with a pertinent anecdote.

"You know, Mr. Edison did not invent the telephone, but he did leave a lasting legacy. . . . But first let me ask you this: What do you say when you answer the telephone?"

Geena did not answer.

"What do most people say when they answer the telephone?" Ellis tried again. He took a drink of water.

"Well, let me start by saying that Mr. Edison was not known to be a patient man. And once, when helping his friend, Mr. Alexander Graham Bell, perfect the telephone, he grew weary of saying 'Are you there?' each time a call was placed. He quickly shortened it to 'Hello?' So we can thank the impatience of Mr. Edison for this wonderful, quick greeting."

A waiter brushed past Geena's back, startling her. She gave a shallow gasp as though she'd been frightened out of deep meditation.

"I'm sorry," she said. "I don't know what got into me. That was very unprofessional of me."

"Oh, no, that is fine," Ellis answered. "What were we talking about?"

"We were talking about my third-grade teacher, Mrs. Banks? Mrs. Banks was the only teacher who truly let me be myself. If there is something I do not like it is someone who tries to be something he is not."

Ellis looked at the pen resting on the table. "Are you not going to write that down?" he asked.

After dinner, Ellis asked Geena to make a quick stop at the twenty-four-hour Walgreens on Cleveland Avenue near his house. They meant only to pick up a bottle of Mylanta but spent nearly thirty minutes perusing the supply of greeting cards, reading their favorites out loud to each other. Geena bought a bag of white-cheddar Cheez-Its and shared it with Ellis as they sampled perfume testers and read the tabloid headlines. Ellis bought a bottle of White Shoulders perfume, which he said was for a gift. Geena paid cash for a plastic heart-shaped pin and attached it to the collar of Safe-T-Man's paisley shirt.

They did not pull up to Ellis's house on Wilna Street until 11:15. It was a good two hours past Ellis's bedtime, and he knew he would have to skip his appointment with Mina's journal that evening. Perhaps the next day he could read one entry in the morning and another in the evening.

Though weary, Ellis did not want the evening to end, and even after Geena put the Excursion in park he did not move to get out of the car. Outside, they could hear the popping of the nightly fireworks from the Waltzing Waters show across the river. Illuminated by the diffused amber light from the streetlamp outside, Ellis closed his eyes and yawned. His hands lay in his lap, palms upward, as if he were doing yoga. Geena had never seen a grown man in such a vulnerable-looking position, and she wondered if Ellis knew that the open palms were receivers for karmic energy.

I just want to take him inside and tuck him into bed, snug as a bug.

Ellis sighed. "Oh, my, this has been most pleasant. Are we finished with the interview?"

"Oh, no. Not even close."

Ellis turned to her, freshly excited. "Really?"

Ellis's eyebrows were the equivalent of a mood ring, although instantaneous. Geena had never seen such animated, telltale brows on an adult. This man would never win a game of poker. He could never tell a convincing lie.

"I'm very, very thorough," she said. "I want to follow you around at work and at home, if that's okay. You're going to be sick of me when we're finished."

Ellis looked at his watch. "Well now, I am a very busy person," he said. "I cannot let this interfere with my work."

"I'll try very hard to respect that."

Geena got out to help Ellis from the Excursion. He slid to the edge of the high chocolate-leather seat, accepted her hand, and dismounted the huge SUV as if it were a carriage.

Safely aground, he looked down at his thighs and tried to brush away the wrinkles in his baby blue trousers. "I think I should go inside and consult my calendar before I commit to anything else. If you do not think it improper, you are welcome to come and wait for me in the living room. It will only take a minute, I assure you."

They were halfway up the walk when Ellis stopped short. "The door is open," he said. "I did not leave the door open. I always lock my door."

He continued up the sidewalk, but Geena grabbed his arm and stopped him.

"Don't, Ellis. Look — the window's busted out."

"Oh, my Lord!"

261

"Let me go ahead of you."

Geena crept up the landing and pushed open the door. She looked to the left of the doorjamb, found the overhead light switch, and flipped it on.

"Police!" she yelled into the house. "You're surrounded!"

It was obvious to Geena right away that the vandals had been young. All but the largest, heavier pieces of furniture had been overturned. The red, spray-painted graffiti on the pale green walls — *fuck U!* — had been spelled out by someone familiar with the typing shortcuts of AOL instant-messaging. Immediately Geena remembered the preteen boy she'd noticed in her rearview mirror as she left with Ellis four hours earlier. He was straddling a motorized scooter a few houses down from Ellis's, and at the time she thought it odd how he watched them drive away, not breaking his gaze until they turned off the street.

"Ellis, you need to come here."

"What has happened?"

"They're gone, but you need to come here."

Ellis stepped up to the threshold of the front door. He brought his shaking hands to his mouth. The color drained from his face as he began to survey the damage of the room. Raw eggs had slid down the walls, leaving trails of shell fragments and yolk. Every framed picture, every knick-knack had been slammed to the floor and shattered into pieces. Someone had peed on the couch and in his TV chair. They had found the Cheerios and All-Bran and sugar in the pantry and threw it about like confetti. And on every wall there were angry, jagged lines of the red spray paint. It was obvious the vandals were no taller than five feet.

Geena took Ellis's hand and led him down the hallway. She turned into the first open door, the Edison Room, and went inside. The tables and their contents had been overturned and smashed. The large portrait of the inventor still hung on the wall, but it was crooked and had been smeared with dog shit. A beige lamp shade with orange fringe, also smeared, had been set like a hat upon the hand-painted plaster bust of Edison.

Geena noticed a teal aluminum baseball bat on the floor.

"Is that yours?" she asked, pointing.

Ellis shook his head.

"Don't touch it," she said. "The police will want it."

As Geena reached down to pick up a decanter cork topped with a small porcelain head of Thomas Edison, Ellis suddenly remembered his irreplaceable treasures, and he left her and walked to the linen closet in the hallway. Ellis counted down to the fifth towel, slipped his hand beneath it, and was relieved to feel the silkiness of the two Ziploc bags. He pulled the journal and test tube from their hiding place to make certain they were intact, then lifted the towel, replaced them, and patted and smoothed the pile of towels once again so they would appear to be fresh and unmolested.

The police came. It helped that Ellis had called them just a week before to report that he had caught the two boys from the river house stuffing a homeless kitten and Mrs. Renfro's miniature dachshund into a mailbox, then tying it shut with rope they'd gotten from a crab-trap buoy.

Wanting to avoid the police, Geena had reminded Ellis to mention the bat and the boy on the scooter, and while they interviewed him, she set about experimenting on the red paint with the cleaning agents she'd found beneath the kitchen sink.

As Geena duct-taped a book to the hole in the door's window, the detective asked

Ellis who she was. "She is my very good friend, Irene," he replied.

After the police left, Geena made Ellis a cup of tea, and they sat down at the pale yellow Formica table Ellis's mother and father had received as a wedding gift. She noticed that his hands were still trembling.

"You know . . . I can stay here for the night. I don't think you should be alone."

"Oh, no, that is not necessary."

"No, I insist. I would want someone to stay with me."

"I suppose you could sleep in mother's room."

"I'll sleep on the couch. I think that's safest until you get that glass replaced. We can do that tomorrow."

Ellis got up to fetch two saucers for their china teacups, brought them to the table, and set each cup into its intended, indented circle. Geena noted that the color was returning to his face.

"I hope you do not put this in your article," he said.

Chapter Nineteen

Dena Rhoades had peeled the moistened labels from three of the Coors Light bottles. Using the wetness from the rings of condensation, she repasted them onto the tabletop all in a row, using her fingers as a squeegee to smooth them out. Any graduate of Sublette High School had practiced the same thing, learning that having the ability to perform such a feat proved one's virginity, as though the untorn paper labels were the equivalent of a young woman's intact hymen.

"See?" she said. "Three times. It must be true."

"Yeah, I'll be sure to tell that to your kids," Barry answered.

Geena's best friend in Sublette, Dena had been stopping by to check on Barry two or three times a week on her way home from the Ramada Inn out on the interstate, where she worked at the reception desk.

"I just feel like she's alive somewhere," she said. "You know how Geena always said to trust your intuition, that intuition was based on real facts? Well, my intuition says she's okay."

Geena's friends and family knew most of the details of her metaphysical beliefs, and though Dot Pangborn referred to her daughter-in-law's theories as witchcraft, Barry secretly sided with his wife. Maybe, he reflected now, he should have been more public with his support.

Geena believed that every thought in a person's brain was simply an electrical occurrence that floated upward as unharnessed energy into the atmosphere — "What do you think an EKG measures? Electricity!" — where it blended with everyone else's thoughts to create a universal mind, and that anyone could access this universal mind, this repository of knowledge, and discover what any living person on the planet was thinking. That's why it was important to meditate, she said, to have quiet time without a radio or TV or other distraction that could cause interference.

She would say to skeptics, "How many times do you get a phone call from someone and you say, 'I was just thinking about you!' . . . How many times have you been in a room filled with hundreds of people and you felt like you were being watched, and you could turn and instantly find that person who was watching you? It's tapping into the universal mind."

She often wondered why someone hadn't invented a device that could harness such energy. And wouldn't it be possible to communicate with the dead if such a machine existed . . . because weren't spirits themselves nothing more than electrical energy?

"Are you still trying to call her cell?" Dena asked.

"Yeah."

"What happens?"

"I just get voice mail. I called Sprint and they said the phone was off. It hasn't been used since she left."

"Not once?"

"No."

"Can't they run some kind of tracerlike thing on it?"

"Not if it's off. Not if she's not using it."

He'd been calling at least twice a day since she'd disappeared, randomly choosing different times because he thought it might improve his odds of getting a hit.

Barry took a drink of his beer and started picking at one of the labels on the table. "It's gonna drive me crazy not knowing what happened," he said.

Dena sighed and slapped her hands on her thighs, as if to jolt them out of a stupor. "So let's just pretend she's okay," Dena said. "Let's pretend she's holed up in some rental house in town, and you and I gotta figure out what to do to get her back."

Barry gave her a quizzical look. "Are you not telling me something, Dena?"

"No. But it's no secret she was pissed off."

"Why?"

"Why do you think?"

"Mom?"

"That's part of it."

"What else?"

Dena got up and walked over to the pantry, hoping to find some Pringles or Doritos or something to eat. All the usual snack foods — Geena loved crunchy, salty things — had been eaten, and she finally settled on a can of cashews and brought it back to the granite-topped breakfast bar where they were sitting.

"If you don't know why she's unhappy, then I'm not sure you deserve her back," she said.

"Shit, Dena! Geena's always had unrealistic expectations of marriage."

It wasn't just Geena, it was all women, he thought to himself. They asked too much of men: Write me a sweet card, build me a brick wall around the air conditioner. Tell me your secrets and vulnerabilities but don't ever cry because I want you to be strong. Take me to Cozumel for the weekend but don't work all those long hours on Sundays. Be ready to kill anyone in defense of your family, but don't hunt, oh, no, don't hunt. Don't you dare kill those precious little animals.

"The man that Geena wants doesn't exist," he said. "Not anymore, anyway."

"So you admit you've changed."

"Of course I've changed. Haven't you?"

Barry pushed back his bar stool, stood up, and started pacing in the kitchen, feeling his beard of four days. He'd always been fastidious about shaving, and Dena was surprised to see flecks of white among the black stubble; Barry was graying early, just as his mother had.

"You try to scrape *your* way to the top of a pile of greedy, conniving brothers and tell me you wouldn't change," he said. "I feel like I've been off to war for twenty years. And I've got a mom who treats wounds with gasoline instead of Bactine."

Barry stopped his pacing to look at a framed photograph on the side of a birch cabinet over the kitchen sink, of him and Geena standing arm-in-arm in front of the ski lodge at Beaver Creek, with raccoonlike faces because ski goggles had protected their eyes from the sun for two days. Barry noted the smiles, which seemed to pop out of the reddened skin like something in a 3-D movie, so white, so big, and these were not smiles created by the muscles needed to produce laughter. These smiles were not by-products of anything. Anyone can smile when they laugh. No, he thought, these smiles were pure. They had formed and survived on their own.

Barry suddenly felt heavy, the way one feels after falling off the boat fully clothed. He sensed gravity in the skin on his face around his eyes, in his hands, and in his buttocks and feet and thighs. How long had it been since he'd felt the lightness that he saw in this picture? Is this why Geena hung it here in this spot where she saw it every day? To remind herself of a baseline of happiness she wanted to maintain in her life?

Or was it more of a memory? Did it remind her of things past — and lost — and, if so, why didn't she take the damn thing down? Why were women such eternal optimists?

After Dena left, Barry collected the beer bottles and trash from their Burger King dinner and threw them away in the trash can beneath the sink. On his way to the bedroom he was stopped by the mound of dirty laundry in front of the washer. Remembering that he'd put on his last clean pair of underwear that morning, he stooped over and indiscriminately scooped up a big multicolored collection of Jockey briefs and blue jeans, socks and towels and T-shirts, crammed them into the washer, added a capful of Wisk, and turned on the machine.

Lupe had been gone for a week now; Barry had fired her. He'd asked her not to wash Geena's pillowcase, but, falling victim to eleven years of habit, she mistakenly did it anyway. That night, he searched the closets of the house for something else that held his wife's smell and was relieved to find her orange-and-black Sublette High School Badgers Windbreaker in the mudroom closet. It seemed odd to keep such a thing in bed with him, so he hung it on a hook on the back of the bedroom closet door and buried his nose in the cool, slick folds of the jacket whenever he got dressed.

Part Two

Chapter Twenty

Judith Ziegler shut the door to her office, turned, and looked at Ellis on the black-leather-and-chrome love seat. She caught herself smiling — inwardly, she hoped. Ellis was sitting in the manner he always did, his hands folded on his lap, his legs rigidly pressed together like the spines of two matching books on a shelf. Judith wondered how any woman, any mother, could resist nurturing this man-child. And as the bubble of this thought burst, she realized the task at hand and quickly grew somber.

"I like your new davenport," Ellis said. "It is very modern."

"Do you want something to drink, Ellis?"

"Do you still have some of that tea with the passion fruit in it?"

"I do."

"I would like some of that, if you do not mind."

Judith disappeared into the closet where she kept a small refrigerator and hot pot, then returned with two sunflower yellow Edison Winter Estate mugs.

"Oh!" Ellis remembered suddenly. "I hope this is herbal tea. I should not have caffeine. Caffeine alters the natural rhythms of the body."

Judith blew across the top of her steaming mug. "I'm assuming this is advice from your new friend?"

"Yes. Irene. She is very knowledgeable about those things. She knows a lot about everything, really."

"Irene . . . I have been wanting to talk to you about her."

"Oh?"

"Yes."

Judith sat down next to him. "Ellis, how long has she been living with you?"

Ellis's gaze turned inward, as if he were computing an equation on a blackboard inside his head. "Nine weeks this Tuesday."

"And it's taking her that long to write an article about you?"

"But it is about my entire life. She is very thorough."

Judith nodded and sipped at her tea. "Yes, but nine weeks is a long time, Ellis. You can research an entire book in seven weeks."

278

In the past few weeks, Ellis had shared with Judith the stories of his new escapades with Irene . . . the ride on the airboat through the Everglades . . . their trip down Martin Luther King Jr. Boulevard in search of ribs and collards . . . playing the slot machines aboard the Casino Del Mar as it bobbed in the legal zone far out in the Gulf . . . taking a yoga class at the Y . . . the massage (his first ever) Geena had talked him into getting at the Hyatt when he'd had a particularly bad day with the arthritis in his right shoulder . . . picking out Tommy Bahama shirts at Fort Myers Beach for Mr. Douglas (on Turner Classic Movies one night they had watched *The Thief of Baghdad* and agreed with one another that Geena's plastic travel companion resembled Douglas Fairbanks in the 1923 black-and-white thriller).

The two of them seemed to be devouring new experiences with a frantic hunger that Judith distrusted.

"Don't you think it's odd that a woman you've never met suddenly pops into your life and stays longer than a Frenchman on holiday?" she asked.

Ellis clenched and lifted his chin. "I do not!"

"You don't?"

"Irene has been a great comfort to me since those awful boys broke into my house."

Judith noticed his folded hands beginning to tremble. She reached over and gently blanketed them with one of her own.

"I would be very frightened without her," he said. "She has a black belt in karate, you know. And she is very handy around the house. She can use a power drill."

Indeed, Geena had done much to restore Ellis's house. After the red graffiti had proven obstinate to remove, she decided to undertake the job of repainting the entire interior of the home.

Though fastidiously cleaned, the bones of the house were in disrepair even before the break-in, and Geena set about fixing things as she painted. She bought a miter box and replaced a rotted-out doorjamb that Ellis had tried painting over. She replaced the ballast in a fluorescent light in the kitchen and the washers in the leaky bathroom faucet.

All the while, Geena snooped through everything. She found the metal Band-Aid box with the hibernating credit cards. She was enchanted by the alphabetized medicine cabinet and the way the socks overlapped in his drawer like fallen dominoes.

She managed to intercept the first SunBank MasterCard statements in the mail, found Ellis's checkbook, paid the minimum amount, and mailed them without his knowing. Ellis didn't record checks as he wrote them, and his signature was an easy one, much like Thomas Edison's, with the leg of the final "n" curving up, then retreating over the entire name like a jet's dramatic contrail.

Judith sighed, then sipped her tea. A drink in one's hands made for easier transitions in conversation, and the hotter the drink, the fuller the glass, the better, because it demanded more of your attention, more opportunity for distraction as you pondered what to say next.

She decided to back up and try again.

"You really haven't told me much about her," Judith said. "Other than she's a newspaper reporter. And that she's from Cleveland. Is she married?"

"Oh, she is married, but it is not a good marriage. He sounds like an awful man. That is one reason she has decided to stay longer. She is taking a break . . . some vacation days . . . and deciding what to do next with her life . . . Oh!"

Ellis set his mug down on the glass coffee table in front of them, then slapped his open palms on his thighs.

"I forgot to tell you the most horrible, sad news about Irene. Her son was murdered last year. Someone threw him off the top of that very high tower in Las Vegas."

"The Stratosphere."

"Yes! I believe so."

"And you believe her?"

"Of course."

"Did you go online to check it out?"

Ellis glared at Judith.

"Well?" she pushed.

"I did not."

"Why not?"

"Why would she lie about such a dreadful thing?"

"Oh, I don't know, let me think of something, Ellis: To get some sweet, unsuspecting old man to take her into his home and treat her to a free Florida vacation? Can you afford all these indulgences?"

"But Irene pays for everything."

Judith felt her momentum thud to a halt, as if she'd just moved to forcefully yank open a door and expose some truth on the other side only to find a brick wall.

"She does?"

"Yes. She does."

"Really?"

"Yes."

"And what about the vandalism? You don't think she had anything to do with that? The timing is very suspicious, Ellis. Is there anything missing from your house?"

Over two months had passed since the night of Ellis's break-in. The neighbor boys who'd done it were charged with a handful of misdemeanors and released under their parents' watch. And although Geena was home with him most times, Ellis now listened for their combustible-engine toys before opening his front door. On eBay he ordered something called BigDog, a motion-activated device that barked a recording of your choice of three dogs, a German shepherd, Doberman pinscher, or an Akita. Ellis hid it in the coleus plants at the base of his front steps, but was forced to experiment with the placement of the sensor because it went off each time a lizard or palmetto bug scampered past.

"Everything is fine," he answered. "Please do not worry about me. I have taken care of myself ever since mother died."

Ellis then looked down at his Snoopy watch that Geena had bought him at Kmart. On a faux blue denim background, the beagle was playing tennis, with the minute hand represented by a racket-wielding arm and the second hand by a small yellow ball that seemed to magically float about the perimeter of the face. ("Actually, it is painted on a clear disk," he explained to Geena. "See? You must look very carefully. You can see it if I hold the watch sideways, like this.")

"I must leave for my eleven o'clock tour," Ellis said.

"Wait," Judith said. "There's one more thing."

She stood up from the couch and walked behind her desk. Ellis was puzzled, troubled by the sudden need for this barrier.

"You're aware of the amnesty program?" she asked. Ellis nodded. One month earlier Judith had announced what she called the Big Thomas Take-Back. With ads in *The News-Press* and in public service announcements on the morning radio talk shows, she told of how the museum wanted to reclaim all the artifacts that had walked off the grounds over the decades. Thieves or their kin could stash their booty in a pillowcase and leave it at the museum gift shop with no questions asked.

"The deadline is tomorrow, Ellis," she said. "After that, there will be no amnesty."

"Oh, yes, I know that."

"Not that you would have taken anything yourself. But just in case there was something your mom might have forgotten to return before she died. I have a complete list of the missing items. Do you want a copy?"

Ellis looked at her warily, waiting, expecting her to say something else, and when she did not, he simply said, "That will not be necessary. . . . And now, madame, my visitors await me."

Chapter Twenty-one

A Tampa Bay Buccaneers stocking cap pulled down to below his eyebrows, Ellis grasped the chrome railing with both hands and avoided looking out into the darkness as he bounced in his seat. Every few seconds the boat's hull slapped against the black water of the Caloosahatchee, and a fleeting blanket of mist would whip over the edge, coating his face. And though Geena had fashioned slickers out of upside-down lawn-and-leaf bags for both of them, Ellis still felt drenched and chilled to the bone.

Every few minutes he yelled out, "How much farther must we go?" But the wind and the whine of the outboard motor ironed out his crisp consonants, melting them into neighboring vowels and making it impossible for Geena to understand. Just as she'd done with Nathan on long car trips when he was a baby, whenever she heard the timbre of Ellis's voice, Geena would look over her shoulder and smile and mouth, "Almost there," even though she couldn't understand what he was saying.

He had never ridden a speedboat, and Geena knew it might frighten him, but the only alternative rental at Club Nautico had been a pontoon boat, and she knew it would never do in a pinch should they require a quick escape.

Geena spotted their destination in the distance, the rectangular cabana at the end of the long pier at Seminole Lodge. They had initially planned on sneaking into the estate with Ellis's key and simply walking the length of the pier to the end, but the restoration work on it had already begun, and there were several four-to-five-foot gaps where rotten boards had been pulled away.

"Can we not do this in the dining room or in his bedroom?" Ellis had asked that afternoon. "We could light a candle. No one will see us from the street. It would be most intimate."

"The more water the better," Geena answered him. "The end of that pier is our best hope."

In all her discussions with Ellis about the Edisons, Geena was most intrigued by the inventor's thoughts on spirits, which mirrored those of her own. Ellis couldn't provide the scientific details she was pushing for, so one evening he brought home a copy of an article from the *Journal of Parapsychology* he'd found in the resource room.

Edison said a human's personality was housed in what he called Broca cells. And when a person died, these cells — looking for a new, viable life-supporting host, as would a leech or louse — dispersed into free space, carrying the entire life history of the dead person. He called them "intelligences" and wrote in 1920 that he was developing an invention that could detect and record the "myriad infinitesimal, immortal monads prowling through the ether of space."

"So don't you see," Geena explained to Ellis that morning at breakfast. "Anyone, anything who has died is still out there."

Ellis, finishing a bite of his boiled egg, cocked his head. A look of concern spread across his face. "But that would mean they are homeless," he said. "Would it not?"

Geena cut the engine as the boat drifted the last few feet to the end of the dock. She threw the line over a piling, pulled it taut, and helped Ellis out of the boat, all the while remembering the summer weekends that she, Nathan, and Barry used to spend waterskiing at Hiawatha Lake. She recalled how her son would climb back into the boat after a run, shaking out his brown hair, his eyes wide with vigor — "Man, did you see that!" — his ribs rising then melting back into his bronzed skin as he sucked in air to catch his breath, the carotid artery in his neck twitching in overdrive.

God, he was so alive!

Geena turned toward Ellis. "Now raise your arms," she said. "Let me take that off."

Ellis did as told, and Geena lifted the trash bag over his head and stuffed it into her kilim-rug purse, from which she then pulled the Ouija board they had bought at Fleamaster's. Geena opened it on the bench, and as Ellis sat down beside it, Geena looked down the moonlit pier toward land. How many photographs among Ellis's Edison library had she seen of the old inventor sitting in various spots along this pier, crouched over, his elbows on his knees as if he were sick, scowling as he looked into the water? She wondered how much of this was truly a love of fishing or rather his desire to plug into an energy source for regeneration . . . because if spirits are actually electricity, then what better place than near highly conductive water to communicate with them? The man had thousands of patents to his name; surely he didn't come up with all those ideas on his own.

"Are you comfortable?" Geena asked him. "We can't do this if you're agitated in any way."

"I would like one of your mints, if you do not mind," he said. "I believe my throat is dry."

Geena pulled a tin of spearmint Altoids from her purse and gave one to Ellis and herself. He'd requested them often, ever since Geena told him that she liked to imagine mints as concentrated tablets of troubles melting away.

They sat quietly on the bench, looking across the Caloosahatchee at the lights of Cape Coral. Ellis finally broke the silence. "I must admit that I am nervous about this. Should we have a license of some sort?"

Geena giggled. "No, Ellis."

"I have never seen a spirit. I imagine it will be frightening."

"We probably won't see one."

He looked at her, quizzically.

"If we're lucky we'll find a spirit guide who will help us talk to Mina, but we probably won't get to talk to her ourselves. We need a middleman, like someone who helps pass your note to a friend across the room when the teacher's not looking. Everyone's got a spirit guide. He's the gatekeeper of the information that comes in and out of the spiritual world and into your mind."

"Oh. I see."

"You sound disappointed."

"No, no. Of course not."

Geena explained how she planned to engage a spirit guide who would in turn field questions from Ellis and Geena, take them to Mina Edison, then transmit her answer back to them through the felt-footed, white plastic pointing device upon which they lay their right hands.

"It'll either creep over to the *yes* or the *no*," Geena said. "If we're lucky, she'll spell out a specific message by using the alphabet, but that doesn't always happen."

Ellis looked down at their two hands resting upon the heart-shaped device. It reminded him of the old Palmolive commercials in which Madge had her customers soak their hand in a small bowl of dishwashing liquid to prove its gentle nature.

"So the spirit guide will move this . . . contraption?" he asked.

"Not really."

"I do not understand."

"The spirit will use one of us. See, she doesn't have muscles, she's not on this physical plane. We're like her puppets. She'll tell one of us the answer, and our subconscious will take over and tell our brains where to move the pointer. Does that make sense?"

Ellis pulled his hand from the device and put it in his lap.

"That's why it's critical we have open, uncluttered minds," Geena said. "So we can feel her message."

She reached for Ellis's hand and coaxed it out onto the board again. "Don't worry," she said. "She'll most likely use me because I've done this before."

"I do not know who my spirit guide is," Ellis said.

"Most people don't."

"Who is yours?"

"I don't know, Ellis. They change throughout your life. I'm kind of out of touch in that area right now. Okay, so no more questions. Close your eyes."

Overhead, a Cessna droned on its final approach to Page Field, a red light blinking

292

on its belly. Somewhere below the pier, a mullet leaped out of the water and returned with a smack. Geena took three deep-cleansing breaths, then spoke.

"We are here tonight to speak with Mina Edison, formerly of Fort Myers, Florida. We wish her peace and happiness. We are friends. Can you help us find Mina? We wish to speak with Mrs. Mina Edison."

In truth, Geena had not practiced a séance since her sophomore year in college. One night after closing, she and her fellow employees at The Living Planet, Mark Silverman and Jennifer Feron, wanted to contact Mark's sister, who'd drowned at age four in a neighbor's pool. Mark wanted to ask if she was mad at him because, instead of playing Atari, he should have been watching her while their mom ran down to Safeway for butter and a sack of flour.

Again and again, Geena and her friends asked the guide to summon the little girl, and nearly an hour passed before they finally got their succinct but gracious reply: No. Geena wondered what could take so long. Perhaps some of the bothersome laws of physics still applied in the afterlife. It was as if their guide was a curmudgeonly, reluctant doorman at a party, and inside that door were billions of people milling about, and they had to convince this doorman to go inside, seek out a particular person from among the infinitesimal crowd, and tell her she was wanted at the front door, then escort her all the way back for a chat. And what if she did not want to come? What if she was involved in a conversation, having already been summoned elsewhere by a different circle of sorry, undeveloped, earthbound humans wanting closure or momentum in their lives? Maybe that was why these moments sometimes fell flat, as it appeared to be doing here now, with Ellis.

Geena let a few minutes pass and addressed the spirit guide again, but again she sensed no response. She remembered the sensation she should be feeling right now as if every centimeter of her flesh had been infused with white, buzzing light, as gas fills a fluorescent bulb. Instead, Geena felt as if she and Ellis were grapes surrounded by cool, blue Jell-O.

She peeked to check on Ellis. He was indeed awake, eyes closed but his forehead wrinkled in concern.

"Ellis," she whispered, so as not to frighten him. As his eyes flickered open, she reached up and gently placed her palm on his forehead. "Relax. Think peaceful thoughts."

Geena set her fingers back on the pointer and closed her eyes.

I should have brought someone who really knows what they're doing.

"We are seeking Mina Edison," she said. "Please guide her to us. We are friends. We want her to know that we love her. Please, let us talk to Mina Edison, lover of birds and flowers, devoted wife to . . ."

Suddenly, with the effect of someone walking out unannounced from behind a curtain onstage, Geena sensed her . . . in the only form she knew . . . in her brunette bouffant, turquoise dress, and lemon-chiffon cardigan from the photograph on Ellis's nightstand . . . and then came the current she'd been awaiting, the warmth rushing into her like pent-up urine, a connection, and the message, expressed not in words but a shapeless bundle of thought . . . Leave my son alone.

"What?"

Leave him be.

"I want to talk with Ellis's guide."

Leave Ellis alone.

"I want to talk with Ellis's guide, please."

I am Ellis's guide!

The last comment came with such force it caused Geena to grimace and pull her hand from the pointer as if it were something hot. The connection now severed, the warmth that had surged into her now ebbed. She suddenly felt cold and empty.

"Oh my God," she said out loud. "Did you hear that, Ellis? Did you feel that?"

Ellis opened his eyes and looked at her.

"Irene? . . . What?"

Did I imagine it? . . . I imagined it.

"Irene?"

Do I tell him this?

"Irene . . . Are you all right?"

Damn her! I just want to give him this one last gift. Oh, Mina, come find us. Shove that nasty, controlling woman out of the way and come and talk to us directly.

"Did you see her?" Ellis asked.

He looked hopeful and expectant like a child, and Geena could not help but reach out and touch his cheek with the back of her hand.

"Was Mina there? Did she speak with you?"

Tell him the truth, Geena: She has no interest in us, Ellis, no interest in you. She's dead. She's moved on to other things. You love a dead woman because a dead woman can't reject you. Go find a flesh-and-blood companion and live the last years of your life with something real. Have sex before you die — it's wonderful.

"What did Mina say?"

"Shit."

"Irene! I have never heard you curse!"

Geena sighed deeply and grabbed both of Ellis's hands.

Oh, hell, what's one more lie? How many times do mothers use lies like Band-Aids? Liar, liar, pants on fire.

"She wants to talk to you," Geena finally said.

His eyes widened. "Mina?"

"Yes."

Ellis brought his hands together in a single clap and held them there in a prayer position. "Oh, this is so exciting!"

And you are so sweet I can't stand it. And I am so awful.

"Are you ready?" Geena asked. "She has some things she wants to tell you."

Chapter Twenty-two

Ellis hit the play button, and the strings of Mendelssohn's "Wedding March" poured forth from the twin, round, black speakers of his boom box. He knew it was one of Mina's favorite songs because she'd played it at her wedding with Thomas, and it would repeat again and again over the next six hours because Ellis had recorded the song sixty-five consecutive times.

Ellis looked in the dresser mirror and straightened his gray-and-burgundy-striped bow tie, then turned to survey the room . . . the fresh organza orchids on the nightstand . . . the pink chenille coverlet he'd borrowed from Mina's bedroom at Seminole Lodge . . . a copy of *Is Death the End?* by John Henry Remmeres, a book that Mina had left on the ottoman in her bedroom . . . and at the foot of his own bed, a stuffed male peacock, Mina's favorite bird, that he'd found from an

Oregon gentleman on eBay.

Ellis breathed in deeply through his nose. Perhaps he needed more perfume. He picked up the spray bottle of White Shoulders that Geena had bought for him at Walgreens and squirted it a few more times over the pillows. Though he wasn't sure which scent Mina wore, this was the one that most reminded him of her, floral and springlike but with undertones of ripe, autumnal maturity.

Geena had gone to Disney World for the day and would not be back until late that night. Ellis was taking his first day off in forty-six years — this, of course, did not include his mother's funeral — and he would need the entire day. If the movie was accurate, this could take several hours.

"I must begin," Ellis said.

The week before, he and Geena had watched *Somewhere in Time*, in which Christopher Reeve falls in love with an actress in a historic photograph, played by Jane Seymour. The actor imagines the photograph speaking to him — "Come to me!" — and he enlists the help of a professor and undergoes some kind of self-induced mental time travel. Dressed in vintage clothes, he lies down on a bed and spends the next several hours repeating things like, "The year is 1921. I am sitting in the theater waiting for the lovely actress, Elise McKenna. . . ." until he is, indeed, transported to that time period, where they meet and fall madly in love.

"Do you think that is possible?" Ellis asked Geena that night at House of Bangkok, a restaurant near the house he had ignored until Geena came to town. Ellis always ordered the chicken satay, timing how long each bamboo skewer of yellowish, curried meat sat atop the small Sterno kettle before flipping it over.

Geena knew what he was thinking. His love of Mina certainly was no secret. He spoke of her all the time, sharing her opinions and details of life, daily, oftentimes hourly. Ellis could tie a Mina anecdote or detail to nearly any topic.

Unbeknownst to Ellis, Geena had read the entire journal her first week in the house. She'd noted with amusement how often he moved his treasure to prevent its detection, just as Nathan had tried to hide his *Playboy*s. Men and their secrets always reminded Geena of squirrels burying their nuts: Certainly they would bother to stash them in holes, but they gave no thought as to where these holes should be, and they'd dig them out right in the open with the world as witness.

Ellis sat down on the bed and picked up the framed photograph, also borrowed from the museum. It was his favorite image of Mina, taken on her wedding day. She wore a pearl necklace and a square-necked white silk gown trimmed with Duchess lace. Over her bosom was pinned a crescent-shaped diamond pendant.

Geena had told Ellis about creative visualization, how if you imagined yourself in a situation again and again, you could program the mind to reach that goal. Holding the photograph in both hands, Ellis now imagined himself standing next to her in this image, she taking his arm and leaning slightly into him.

The "Wedding March" masking all sounds from outside, Ellis slowly lifted his legs onto the bed and lay on his back. He closed the journal, set it beside him, then rested his arms at his side.

"I am coming, my love," he said, and he closed his eyes.

Geena knew the project would take all day, that she had time for just one run to Home Depot, so she carpeted the floor of her Excursion with sixteen plastic bags of topsoil and, on top of this, all the tropical foliage it would hold. A dieffenbachia spilled over from the backseat, tickling her neck as she drove. Safe-T-Man had been turned sideways and squeezed between two five-gallon ginger plants. She had baby spider ferns and orchids, impatiens and Hawaiian ti plants that looked like magenta cornstalks. On the roof, a white arbor lay on its side, tied down with yellow rope she'd bought and cut up in the parking lot.

"We're like Noah's ark, Mr. Douglas," she said. "A vegetarian Noah's ark. I hope you're not too uncomfortable. We're almost home."

Ellis is going to be so surprised!

She'd told Ellis she had gone to Orlando and would be back by the time he got home from work, so to maximize time and energy Geena laid out the plants and bags of topsoil onto a slick, dark green plastic tarp and, as a mule would pull a heavy load, dragged it all in just two trips from the driveway into the backyard. She found a shovel in the shed behind the house and spent the next three hours creating a garden from scratch beneath the shade of a sea grape, a much more hospitable environment for the delicate orchids Ellis had tried to grow in vain. (Geena had spent an hour studying the gardening magazines at Home Depot to acquaint herself with the plants of the region.)

For a tiny pond, she set into the soil an upside-down, black plastic lid of a Rubbermaid trash can, then planted a few small maidenhair ferns along part of the edge to create a more random, natural shape. At the front of the garden Geena erected the trellis as an entryway and planted two crimson mandevilla vines at the base.

God, how I wish I could plant these tropicals at home. . . . They might do all right in the living room with that afternoon light. . . . I wonder if Barry's watering my plants.

Four hours after beginning, sweaty and exhausted, Geena trudged inside to take a shower. She sang a Frank Sinatra song — it had been Ellis's turn to choose the CD for dinner that previous night — but in the middle of the silence of drinking she stopped swallowing. There was music playing in the house, back by the bedrooms.

Geena felt the muscles of her throat tighten. She set down the Coke, pulled a butcher knife from the wooden block on the counter, and crept toward the hallway. The sound was coming from Ellis's room, but the door was closed. Geena detoured her way around the creak in the wood floor outside Irene Norton's old bedroom, where she slept, and crept closer to Ellis's. Inside, she could hear a muffled voice.

It's Ellis! . . . Oh my God — is he sick?

She pressed her ear against the wooden door to listen.

". . . year is 1886. I am at Seminole Lodge with my new lovely bride, Mina. The pelicans are flying overhead, and the jasmine perfumes the air."

"Oh, Ellis," Geena whispered. "Oh, no."

Geena tried the doorknob — it was unlocked — and slowly pushed until there was a fist-size gap and she could see inside. She could tell that he was near the end because his voice had taken on a slight anxious edge, and it was growing raspy. How long had he been at this?

Ellis had set his three-way reading lamp on the lowest wattage, and he was bathed in soft yellow light. He had pressed his gray, tropical-weight wool suit and greased and combed his hair straight back in the fashion of the black-and-white film actors she knew he admired, a style she'd not seen on him. And, if Geena wasn't mistaken, Ellis had also helped himself to a bit of her blush, which she'd offered to him in the past when he looked pale.

". . . In ten seconds I will open my eyes and Mina will be waking me up from my nap, in the year 1886 in Fort Myers, Florida. I will open my eyes and we will look at each other with deep love, and we will go and partake in a lovely lunch on the veranda."

God, Ellis, can you get any more delusional? Stop living in the movies. Stop lying to yourself. . . . And ain't I the pot calling the kettle black? Who's got the blow-up doll in her car dressed up like her dead son?

God, how crazy this is. How crazy all of this has been. What the hell am I doing here?

Ellis lay very still for a moment before his eyes flickered open and looked at the ceiling for the first time in five hours, and when he recognized the crownlike, stainless-steel light fixture as the one in his room on Wilna Street, he sighed, lay very still for a moment, then finally rolled his head leftward, toward the door.

"Irene," he said sedately, as if he'd just awakened from surgery. "You are home already."

Saying nothing, Geena crawled into bed beside Ellis and lay down.

"I feel very foolish," he said.

Geena reached for his hand and gently squeezed. "No one should feel foolish for taking a brave journey into the unknown," she answered. "You were going to leave me, weren't you Ellis? . . . Why?"

"You will not be here for much longer. . . . I do not want to be alone again."

Geena rolled onto her side, laid her arm across his chest, and rested her head on his shoulder. It was bony and hard, and she couldn't help but compare it to Barry's.

"You are lucky," Ellis said. "You have your husband to go back to."

You silly man. Can you read my mind?

"I can't go back," Geena said. "You have no idea what I've done, Ellis."

She felt him shift his head and look down toward her. "It cannot be that bad."

"It is. I haven't told you everything. They'll never forgive me."

Nor will you.

"But, Irene," Ellis said, "you are the one who told me that nothing lasts forever. No one can stay mad forever."

"Please . . . don't call me Irene."

"I beg your pardon?"

"Never mind."

This poor man is so alone. I don't want to be this alone.

That night for dinner, Geena drove the two of them out to Captiva Island and their favorite restaurant, the Bubble Room. They liked its junky, tropical-Christmas decor and the waiters dressed in Boy Scout uniforms and the toy train that ran on a track suspended from the ceiling, chugging throughout the restaurant like blood in a circulatory system.

Ellis ordered his favorite dessert of red velvet cake with butter-cream frosting. He'd started eating sweets about a month ago, for the first time in his life, finally allowing Geena's coaxing — "Don't deny yourself such a simple pleasure of this world, Ellis, you never know how long you're gonna be around" — to override Irene Norton's embedded motherly advice.

Geena loved watching him eat dessert. It seemed that after every bite Ellis had to remark on the pleasure washing over him: "Oh, my. Oh, my goodness. This is so creamy." And those eyebrows! Up and down, up and down, nodding their approval.

The waitress brought the check. Geena intuitively reached for the stolen MasterCard and handed it to her. Throughout all these weeks she'd been careful to make every dinner reservation in Ellis's last name. This way, if an overly friendly waiter read the name on the card and addressed her as Mrs. Norton, she could explain the mistake to Ellis.

The waitress had turned and started to walk away.

"Wait," Geena said.

"Ma'am?"

Geena leaned over her chair, toward the floor, and reached into her purse again. "I gave you the wrong card," she said. She unzipped the rearmost compartment of her wallet and pulled out her American Express.

"Here," she said, handing it to the young woman. "This is the right one."

Ellis looked at her and furrowed his eyebrows. "Have you reached your limit?" he asked her.

Geena folded her soiled pastel-blue napkin and smiled. "Yes," she answered. "I've reached my limit."

I can't do this anymore to this poor man. And now what? What happens next? I'm throwing myself back into the real world, right at their feet, like a body that's washed up on the beach.

I need a plan, I need a plan. . . . I'll get a job in a florist's shop and pay him back and start over.

Chapter Twenty-three

The doorbell rang, and Barry, still in his white Jockey briefs at ten in the morning, hurried from the kitchen table into the bedroom to get his robe. He was expecting the FedEx man and the final signed contract for a deal that would be the largest single transaction in Centennial Realty's history. After sitting empty and idle for two years, the old Fort Morgan airport was being sold to Pushway Leisure Industries of North America, Inc. If all worked as planned, the company's first golf carts would roll off the line within the year. Barry's commission, even after his parents' take, would be nearly a million dollars.

Barry swung open the front door.

"Barry, why aren't you at the office?"

"I'm waiting for FedEx."

"Why don't you wait at the office? You're spending too much time at home. Your father said so."

"Because they're delivering it here. Any other questions?"

"There's no need to get nasty with me, Barry Allen Pangborn. Aren't you going to invite me in?"

Barry glared at his mother, then moved aside and gave an exaggerated sweep of his arm to welcome her into the foyer. Dot walked in, her navy Ferragamo heels clicking on the slate floor.

"Lupe told me you fired her. Care to tell me why?"

Barry shrugged.

"That wasn't necessary, Barry. The Nuñez women have been with the Pangborns for nearly thirty years. . . . Your house looks clean, though." Dot looked around the great room, then walked into the kitchen. "What have you been eating?"

Barry had not spoken with his mother for nearly a month, after tracing directly back to her a rumor that Geena had withdrawn three hundred thousand dollars and fled to Puerto Vallarta with a salesman from the John Deere dealership in Limon. (Barry called the dealer to make certain no employee had inexplicably quit and disappeared.) She'd even asked Lonnie Buol at the First National Bank of Kit Carson County, of which the Pangborns were the largest shareholders, to forge a withdrawal form, which she strategically shared with a select few, talkative friends.

"Geena's right, Mom," Barry said when confronting her. "I could describe you to a stranger and he wouldn't believe me. You're a caricature of evil."

"We had to put closure on this, Barry. I am thinking of the family."

"I'm part of this family, Mom. Don't you think that lie reflects on me?"

"People know the two of you weren't happy, Barry. You argued in public all the time."

This comment proved to be the equivalent of a shove into a labyrinth, and Barry found himself spending his evenings wandering, turning, retracting his steps, trying to track the decline of their happiness.

He pulled out the scrapbooks Geena had made, chronicling each year of their lives together. She'd saved everything . . . a piece of dress caught in the car door on their third date . . . the receipt for their first *Rocky Horror Picture Show* . . . the speeding ticket he'd gotten when she was pleasuring him as they drove down I-25 to a Sting concert in Boulder.

On one page Geena had saved all of Nathan's baby teeth, gluing each one onto a large cartoonlike diagram of a mouth, with little explanations of where and how they fell out. A lower bicuspid was missing, and the note explained, *Lost while staying with Dot. She threw it away! Arrgh! Gotta love that woman!*

Barry looked through all seventeen volumes twice, the first time letting the contents pleasantly waft over him without introspection, just as one would enjoy the smell of fresh caramel corn or brownies in the oven.

But Barry, who majored in business administration and minored in logic, then set about scrutinizing the contents of each scrapbook, chronologically, trying to gauge the intensity of smiles . . . but everyone smiled for photos, he soon realized, so maybe that wasn't such a good barometer after all.

He remembered something Geena had said about reading body language because people often tried to mask their feelings on their face but often forgot about the rest of their body, an insight that had since helped him in many a land deal.

That's what he loved about his wife. Geena saw and mentioned things to Barry that would have swept past him like a speeding truck on the interstate, never to be seen again. She knew the strangest facts, like which parts of the tongue tasted salt and which parts tasted sweets. She could name the running backs of the Broncos and knew how to spin a piece of wood on a lathe. Geena knew something about everything.

He noticed in the photos that sometime in Nathan's second or third year, his wife changed the way she embraced her husband. In earlier shots she nearly always had two hands on him as if he were a fish that might slip away, but in later photographs it was a single arm around the shoulder, a hand in the hand. Was this a sign of a growing security on her part or detachment bred by disenchantment? How could he tell? Why could he not see this? Geena had once told him he'd developed blinders over the years for the same reason a ram grew horns. There was so much he could not see, so much he could not answer. Why had he stopped reading the *Rocky Mountain News* three years ago? Which had changed — the content of the paper, under direction of a new editor, or the interests and filters through which he now saw the world? How could someone know these things?

Yet this he knew for sure: Something

happened long before Nathan died, and it wasn't entirely his fault.

"What do you want?" he asked his mother. "Why are you here?" They were sitting at the kitchen table. Dot had piled up and moved the scrapbooks.

"I'm worried about you, honey. I want you to get on with your life."

Indeed, Barry had been missing from the family landscape. He no longer joined them for what everyone considered to be compulsory Sunday dinner at the Hoof and Horn, the restaurant adjacent to the sale barn. He did most of his phone work from home. Though he wasn't sure why, he hadn't even told any of them about the big deal he was closing that week.

"You all think I'm losing it, don't you?" he asked his mother.

"Well . . . you have stopped cutting your hair."

Barry unconsciously felt at the nape of his neck, where his black hair had started to curl upward. Geena liked his hair longer and would occasionally ask him to return to the style of his younger years.

"And you gave Marcy two weeks off just so she could help her daughter with her baby? Who's going to answer your phones for you?"

"I'm trying to keep things in a healthier perspective, Mom."

"And what is it with the clogs, Barry? Where did you get clogs?"

"Geena bought them for me. Nathan had a pair just like them."

Dot raised her eyebrows. "You're not in college anymore. Do I need to remind you of that?"

Barry toyed with the idea of telling her what he'd done the previous Tuesday in Denver — just to see her reaction. He had driven up to the downtown Westin in Denver to meet his buyer and sign some documents, and on the way home, driving down Colfax Avenue, Barry passed a sign for a psychic, a giant yellow-neon hand with a large blue human eye painted in the center. He passed it but fifteen blocks later made a U-turn.

In a small room with bloodred fabric draped over the walls — Barry felt as if he'd stepped into some giant uterus, a thought that pleased him because he knew Geena would have said it first, out loud — Madame Keech asked a series of questions and then sat back, palms up and resting on her crossed thighs in her purple crushed-velvet recliner in the corner. It was nothing like the experiences he'd shared with

Geena in the past, in which the mediums seemed more concerned with putting on a show, swirling their hands about a glass orb and blabbing out some schtick about energy and vapors and so forth.

Instead — and this actually gave her credibility in Barry's mind — Madame Keech was silent, the only movement being an occasional deep breath or a tight squinting of her already closed eyes.

After eleven minutes she opened them. "Here is what I know," she said. "And it is not much. I'm very sorry. I will only charge you half price."

"What did you see?"

"I saw a handsome old woman . . . and a lovely house. There were many birds. It was on the water somewhere. Also, an old man in a wheelchair, very grouchy. He looked familiar to me, but I can't think of who he was."

"Where?"

"I don't know. . . . But there are palm trees."

"So she's alive?"

Madame Keech shook her head. "I'm not sure," she answered. "I think the energy would have been different if she were dead, but I don't know for sure. I'm sorry."

In Barry's kitchen, Dot had gotten up to

help herself to a glass of water. "Barry," she said. "Promise me you'll get your hair cut. I want things back to normal."

Barry smacked the table with both open palms, causing his mother to jolt and toothpicks to jump like exploding popcorn from their cranberry-glass holder.

"Jesus, Mom! Did it ever dawn on you that I just might be grieving here?" The veins in his flushed neck swelled with blood.

"She ran away, Barry."

"And you do remember that I had a son who died eleven months ago? Hmm? Has that one slipped your mind?"

"Of course I remember. I can't believe the way you're talking to me."

Long, long overdue, Barry thought. If I'd done it sooner, my wife might still be here with me right now.

Chapter Twenty-four

"It is almost time to go, Irene," Ellis yelled through the bathroom door. "Will you be ready soon?"

"Yes, Ellis. I'll be ready."

"Is the dress giving you problems?"

"No."

"Are you sure it will be nice enough? Will it be appropriate?"

"Yeeeees, Ellliiiiis."

Much to his dismay, Geena had found her gown at the Goodwill store in Naples — "Why spend so much money on something I'm only going to wear once?" — a Badgley Mischka, sea-foam green with randomly placed clear sequins and long, clinging sleeves.

Ellis had changed into his rented tuxedo two hours earlier and was killing time on eBay and practicing his dancing with a Glenn Miller CD. He was fox-trotting with an imaginary partner when he heard the bathroom door open.

"Irene! Oh, my Lord! Look at you!"

"Do you like it?"

"Oh, yes!"

Ellis walked up to scrutinize her hair, which she had returned to her original blond color and pulled into a tight up-do.

"Those are coquina shells!"

A few weeks back, Geena and Ellis had taken a beach walk on Sanibel. As they were sitting at the surf line, Geena noticed how the small, subtly colored fingernail-shaped mollusks washed up by the thousands in each wave, and as the water receded and beached them, they would sit for a short while as if stunned, then suddenly realize, en masse, that the water had drained away. Their tiny, clear gelatinous legs would poke out from the shells and they'd all start digging like mad, pulsating in motion, disappearing within seconds. "It looks like they're melting into the sand," Geena had said.

This was exactly the impression she'd tried to re-create in her hair, twenty-two coquina shells, all in various phases of their mad dash toward safety. She had started with about fifty but thought it too much.

"How do those stay in?"

"A lot of hair spray. You don't think it's too whimsical?"

"Oh, no! You look like a princess from a fairy tale."

Geena wanted to arrive early because she had elaborate plans for the table. Ellis had described how each family brought their own dinner and decorations, and that there was a competition for a traveling trophy, called The Seminole, awarded to the most outstanding table.

"What do you mean 'outstanding'?" she asked Ellis. "Do they mean extravagant or unique?"

"I am not sure."

"Fine, then. We'll make sure we're both."

Geena knew exactly what she wanted, a spread just like Mina would have made at a Fourth of July picnic at Glenmont, the Edisons' mansion in West Orange, New Jersey.

Ellis fished all of his mother's silver from the top shelf of the hall closet, and Geena was thrilled to find silver goblets, eight of them, just enough for everyone at the table.

Geena scoured Lee County for rental candelabras, and when she was just about to give up and rethink her decor theme, she remembered reading an article weeks ago in the travel section of *The Palm Beach Post* about the antebellum charm of Tallahassee. She drove the six hours north and not only found three four-foot-high silver candelabras but also a collection of silver serving dishes and napkin rings made of silver cherubs.

On the way home, Geena bought ten yards of white silk at a wholesale fabric shop in Tampa. She would drape this around the candelabras and let it fall to the floor in spots, like trains of wedding gowns. In the center of the table would stand the stuffed peacock and an immense crystal vase, bursting with fresh tropical flowers.

She found gold-colored chargers at the outlet stores out by the university and faux-crystal flutes at T.J. Maxx. Ellis worried that people would discover they weren't real crystal, but Geena reassured him that no one would know the difference.

As they were finishing the table, Judith arrived with the five employees who worked in the mayor's office. She wore pearls and a knee-length black tuxedo suit, and, like Geena, had her hair in an up-do. Ellis could not help but stare; it reminded him of the times when he was small and he would see his teachers out of their school environment, shopping in his mother's store.

"Ellis, you're wearing tails!" Judith said, and she leaned into him and kissed him on the cheek. "And you must be Irene." She offered her hand to Geena. "I can't believe we haven't met."

"Yes, it's hard to believe," Geena said.

"It certainly is," replied Judith, raising her eyebrows.

She's on to me. I can tell she's on to me.

"Excuse me, please. I need to get the food ready."

Ellis had chosen the meal of fried chicken, dinner rolls, deviled eggs, and celery with cream cheese smooshed into the half-moon hollow centers and topped with raisins. For dessert Geena served apple dumplings, Thomas Edison's favorite sweet. Throughout the meal, she poured champagne for all. Geena had picked a sweeter, cheaper variety because she knew Ellis would like it better, and he did indeed. By the time the coronation began he was enjoying his second flute of bubbly drink. His cheeks were warmed and flushed, and his smile perpetual.

"Are you having a good time, Ellis?" Geena asked.

"Lovely. Just lovely."

Ellis had insisted that Geena and Judith flank him at the table, and as each young man and woman of the Court of Edisonia was introduced, he would whisper commentary on the families they represented.

"The Hardemans . . . Now the Jerry Hardemans used to own the dairy next to *The News-Press.* I am not sure what they are doing now because, as you know, the dairy has been torn down."

A tall but chubby brunette was announced as Jennifer Anne Hartupee. Judith leaned into Ellis.

"Hartupee . . . as in granddaughter of Mary Jayne?"

"Yes, of course," he answered.

After the coronation and dinner, the dance began. With Geena on one arm and Judith on the other, Ellis milled about the entire banquet hall, all the while luxuriating in the comments about his young escorts and elaborately decorated table.

Overhead, silver, gold, and yellow streamers attempted to disguise the Quonset hut–like ceiling, which was blemished with cumulus-cloud-shaped, tea-colored stains from many a tropical storm. A purple carpet runner dissected the hall, stretching from the main door all the way up to the thrones, and Geena could not help but notice that Ellis led the three of them onto this rug whenever possible as they flitted from table to table.

At table number 6, Ellis introduced Judith and Geena to the Meekers, owners of the Cadillac dealership that had been in the family since the thirties. That past year they had finally managed to coax their only son, Robert, back home from northern California to take over the business. His bow tie was speckled with yellow smiley faces, and the elder Mrs. Meeker frowned at her son when Judith complimented him on it.

At table 11 they talked with Dickie Stallard, a native son who had been commissioner of the Lee County Mosquito Control District for the past forty-seven years. Joining him at his table were Ben and Marga Wilcox, who owned motels out on Fort Myers Beach. (Ellis later explained to his escorts that the family had recently sold its holdings and erected for themselves the first granite mausoleum in all of Lee County. "I have seen it," Ellis said. "It is very garish. I believe it makes them feel like royalty.")

They finally came to the Hartupees, table number 9. Mary Jayne, wearing a red-sequined gown, immediately stood up. Like an out-of-town grandmother testing her grandchildren's loyalty, she opened her arms in invitation to lure Ellis away from his escorts. He dutifully stepped forward, took her hands, and she leaned into him, kissing both his cheeks.

"Ellis! I'm so glad you decided to get a table this year. And your table! You'll surely win the Seminole."

"Thank you, Mary Jayne," he said. "I would like to introduce you to my friends. This is Irene Wolff. She is a reporter with the *Cleveland Tribune* newspaper and is writing an article about me . . . so you had better be careful what you say around her or it might show up in a major metropolitan newspaper.

"And this is Judith Ziegler, chief executive officer of the Edison Winter Estate."

"We've met," Judith said. "Haven't we, Mary Jayne? Very nice to see you again."

"So are you enjoying your first coronation ball, Miss Ziegler?" Mary Jayne asked.

"It's lovely," Judith answered. "And very interesting. I'm still trying to decipher the local culture, as you're well aware."

"Yes . . . so . . . do you plan on getting your own table in the future or do you plan on still being here next year?"

Judith forced a smile. "I've promised Ellis a dance," she said. "Would you please excuse us? . . . Oh, and your granddaughter is lovely. I'm so sorry she didn't get the crown. Perhaps next year."

Judith turned toward Geena. "Do you mind?" she asked.

"Not at all."

When they got to the dance floor, a string quartet from Edison Community College was playing a piece by Mozart. Ellis pulled a pair of white gloves from the inside breast pocket of his rented tuxedo and put them on. Judith wondered if they were for effect or if he didn't like the intermingling of body oils and germs. More than once she'd seen him open doors with a handkerchief or pencil.

"Madame?" Ellis said, holding up his hands for Judith to take.

"I've got one small confession," she said. "I don't know how to dance."

"But this is only a waltz."

Judith shrugged her shoulders and shook her head.

"You truly do not know how to do the waltz?"

"I was always the fat girl sitting at the wall, Ellis. I've danced with maybe five men my whole life."

Ellis imagined her as a high school girl, sitting in a chair with her arms folded in her lap, perhaps kicking an errant balloon that rolled in front of her chair, trying very hard to look content and not interested in the goings-on of the dance floor. She could be maddening as a boss, but he thought right now that they might very well have been good friends back then. Both of them appreciated beauty and intelligence. Both were being raised, alone, by their mothers. Both had a deep love of history, and they didn't seem to care at all what others thought of them.

Ellis smiled and wiggled his gloved fingers, beckoning her to join him.

"And I was always the skinny boy sitting at the wall," he said. "But that is the past, and the present calls for a waltz. . . . May I?

"Okay . . . now . . . we are going to step in the shape of a rectangle by counting in threes. I move forward with my feet — that is called leading — and you move yours backward. . . . Are you ready?"

Midway through the dance, Judith was comfortable enough to look up from her feet and smile at Ellis.

"That was not a nice thing to say to

Mary Jayne," Ellis said. "One does not get a chance to win the throne the following year. Her chance is over."

"I know, Ellis. I was rubbing salt in her wound."

"But why?"

"Have you heard the rumors she's been spreading about me?"

"I have not," he said, and stopped dancing.

"Well, there are plenty."

They walked to the edge of the dance floor. Ellis looked around to make sure no one was listening to them.

"Please tell me. I have not heard them."

"I'm not going to dignify them."

"I would like to know. Really."

"All right. There's the one that says I'm being investigated by the IRS for my payroll ledger."

"No!"

"Oh, yes . . . and one of the more salacious, one of my personal favorites, that I'm a lesbian and my partner is one of the waitresses at the Banana Leaf, *and* that we were caught making love on an inflatable raft in the Edisons' swimming pool."

For the first time all night, Ellis's smile melted. He started to shake his head. "That is not right," he said. "She should not be saying things like that. She of all people."

"What do you mean, 'She of all people'?"

Ellis looked at her with wariness.

"It is nothing."

"Oh, Ellis, you're a horrible liar! What is it?"

Ellis shook his head and nervously fumbled with one of his silver cuff links. "No."

Judith grabbed both of Ellis's forearms and squeezed them as would a parent, gently but with authority, delivering a hint of necessary pain that might, someday, help save his life.

"This lady's crazy, Ellis. She wants me fired. She will stop at nothing. If there is any information that can help, then please share it. You can swear me to secrecy."

Ellis sighed and shook his head. Was this what happened when you intertwined your life with the lives of others? Was this what it was like to have close friends? Must you always inherit their problems, and was it true that their happiness and livelihood could hinge on something you said or did or simply knew?

Ellis remembered a scene from the movie *Being There*, in which Peter Sellers plays a sheltered gardener not accustomed to high drama in his life, and when he suddenly finds himself plunged into a situation of chaos, he reaches for the television remote control and points it at the people who are causing the horrible friction, trying to click them away.

Ellis thought of how he often hid behind one of his couch pillows during such a scene, clutching it as if it were a floatable seat cushion from an airplane and hiding his eyes when necessary. Oh, to have that pillow right now! . . . and to regain the control he once had in his life! Thomas Edison's doctor had said one reason the inventor lived to be eighty-four, despite his horrible diet and chronic sleeplessness, was because he was so adept at controlling his environment. He did as he wanted, when he wanted, damn everyone else, and it was a mantra that had successfully guided Ellis through so much of his life. Do not bend, do not give in, do not intertwine with the emotions and problems of others or you risk drowning in anxiety and sadness and regret. The inventor himself said, "The best thinking has been done in solitude. The worst has been done in turmoil."

But the estate! The future of Seminole Lodge might very well be in his hands.

Ellis had begun to trust Judith's abilities and vision. He had taken to stopping by her office at the end of each day, and she would update him on the improvements she was making. Occasionally he even asked her about her son, though she rarely said much about the boy. Ellis now knew very well that Judith would make Edison's tropical retreat the envy of museum curators everywhere, and that she would help shepherd the sacred Victorian lifestyle and its manners and thoughts into the modern world, transmitting them to the vulgar, vacuous cultures of today like the beam of a lighthouse . . . and perhaps true civility and chivalry could survive the millennia.

Mina herself had told him at their séance: No Holidazzle. Those were her precise words, she spelled it out. And if Mary Jayne were not shot down before Judith Ziegler was, then Judith's wishes might very well blow away in the wind. This would be Ellis's sad legacy.

"Judith, I must tell you something that nobody but two people in the entire world know."

"Yes?"

"Mary Jayne Hartupee . . . is not a Bivens."

"I'm sorry?"

"Bivens is her maiden name. You do know the name? They are very large landowners. They built the Twin Palms Mall. They are one of the oldest, wealthiest families in Fort Myers."

"And she's not a Bivens? What are you saying, Ellis?"

"I am saying that Mary Jayne is my half sister."

"What?"

"Mary Jayne's father is not Lloyd Bivens. Her father is my father. That is why my mother made him leave town. He was committing adultery. Of course, no one knows this. If you do not believe me, I can show you some photographs of my father. She looks quite like him."

"Oh . . . my . . . God."

"I have their love letters. Mother saved them because she thought they might come in handy someday."

"Ellis!"

"I am not even certain that she knows. Perhaps her mother did not tell her. . . . But I suspect she does because she has always been very nice to me."

"May I borrow the letters?"

From afar, Ellis watched Mary Jayne Hartupee dancing with her husband, sharing comments and laughter with other women as the couples glided past each other. Ellis liked how her long fingernails matched the red of her dress, though he now remembered how his mother had said that red was an inappropriate color for a lady to wear . . . as an accent, yes, but never more than that.

Perhaps Mary Jayne was not that awful of a person — after all, his mother did leave her in charge of Holidazzle — but he knew now that they both had been horribly misguided. Seminole Lodge was not meant to be a dollhouse for their play. She deserved dignity, and while Mina might have appreciated having some twinkling white lights hung on the porch and wrapped around the occasional trunk of a royal palm, she most certainly would not — in fact, did not, according to what they'd learned in the séance — approve of turning the historic home into something akin to the It's a Small World ride at Disney World.

"That will not be necessary," Ellis said to Judith. "You do not need the letters. I will take care of this."

Chapter Twenty-five

After months of reviewing her inventory and the Edison collections in Michigan, New York, and New Jersey, Judith Ziegler knew of every item that should be — and wasn't — resting securely among the leafy, fragrant confines of the Edison Winter Estate. Everything. Down to the last crispy sprig of goldenrod in the laboratory, to Mina's extra-large, black-and-red palm-frond-pattern swimming suit from Irene Norton's Dress Shop, to the pieces of organic black rubber that, now dried and cracking from old age, rattled about the bottom of test tubes like leeches long dead.

In several trips to the Northeast, Judith had read nearly all of Mina's writings, but what seemed to be missing were the day-to-day details of her life as a young newlywed, especially during those early, short winter days spent in Fort Myers. She was certain there was a missing correspondence; it was just too important of a period in the life of a young bride for whom writing seemed as critical as breathing. Judith had heard anecdotes of a woman struggling to duplicate the garden-party life of wealthy New Jersey in the frontier of Fort Myers, much like Carol Kennicott, the East Coast bride in *Main Street* who tried to plant the seeds of culture in her new, small-town Midwestern home.

Repeatedly, Judith thought of Ellis and his inexplicable about-face, his defection to the other side, his new knowledge of Mina's emotional landscape.

In fact, Ellis's tours of Seminole Lodge had become so laden with the details of Mina's wintertime life in southwest Florida that Judith pulled him off his normal duty and assigned him to a new once-a-day tour entitled Behind the Bright Ideas: The Woman of Seminole Lodge. Thrilled with the new task, Ellis suggested they give free orchids to every woman on his tours. Judith compromised by offering color postcards of the white, Georgia O'Keeffe–like *Richard Mueller* that lived in a bough of the sea grape off the guesthouse porch. Ellis had assured her that it had been planted there by Mina herself and not by some passing egret or overzealous member of the Lee County Women's Club.

In her effort to improve the quality of the tourist's experience at the Edison Winter Estate, Judith continued to import experts from New Jersey and New York to secretly audit the tours, including Naomi Price, curator of the Mina Edison collection at the Chautauqua Institution.

"I'm not sure if it's all accurate, but he certainly captures her personality," Naomi reported to Judith of Ellis's tours. "He takes great liberties in expressing her personal thoughts. I have to say, he does know the botany, though."

"You know her journals and travelogues," Judith said. "Don't you think his tours sound as if she'd written them?"

"Yes. Exactly."

"And how can that be?"

Naomi reached for one of the last few lemon balls in Judith's new electric-aqua, cube-shaped decanter on her desk. She pulled the ends with her fingers and watched the clear cellophane slowly twirl open.

"Maybe he's just in touch with his feminine side," she said.

"No," Judith replied. "It's just too pitch-perfect. I know these things, I know dialogue. My parents were actors."

"Did you ask him what his source of information was?"

"Of course. Several times."

"And?"

Judith reached for a cherry ball, the last. Unlike Naomi, she simply pinched on one end, effortlessly squeezing it from the cellophane as if it were a gob of dried toothpaste blocking the flow. "He says it's from a source on the Internet. But he won't let me pin him down on it. He could be remembering her from his childhood. He must have known her and spent time here. He's mentioned seeing her with his mother, but I don't think he could remember such detailed conversations and comments this late in life. Frankly, I haven't pushed it because his tours are so popular. I had someone in here last week from *Le Monde*."

Naomi stood up to leave. "Well, I'm going. I want to enjoy some of Sanibel before I head back tomorrow. What time in the morning?"

"Six forty-five. Meet here."

"And what does one wear to a bust? Black?"

"Sensible shoes," Judith said. "We're gonna be scattering like mad ants."

337

The living room was dark except for the light on the corner table, a lamp with a big cylindrical white shade that had somewhat yellowed over the past half century and smelled like formaldehyde when it got too warm. Although Geena liked watching movies in the dark, Ellis preferred to keep a light on, especially when the choice was even the least suspenseful, as was this evening's: *The Man Who Fell to Earth.*

They took turns picking movies, alternating their picks on Netflix.com. The previous night they had watched *On Golden Pond* with Katharine Hepburn. Geena had chosen tonight's film, in which David Bowie plays an alien whose spaceship crashes to earth, where he proceeds to sell his gold jewelry and hire someone to build a worldwide megacorporation.

Ellis fell asleep within twenty minutes, his hands resting on his lap, his head leaning straight back. His mouth had dropped open, emitting the dry, raspy sound of the suction wand that dentists use. Because she was the only one watching, Geena took liberties with the remote, replaying spots in the first third of the movie in which Bowie seemed to be slightly off-balance or afflicted with a subtle case of vertigo. He was gaunt and pale and dressed in black, his face revealing a slightly pained and bewildered look as he traversed the landscape of a strange new world, walking tentatively, as one does on ice.

I know just how you feel, buddy. I've been there. God, I've been there!

So much of the past year was unclear to her now. Time had passed, but she'd reaped and stored none of the physical details from living it. It reminded Geena of how she used to drive to Denver with the cruise control on, and her mind would check out and go somewhere — where? — and twenty-six miles later, like a yo-yo returning to the palm, she would snap back and wonder what medical miracle had kept her eyes seeing, her muscles moving.

Geena now remembered a trip she'd taken to New York with Barry. This was sometime after Nathan's death, but she could not recall the shows they saw, the hotel they stayed at, whether they went shopping.

She recalled the wreck of the mail truck outside Atlanta, but could not remember how that bag of mail got into her car, that bag of mail that was still in her car. And what was the final straw that had pushed her to flee in the first place? Obviously Dot's nasty prodding. Obviously something Barry did as well . . . not standing by her side as he should have . . . but what could have been so awful as to shove her off into a world, all alone, like this?

Geena looked over at Ellis, who was now mouthing unintelligible words in his sleep.

Lord, what is this man dreaming up now? He's the crazy one — I'm not.

She got up from the couch, slowly so as not to wake Ellis, and went into her room. She pulled a shoe box from under the bed, opened it, and retrieved the three months of SunBank MasterCard bills she'd intercepted and hidden from her host.

Geena sat on the bed and began reading through them, line by line, looking for clues that might give meaning to these cloudy months of her life. She noticed a southward movement, obviously. . . . Macon, Jacksonville, Daytona, Miami . . . and several charges at different spas and nail places along the way. Geena remembered buying the sundresses at a Dillard's in Jacksonville — she was wearing one now, after all — but what was the $45.89 purchase at Welton's Surf Shop in Flagler Beach? What did she eat at Ed and Netty's Lobster Shack in Stuart?

She thought of the story she'd read in the News from the North section of *The News-Press*, about some young farmer in one of the Dakotas who got his hand caught in a rock-picker with no one nearby. After three days of no food and water he grew delirious, and his subconscious mind knew that he would die if he did not use his pocketknife to cut off his own arm. The young man began to hallucinate that he was at a barbecue at a Mexican resort and that he was cutting some beef apart for guests, and it was a horrendous, tough piece of meat, which he carved at with a vengeance, all the while actually cutting off his own flesh and bone until he was free. Then he got into his pickup and drove himself to the hospital.

How does that happen? How do our minds lie to ourselves so we can do what we have to do? . . . And why in the hell did I have to do all this?

Geena reached into her big purse and found her calculator. As she began adding up the total of the bills, she was soon interrupted by a noise outside. Geena was set to ignore it — a fat, swaybacked possum, crippled by a car, had been rooting through the metal trash cans in the evenings — but when she heard the muffled sound of children laughing, Geena shot off the bed and hurried to the window. She could see that the dome light of her Excursion was on, the door open.

Geena raced to the kitchen, flung open the back door, and ran out to the driveway. In the glow of the amber lights that illuminated Wilna Street she saw the two devil children from the river house sprinting barefoot across the grass. In the arms of the elder boy, his rubber head bobbing to the beat of the boy's strides, was Mr. Douglas.

"Stop!" Geena yelled. "You little shits!"

The boys had stripped him of the Hawaiian-print Jams she and Ellis had bought at a surf shop on Fort Myers Beach and thrown them on the ground, and as Geena sprinted after them she could not help but notice Mr. Douglas's newest acquisition, something that appeared to be a semi-erect penis bouncing in his white briefs.

Suddenly the source of this anatomical correctness made itself known; Geena saw the rounded tip of a clear-glass test tube poke free from the underwear's fly. With each stride the tube grew in length, and within seconds nearly all ten inches of it had slipped out, and as the boys crossed the Eagans' driveway the paraffin on the cork finally lost its grip on the cotton, and the tube fell from the safety of Mr. Douglas's underwear. It dropped to the concrete and shattered.

Geena stopped at the glittery mess of shards, catching her breath, and looked up to notice the boys disappearing with Mr. Douglas behind the green house on the corner of Wilna and McGregor.

"You little bastards!"

"What has happened, Irene?"

Awakened by her shouts, Ellis was walking down the sidewalk, toward her. He'd not noticed the empty backseat of the Excursion.

"They stole Mr. Douglas."

"Oh, no! Where is he?"

"Gone."

Ellis then noticed the shattered tube on the pavement, and when he recognized the paraffin-coated stopper he gasped and brought his palms up to his mouth. "Oh, my Lord," he said through his fingers. "Oh, no. This is horrible."

"When did you stuff the test tube in his underwear, Ellis?"

"Oh, no."

"What was it anyway?"

Nervous from Judith Ziegler's recent repeated queries for any Edison artifacts he might have had at home, Ellis had begun harboring Mina's bagged journal on his person, tucked into the elastic waist of his boxers, in a navy blue, felt Crown Royal bag with gold fringe that he and Geena had found for five cents at the St. Vincent de Paul Thrift Shop that now occupied the old Eckerd drugstore near his house. Like a family in the federal witness protection program, the tube had been shuttled from hiding place to hiding place. Recently convinced of the undetectable, inviolable safety of a grown man's undergarments, Ellis finally chose the intimate confines of Mr. Douglas's Calvin Kleins.

He slowly crouched down to the driveway and picked up the stopper, still stuck in a ring of jagged clear glass that looked like a crown for some tiny snow princess. Closing his eyes, he brought it to his nose and sniffed at it.

"Ellis, answer me," Geena said. "What was in the tube? You've been hiding that thing all over the house."

With a sad, wrenching look of anguish upon his face, Ellis shook his head. "Oh, I am a most unworthy shepherd of history. . . . This can never be replaced."

"What are you talking about? It was empty."

He told her the story. Geena, growing increasingly impatient with his constant reinventions of reality, did not believe him. Yet the sadness on his face reminded her so much of Nathan. She saw this now, his resemblance to her son, not just in the way they both used their eyebrows as an expressive second mouth, but also in the face structure itself. They had the same cheekbones, the same fleshy earlobes that were the envy of women.

This moment on the Eagans' driveway reminded Geena of the time their bulldog Hercules got run over by the water-softener deliveryman in their driveway in Sublette. And just as she did on that day with Nathan, Geena took Ellis in her arms to comfort him. He laid his head on her shoulder, his nose pushing into her neck. Ellis sniffled. Geena knew he was crying, and she patted and rubbed his back.

"Maybe I can glue it back together," she said.

Ellis lifted his head to look at her. He wiped his nose with the sleeve of his cardigan. "Oh, no, that will not be necessary, Irene. It is gone forever."

Ellis laid his head back down. The two of them, embracing, unconsciously began to rock, the weight shifting from left feet to right as if they were slow-dancing.

An ambulance bound for Lee Memorial, sirens blaring, passed by on McGregor, and as the sound melted away, Geena heard in its quiet wake the parrots overhead, coming home to roost for the evening. She thought of how the first of the robins would have returned by now to eastern Colorado, and of the brown blanket of moist, compressed elm leaves in the back field, formed by a winter's accumulation of heavy, wet snow, and how it gave way to the thousands of green, squeaky-clean shoots that would soon be daffodils and tulips and hyacinths. Geena planted hundreds of new ones every year, and Barry would laugh at the manner in which she did so, tossing each bulb backward, blindly, over her left shoulder, then digging its new home in whatever random spot it happened to land upon.

Ellis pulled away from Geena and looked at her. "I am sorry about your loss," he said. "I am afraid he will not be back."

Geena wiped away his tears with her thumb. "No, you're right," she said. "I can't replace him. But things always come back in one form or another, don't they? We've learned that, haven't we?"

She took his hand and they walked back

to the house. The dog-bark machine was silent as they approached the steps of the porch.

I've got to show him how to change those batteries before I leave.

After they parted for the night, Geena was lying awake in bed, the dregs of adrenaline still trickling through her veins. She decided to clean out her purse and dumped the contents of it on the bed.

Geena picked up her cell phone. She flipped it open, and the green panel of numbers glowed for the first time in months. She looked at it for a few moments and then, using both thumbs, quickly pressed out her phone number in Colorado.

Barry answered after three rings.

"Hello? Hello? Can I help you?"

The voice she remembered as terse and angry instead sounded expectant and kind and vaguely vulnerable.

Hopeful?

Not wanting him to hang up, Geena cleared her throat as bait.

"Hello? . . . This is the Pangborns."

He said "the Pangborns" plural!

"Who's there?" he asked. "Can I help you?"

Yes! Yes! You can help me!

"Hello?" he said again. "Hello?"

Geena had almost forgotten the sensation of the deep, buzzing vibration of Barry's voice on her phone, and she impulsively brought the earpiece to her mouth and closed her eyes so that she could feel her husband's words on her lips: "Hello? . . . Is anybody there?"

Chapter Twenty-six

Barry dropped into the cordovan leather couch in his father's office and began stroking the slick surface, still new and free of creases.

"When did you get this?" he asked.

"Not over there," Brit said. "Over here, at the desk. I don't wanna have to yell across the room. . . . Your mom found it somewhere."

As Barry moved to the chair opposite his father, Brit brought his feet up onto the glass top of his walnut desk. He crossed his legs, and the recessed halogen lights above cast a shine upon his polished, tan boots. They were new, and Brit stopped to admire them. These had a more rounded toe than most of his boots, with an unusual stitching pattern of interlocking squares that looked Mayan-like in design. In the middle of each square was an inset piece of turquoise with his favorite hue of the stone — a slightly more greenish tinge than the more common, popular sky blue — marked with tiny black fissures that looked like the spider veins on middle-aged ankles.

He brought his hands behind his head, interlocking his fingers to make a hammock for his skull. Brit had a habit of doing this. Barry remembered that Geena had always said it made him look like a cobra rearing up for battle. "So how are things goin'?"

"Fine," Barry answered.

Brit craned his neck forward to look at his son's feet. Barry had changed into boots for the meeting with his father.

"You're lookin' pretty casual nowadays."

"I'm working more out of the house."

"We don't see much of you anymore. Your mom misses seein' you for Sunday dinner. Any reason you not showing up?"

"Been busy. What did you want to see me about?"

Brit began drumming his fingers on the table in two-second intervals. Barry had wondered for years if the cause of this customized, predictable cadence was the lugubrious, flashing red light atop KGIR's radio tower, which could be seen, pulsing at the same beat, outside

Brit's north-facing picture window.

"It was a cold winter this year," Brit said.

"Yes . . ."

"Your mom doesn't like the cold much. Makes her crabby."

"What are you getting at, Dad?"

"A month in Arizona wasn't enough this year."

"What are you saying?"

"Jesus, Barry, what bug is up your butt today? Be patient, okay? I've got something to tell you. Your mom and I are gonna start spending half the year at the Scottsdale house."

"Which means what?"

"Which means, you impatient little shit, that Jerry's gonna be in charge."

Barry shot to his feet. "Jerry!" He walked over to the window, then pivoted on his heels to look at his father. "Jerry?"

"Yes, Jerry."

"But Jerry can't sell a gold mine to a pauper."

"Jerry's the oldest. It's only fair."

"Jesus! . . . Jerry!"

Barry grabbed fistfuls of his coarse black hair at the sides of his head, slowly tightening his grip, and when he reached the point at which he could bear no more, he stomped his foot on the Navajo rug.

"Shit! I can't believe this. I can't believe you'd do this to me."

"See? There you go again. Stampin' your damn foot like a little boy. Frankly, Barry, your mom and I don't think you have the maturity to run this company."

Barry looked at him with surprise. "How can you say that? Didn't that airport deal mean anything to you? I make more money than anyone in this family."

Brit brought his feet down from the desk to the floor. "It's more than making money — it's dependability," he said. "And I'm afraid you ain't got it, son."

"How can you say that? I'm the one you always go to. I'm the good son. I do everything you expect me to do. I'm chairman of the Kit Carson County Republicans, and I'm not even a damn Republican!"

Brit raised his eyebrows. "Excuse me?"

Barry sat silent for several moments, and then, sensing that enough of the weight on the scale in his mind had been moved to one side, and the creeping movement downward now appeared to be irreversible, he said, "I haven't voted for a Republican president my whole life. I voted for Clinton. Both times."

"Well, that certainly is news to me."

"And did you think I really wanted to go to friggin' redneck Colorado State? No. Negative. I wanted to go to Boulder, but I knew you'd shit a brick."

"Now, Barry . . ."

"I can go on and on, Dad. No, I do not like to hunt. I don't believe in Jesus. I'd rather be out shovelin' cow patties than go on our asinine Brit's Boys gambling trips to Reno every year. I've lived my whole life being someone I'm not just to please you and mom. And then I tried to get Nathan to do it, and look where that got me. My son died, hating me, Dad. Do you know how that feels?"

Brit, silent, scowled at his son. His face was flushed.

"I asked you: Do you know what that feels like? No one gets over that. How do I get on with my life after something like that? . . . And Geena . . ."

Brit stood up from his chair, walked over to the window, and watched Marie, one of the front-desk secretaries, getting out of her mud-splattered green Blazer with three sacks of food from Burger King. Dot, who monitored her husband's cholesterol as if it were her own, was shopping in Denver for the day, buying a Lalique vase she would tell her husband she bought at Target. Brit had taken advantage of her absence by ordering two double bacon cheeseburgers and a large order of fries. Seven years after supposedly giving up cigarettes, he also still sneaked his smokes in the bathroom at the office, where he kept a supply of Listerine and Lysol spray in the medicine cabinet. All the Pangborn men lied to their wives, and the wives to their husbands, and these small lies seemed to desensitize them for the larger ones. With Dot and Brit as an example, they all learned that life was easier — emptier, Geena had always said — if everyone smiled and nodded, harboring true opinions as dark secrets, then going about their way to do as they pleased. It's why the others appeared to be content while Geena and Barry were arguing, refusing to abandon truth, oftentimes their desires and goals clashing and sparking, occasionally producing a fire large enough for the family to stand around and raise their eyebrows, tsk-tsking. But still they stood there, mesmerized and enjoying the heat of passion produced by an honest-to-God, pulsating disagreement.

And yet he realized now that he, too, had been lying to his wife for too long. Just as a child loyally votes his parents' party affiliation in a mock election at school, Barry had been taking a side he didn't truly believe in. Somewhere along the way, his and Geena's discussions had spun into arguments that had settled nothing but disturbed everything because there was no truth or conviction on his part.

"You know," Brit said, "that woman . . . she ruined your life. You'd respect me and your mother more if it hadn't been for her."

Barry stood up to leave. "I haven't heard you speak her name in five months. I want to hear you say it."

"Don't be an ass."

"Come on — say it."

"You're crazy."

"You can't. You won't. You want to pretend she never even existed. What a warped sense of reality you have."

"That's no way to talk to your dad."

"Say it."

"Get the hell outta here."

"Say it. Gee-na, Gee-na, Geeeee-nuh. See my lips, Dad? Geen-nuh. Let me help you here: Geena rhymes with hyena."

Barry left the office, stopped by 7-Eleven for a frozen burrito, then returned home. Another five inches of dry snow had fallen since he left that morning, and as he walked from the garage down the flagstone driveway, his boots made a crunchy squeaking noise that comforted him.

Like half-submerged porcupines, the slender, silver-green spikes of the yucca plants poked out from the snow beneath the mailbox. Barry immediately thought of the quarter-size red Christmas balls Geena would stick on the end of each spike every year.

Barry leafed through the day's mail on the way back to the house, throwing all but a few envelopes into the trash before coming inside. He turned the television to ESPN — *NFL Rookie Watch* was on — and sat on the couch with the American Express bill in his hand. One of his brothers had been the victim of identity theft the previous winter, and Barry had since looked over every charge of his credit card bills. Usually the American Express statement was their longest, sometimes seven or eight pages, but ever since Geena had disappeared, and Barry hadn't been to Denver except for one business trip to get a contract signed, the last few statements now fit on just two pages.

As he stole glances of the Steelers' Ben Roethlisberger, Barry weighed the envelope in his hand; it seemed thicker this month. He wondered if they'd stuffed in another flyer for travel insurance.

He tore it open and began reading line by line this diary of his consumer life for November . . . $64.35 to B & B Dry Cleaners . . . $125.33 to Melcher's Family Department Store . . . $37 to Tamco Ace Hardware . . . $36.43 to Riddick's Texaco . . . $14.22 to the Golden Corral in Fort Morgan.

Barry brought the second page to the front, expecting it to be blank, but when he saw it full of itemized charges . . . and then the third page . . . and the fourth . . . his breathing grew shallow and quiet.

Geena's card had been resurrected on the southwest Gulf Coast of Florida, and someone appeared to be using it in the same energetic, eclectic tradition of his wife. There were charges from Island Girl Boat Charters, Publix grocery store, the Lazy Flamingo, Thai Gardens . . . and what did someone buy at a place called the Bubble Room?

And what did it mean? Had someone found her purse in a ditch someplace in Oklahoma or Georgia? Didn't all criminals end up in Florida at one time or another, as if the weight of their crimes were too heavy to bear and they fell downward, like marbles, into that peninsula of hedonism, the underbelly of the country?

Barry got up to call American Express, and as he held for a live representative, pacing the kitchen, he blew his nose in a dirty kitchen rag and looked again at the two pages of charges. There were three at a Nordstrom. What kind of criminal would shop at a Nordstrom? And a Michael's craft store?

Like the tiny pins in a lock as they fall into place, one by one, on the juts and grooves of a key being pushed into the dark, metal hole, a hazy picture of hope began to click into place. There were the three different charges to Home Depot, which Geena loved so much she'd bought one of the HOME DEPOT — MY TOY STORE bumper stickers. There was the $6.34 charge at Ben & Jerry's Ice Cream in Bonita Springs (Geena's favorite flavor was Cherry Garcia; Barry had no idea the company had retail outlets) and two charges to a Pizza Hut To Go in North Fort Myers (even though she preferred the ubiquitous Domino's, Geena refused to buy there because she didn't like the antifeminist, antichoice leanings of the companys' Catholic founder).

And then a new wave of skepticism and

reason — those persistent, adult scourers of youthful optimism — washed over him and toppled his wobbly structure of hopeful thoughts. Surely he was playing mind games with himself, a sick, grieving man in search of answers, in need of hope. Perhaps his mother was right — he needed to move on and forget about her.

The American Express rep came on the line, and Barry queried her about the use of the card.

"There's been no question of theft," she said. "The spending pattern fits her profile."

"What other charges have been made since the statement was issued?" he asked.

As the woman pulled up a different screen, Barry could hear the muffled voices of other reps talking in adjacent cubicles.

"There was one four days ago at Boca Bargoons Fabric Warehouse in Fort Myers . . . and there's one for Florida Nails in Fort Myers, posted on Thursday, the twenty-first."

Barry's hopes sank as he envisioned Geena's unpainted, short nails, the one on her left thumb permanently split by a tiny canyon from the time it was sliced by a band saw in high school shop class. She was the first young woman to ever take shop at Lupton Valley High School, after organizing a petition drive and forcing the school board to allow females.

Still, something was nagging at him, and Geena had always told Barry that a nagging feeling was nothing more than the enlightened subconscious mind trying to poke its way into conscious thought with a message, like an uninvited courier knocking at the door during naptime.

Barry hung up, went into the den, and logged onto the Internet, and after typing in his password on the Cingular site, he clicked on your account and then Geena's phone number.

A list of phone calls began to form on the screen in that reluctant, haphazard manner in which dial-up modems dump information: part of a graphic here, another part there, two lines of information up top, five lines in the middle, the overall message unclear until all the pieces are in place, like a puzzle.

The calls had been dialed within the Florida 239 area code, all of them in the last eight days, all of them less than five minutes in duration . . . calls, he thought, that were made by someone who minimized her time on the cell phone because she worried about their deleterious impact on the psyche's energy levels.

And then he saw it, midway down the page of calls, in the sea of 239s, a 719.

Sublette's area code.

And his telephone number . . . *their* telephone number.

Chapter Twenty-seven

When Judith Ziegler was associate curator at Monticello, a vitriolic national TV talk show host resurrected the rumor that Thomas Jefferson had enjoyed an enduring love affair with one or more of his slaves. And though it was news that had been re-gurgitated and chewed upon and swallowed time and again over the last century, Judith, fresh out of Wellesley and twenty-three and new on the job, saw opportunity.

It was no secret that historic sites and museums were being left behind to drown in the foamy wake of America's speedboat culture — admission numbers were down everywhere, and the future looked even bleaker — and Judith thought that if the Monticellos of the world did not continu-ally prove their pertinence to the present, then they would grow obsolete and unim-portant and, thus, be discarded like twenty-six-volume encyclopedia sets, passenger trains, and the human appendix. So, with the reluctant support of her boss, Judith quickly organized a symposium entitled American Sexuality in Black and White: How and Why the Races Come Together Beneath the Sheets.

Within days, angry letters filled the op-ed pages of the *Richmond Times-Dispatch*. The VFW post in Charlottesville quashed its fund-raiser that would have helped restore the kitchen of Monticello. The Daughters of the American Revolution, some of its members on canes and in wheelchairs, protested outside the grassy entrance of the former president's white-domed Virginia home.

In a compromise, Judith dropped the last three words from the title, but still she got threatening phone calls, and someone scrawled *nigger luver* in the black paint of her Volvo. What finally saved her was the attention Monticello attracted throughout it all. Oprah Winfrey invited Judith to Chicago to discuss interracial love stories from throughout history. Whoopi Goldberg and Richard Gere asked to participate in the symposium.

"And now," Judith thought as she sat in the darkened chambers of the Fort Myers City Council, "now I'm fighting a bunch of stupid ladies about their plywood snowmen. This is not progress."

Though the Edison Home was item seven on the agenda, Judith had arrived early so she could save front-row seats. Ellis would be joining her. All her adult life, from college onward, she had chosen the front row. Judith believed that if you exhibited active listening, with nods of the head and furrowing of the eyebrows that showed not only ingestion but also careful digestion of their words, then the speaker would unconsciously feel flattered and beholden to you, the listener, because you'd made them think they'd fed you something nourishing and important, something that had changed you in some way. Really, it was nothing but blatant flattery, an act that tipped the balance of power from the talker to the listener. She couldn't understand why more people hadn't figured it out.

Again, Judith looked over her shoulder, toward the door that opened to the much lighter hallway. Ellis had been talking with Mary Jayne Hartupee for five minutes, and Judith was dying to know what was being said. Each time she turned to look, there was a different expression on Mary Jayne's face: impatience, skepticism, anger, sadness. At one point her eyes appeared to well with tears. Judith thought: I hope he's doing what I think he's doing.

Ellis had considered breaking his promise to accompany Judith to the city council meeting; he was incensed when he learned of Larry Livengood's arrest.

Larry called to tell Ellis what had happened after his sister posted bail and drove him back home to Passaic Avenue. He'd refused to cooperate with the detectives, so they searched his house from attic boxes to underwear drawer, all the while Judith checking off from her list the recovered items. They included, among others, two leather-bound experiment logs from the laboratory; a white porcelain bedpan, which Larry had been using to store his matchbook collection; framed photographs of the inventor and his first wife, Mary; a collection of Thomas's monogrammed, India-silk handkerchiefs, each a yard square; a chrome General Electric toaster that Larry was using as his own; a badger-hair shaving-cream brush, the bristles splayed outward from years of lathering the inventor's white-whiskered cheeks. In all, they recovered three large boxes of stolen booty.

"Did they find the test tubes?" Ellis asked.

"Hell yes, they found 'em. They took my whole house apart, Ellis. It's a goddamned wreck."

"Oh, my Lord! Are you going to prison, Larry?"

"Those things were given to me, Ellis. They can't send you to jail for accepting gifts. All those things belong to me."

Fear shot up in Ellis like a geyser. "Did you tell them I have one of the test tubes?"

"No. And take care of that one, Ellis. It's the last one Fort Myers has got. She's gonna ship the others up to New Jersey, just watch her."

Ellis called Judith immediately, and she came and picked him up and took him to the Village Inn on Cleveland Avenue. It took her an hour, two cups of hot chocolate, and a piece of French silk pie to calm Ellis down.

"So you are telling me that Larry is lying," he said.

"Yes, Ellis," she answered. "He stole the artifacts. They belong to the people of Fort Myers, to whom Mina left the estate. They were not intended to be personal collectibles. Frankly — and I'm trusting you won't pass this information on — he stole a lot more than artifacts."

"Have you found everything that was

missing?" Ellis asked.

"Not everything, Ellis. Why? Is there something I should know?"

"Oh, no," Ellis answered, and he thought of the cork stopper and shards of thin, clear glass now stowed in a dark brown sock in his bedroom bureau. Everything else he had managed to sneak back into the estate without detection, and if it was an item whose ownership was uncertain, such as the African-looking, ebony-wood spoons from the sideboard in the dining room, he brought them as well just to make sure nothing was left behind.

And the journal . . . what to do about the journal? Did anyone even know of its existence? Ellis still did not know who had put it there. He had eventually asked Judith if he could read the list of missing items, and there was no mention of any journal.

He knew he did not dare return it. Oh, the secrets within those pages! Perhaps no other person in the world knew so well the heart of the young bride from those first, few, self-doubting, and almost frantic years of marriage to Thomas. Indeed, the Mina of textbooks and museum exhibits was a buxom, opinionated woman who once visited the Buckingham Air Base east of Fort Myers during the war and, after watching a demonstration of a soldier firing a 50mm machine gun, said, "I'd like to try that" — and she did. The Mina of record was known to summon the mayor and other civic leaders as if they were her children or the staff in her own home. She called them the Roundtable of Fort Myers, and they would meet at Seminole Lodge to discuss the crying needs of civic reform, including, at her insistence, plans to help eliminate unnecessary street noise on the increasingly car-laden McGregor Boulevard.

And, of course, most historians knew of her tireless cheerleading for housewives. In interviews and speeches Mina often elevated women and their oft-overlooked caregiver contributions to society: "Mothers speak of the work of the home as drudgery, but I feel that one can create real art in handling linen and dishes. A linen closet properly kept is a joy forever. I would like to change the word 'housewife' to 'home executive'. Who is more executive than the homemaker? She is priceless to her husband. Could he find or afford anyone to fill such a position? I think not."

Ellis had fallen in love with a young bride who seemed as delicate and vulnerable as the orchids she so revered. And while he adored this secret side, Ellis knew that if it were thrown into the arena of modern culture, the media would sniff it out and tear it apart like famished hyenas, just as they'd done with Rock Hudson and his homosexuality, just as they'd done with Marilyn Monroe and her love affairs with the Kennedy boys. Ellis already was painfully aware that he'd carelessly lost one of her husband's sacred last breaths taken on this Earth. He vowed not to lose Mina's dignity as well.

From the corner of her eye, Judith saw Mary Jayne Hartupee walk into the darkened council chambers. She bent down and whispered to two women sitting near the front, and they reared back with perplexed looks.

She whispered some more, urgent and rapid, then turned and walked from the room. The women quickly collected their purses and notebooks and manila envelopes, including one that had PETITION written on it in thick black marker, and followed her out.

Ellis then appeared beside Judith, smiling with an expression that balanced between satisfaction and smugness.

"I think we can leave now," Ellis said. "Our business is done here."

"What happened?"

"Mary Jayne will not be speaking to the city council about Holidazzle. In fact, I am pleased to tell you that there will never be another Holidazzle."

"Ellis! What did you do? Did you blackmail her?"

Ellis smiled. "I would not be a gentleman if I spoke about it. Shall we go?"

"Are you serious about this?"

Ellis smoothed out the wrinkles on the thighs of his khaki Dockers. "Oh, yes. Mary Jayne will never bother you again. She is going to resign from the museum board."

"Ellis! You're kidding."

"I am not."

"I don't know what to say. . . . Can I take you to lunch?"

"I would like that very much, but I am afraid I cannot. There is something I must plan for."

Judith dropped him off at home, and when she saw Geena's patchwork-colored Excursion at the curb, she remembered the task she'd overlooked amid the joy and surprise of the last hour. Judith knew for certain now that there was no such newspaper as the *Cleveland Tribune*, not even in the form of an e-zine or obscure alternative weekly. Surely web-savvy Ellis knew this.

Surely by now his vanity would have forced him to search out the site of the newspaper that wanted to feature his life story.

Yet perhaps he was hiding the truth from her. Perhaps this truly was a cross-generational love affair, and Ellis was too embarrassed to let anyone know. She'd seen them hold hands and lock arms, and there was a new, sated, more nourished look about him now, with that ruddiness in his cheeks and a few extra pounds filling in the sunken, shaded dents of his thin frame. Judith thought it uncanny that this would happen to Ellis; she'd noted a similar evolution with the dead woman he loved so dearly. Looking through years of photographs, Judith could clearly chart the metamorphosis of a thin, ashen, and solemn bride into the middle-aged, smiling matriarch, pink and robust and juicy as a peach ripened in the sun. And she wondered now: Had Mina learned to accept and embrace her often-oblivious man, shortcomings and all? Or had she grown to love herself in spite of him?

Chapter Twenty-eight

Frowning, Ellis walked among the candy-colored kayaks lined up on the ground like bodies recovered from a disaster. "I am afraid none of these will do," he said. "For my task I need one that is not so brightly colored."

"It's for safety," said the teenage boy, his dark brown ponytail pulled through the back hole of a Caloosa Outfitters baseball cap. "They're painted bright so you don't get hit by a boat." His skin was dark beyond tan. Ellis wondered if he was from the Miccosukee Reservation. Perhaps his father was one of those large men who wrestled the alligators at that festival every year in the Everglades.

Ellis walked over to the more subdued canoes, some of them silver, others caramel tan and navy blue and the color of Christmas trees.

"If the kayaks are painted brightly for

safety, then why are these canoes painted to blend in with nature?" Ellis asked.

The young man shrugged his shoulders. "Good point. I don't know. . . . Then why don't you rent a canoe?"

It was tempting, but Ellis leaned away from the idea because he had never piloted a canoe before. The only time he'd paddled was with Geena, when they rented a double kayak at the Four Mile Cove mangrove preserve across the river from his house. He knew how to place his heels in the indentations pressed into the plastic body. He'd learned how to pull the vessel in and out of the water using the white PVC-pipe handles that hung, like earrings, from short black ropes on the ends of the boat.

But a canoe . . . how did one sit in a canoe, and which end was the front? Where did one put his feet? The single paddle did indeed appear to be simpler in design, but what happened if someone paddled for too long on one side?

No . . . a kayak it would be. The only other option Ellis had considered was the speedboat they'd rented for their nighttime trip out to the end of the Edisons' pier, but maneuvering something so large and motorized all by himself seemed even more impossible than swimming the half mile out to the spot in the channel where he needed to go. Besides, the kayak would provide a leisurely, moonlit ride, and though Ellis was somewhat unnerved about taking the trip alone, he also was looking forward to it. He could not wait to tell Geena what he'd done all by himself.

Ellis tried to visualize one of the apple red or neon green canoes on the Caloosahatchee at night. If the moon was half full, as tonight's would be, could someone see him in the channel from either bank, or from the concrete bridge that arced across the river like the skeletal back of an immense brontosaurus?

Red or green? He wondered which one Geena would pick. And then, as if she'd answered his call, Ellis got an idea. He would wrap the boat in dark green plastic trash bags and masking tape. Yes! That was it! That's exactly what she would do!

Since the green did not appear to be a naturally occurring color — indeed, it seemed to have a nuclearlike glow to it — Ellis chose the red. He rented it for a night and a day and asked that it be delivered to the end of Poinciana Street.

"Just dump it at the end of the street?" the boy asked.

"Please set it under the large banyan tree in the spot of grass beside the river. There is a bench there."

"Won't it get stolen or something?"

"Young man, that is a reputable neighborhood with fine homes and fine families . . . the founding families of Fort Myers. We do not have a problem with vandals. The kayak will be fine, I assure you. I would take it with me now, but there is no room in the taxi for it, as you can see."

That night, Ellis changed into his tennis shoes and put on a Fort Myers High School sweatshirt. On the front was a cartoon illustration of his alma mater's mascot, the Green Wave, depicted by a towering, curled body of water poised to crash upon a group of tiny rival mascots below, including a Red Devil, a Florida panther, a Seminole Indian, and a peg-legged pirate, all fleeing with expressions of terror.

Before walking out the door, Ellis felt again at his waist for the now familiar silky-slick sensation of cotton slipping across a Ziploc bag. The journal now had company; he'd also brought along the old love letters that Mary Jayne Hartupee's mother had written to his father years ago, the very illicit correspondence that Ellis had threatened to reveal if she did not agree to abolish Holidazzle.

He walked the eight blocks to Poinciana, and as he turned off McGregor and looked toward the water, he was relieved to see the red kayak resting beneath the banyan, a white receipt taped to the side and flapping in the cool air that swept off the river. The wind had picked up, and Ellis hoped it would not hamper his efforts.

Yet Ellis's enthusiasm crashed when he got to the boat and discovered he'd forgotten to ask them to bring a life preserver. He did not dare venture into the river without one.

Geena had gone to Miami to shop for the weekend — Ellis thought it strange that she was staying away overnight; she'd never done that before — so he had plenty of time to walk home and find something . . . but what?

He began his search in the garage, then moved to the kitchen, then beneath the beds. He'd lived in this house as a coastal Floridian since he was two years old — surely there was some sort of flotation device somewhere. Ellis toyed with the idea of strapping one of the foam couch cushions onto his torso with a belt, and wondered if he could fashion a vest out of duct tape and Ziploc bags blown up like balloons.

He found his solution in the front hall closet, a hunter orange, quilted, down-filled coat that Geena had bought for Mr. Douglas at some thrift store. Ellis took it off the hanger and held it up. It certainly was light, and it looked as though it would float; the quilted compartments appeared to be filled with air. And wouldn't something made for hunters, something in this safety-orange color, wouldn't it be constructed for both land and sea? Of course, the garish color was all wrong, and his efforts to camouflage himself and the boat would be for naught, but Ellis realized this was his best choice. He put the coat on, zipped it up, and walked back to his kayak on Poinciana, which seemingly glowed beneath the streetlights of McGregor.

He had imagined this moment more than once. It would be just like the scene from *Titanic*, in which the old-woman survivor from the fatal wreck is summoned out to sea by the salvage divers, who want her to help them find the rare blue-diamond necklace that went down with the ship, the very necklace her lover had given her hours before the collision with the iceberg.

In the predawn of the morning, when the divers were scheduled to go down and crack the barnacle-encrusted safe in the captain's quarters, the woman snuck out of bed in her bathrobe and walked to the edge of the research vessel. Her hands balled into fists and, resting them atop her chest, she stopped at the edge, closed her eyes, and breathed in deeply, as if she'd come out to meditate in the crisp sea air. With moonlight glittering on the water, her hands then bloomed open, revealing the sought-after diamond necklace she had managed to save that night — no one in the world knew she had it, just as no one knew Ellis possessed the journal — and with a startled, quiet, small yelp of both elation and regret, she tossed the necklace into the ocean, never to be found again, finally, properly, burying at sea her love for the man she lost that night in 1912.

Ellis paddled against the breeze, the hull of his kayak bouncing and slapping atop occasional random waves. His feet were cold because he had stepped into water up to his ankles when launching. In his lap lay the plastic bag with the documents and a few rough, fist-sized limestone rocks he'd picked up from the bank.

The current kept trying to push Ellis to the right, and he found that he had to paddle nonstop on that side or he would quickly veer off course. His arthritic shoulder ached, and it was very hot and moist inside the insulated jacket. Ellis's breath grew labored. His heartbeat throbbed in his ears. He could taste the iron tang of blood because he'd bitten the inside walls of his cheeks. He wished now that he had told Geena of his plans so she would be here to help him right at this challenging moment.

Ellis passed a yellow Styrofoam float that marked a crab trap on the sandy bottom below. Did this mean he was getting closer? He looked ahead and wondered how much longer it would take him to reach the channel.

Only the channel would do. Though the murky, two-mile-wide Caloosahatchee appeared to be the depth of a frigid, blue-black Scottish loch dug by a glacier, a man could actually wade across the entire width, save the channel, of course, which had been dredged time and again over the years so that barges could carry oil upriver to the power plant near Alva. Ellis remembered the summer day in 1960 when Hurricane Donna blew ashore. The huge storm was situated in such a way that, instead of pushing a wall of water inland and flooding everything in sight, the inverse occurred. Ellis, his mother, and their neighbors watched in awe as the immense river was sucked dry, the water pulled out to sea, just as God had done for Moses and his people when they fled Egypt, exposing a mucky, flat expanse littered with lumber from collapsed docks and rusty lawn furniture and metal gas cans and bottles and tires and marooned manta rays flapping in vain in the greenish muck. Within minutes, the eye of the storm passed, and, as if some huge magnet had suddenly been reversed, the water came rushing back into the river. A neighbor had looked at Irene Norton and said, "I'm not tellin' no one. Who would believe us?"

Ellis paddled onward. Though he'd pondered it many times in the past week, he again wondered about the depth of the channel and whether it was deep enough to swallow and irretrievably hide something as small as his Ziploc bag. He'd heard stories of catfish the size of grown men living among the detritus on the bottom, and he wondered if they might mistakenly eat it. Ellis had toyed with the idea of burning the letters and journal, but that seemed too violent an act. He liked the idea of knowing that this surrogate heart of his beloved would lie, forever, just a mile away.

The channel . . . oh Lord, how long would it take to reach the channel? Ellis felt the sting of blisters forming on the inside of his thumbs. New, stronger gusts of wind were buffeting him, as if fresh reinforcements had been called in to stop an advancing enemy. Feeling dizzy, Ellis remembered the advice of Jane Fonda in the workout tape that he and Geena had found at the Goodwill store in Punta Gorda — "Don't forget to breathe" — and he concentrated on taking deeper breaths. He slipped his thumbs to the other side of the oar's bar, and though this made progress slower, it allowed him to forge ahead.

Finally Ellis came to the channel marker, a reflective red triangle set atop a guano-splattered wooden piling. In what seemed like a kiss of welcome, Ellis's kayak bumped against it. He had stopped paddling, and he knew that if he did not anchor himself in some way to this post he would drift out of the channel within seconds, and he certainly did not have the energy to return.

"Oh . . . oh . . . Oh, my Lord."

Finding nothing to fasten around the pole, he finally decided to lean rightward, into it, so that he could wrap his arms around it and rest until he regained his strength, but when his center of gravity crossed over the edge of the kayak, he felt it begin to tip, and instead of falling back into the boat, Ellis panicked, instinctively grabbing for the more stable, landlike option.

With his hands wrapped around the piling in a white-knuckle hug, Ellis's legs were left dangling on the boat like a rag doll's, and when he tried to find his footing, pressing on the boat's side, he hastened the capsizing. As the boat fell over onto its back, it hit Ellis's heels, pulling off one of his tennis shoes.

"Oh!"

Clinging to the piling with his arms and legs, Ellis tried to spot the Ziploc bag as it drifted downward, into the dark, but all he could see was his white shoe, bobbing in the green water like a dead fish.

Buoyed by the water — he was submerged from his navel down — Ellis could hold on, though he still found himself creeping downward, and as Ellis suddenly realized he might die out here, alone, he felt panic rise in his throat and spread through his chest.

Then Ellis felt the orange coat, which had been pushed upward and now was gathered in plump rolls beneath his chin. The life preserver! Of course! He would be fine! This was not the North Atlantic after all, it was a subtropical river. Though it might take him all night, Ellis would make it back in fine condition. All he had to do was lie on his back, flutter-kicking whenever possible, and within ten minutes he would be out of the channel and standing on the firm, sandy bottom of the river. Then he could happily walk home, his brave act of chivalry complete.

Ellis counted to three, loosened his grip, and slid the rest of the way into the water. Instantly he knew something was horribly wrong. The coat . . . it was not floating . . . in fact, it felt heavier, substantially heavier, as if someone had thrown a sopping quilt over his shoulders. What was wrong with the coat? Had he overlooked something? Should it have been blown up in some way?

Best as he could do in the water, Ellis felt around for a rubber nipple or some sort of string to pull, all the while frantically bicycling his legs. Though he'd never learned how to swim, he suddenly tried to do the crawl stroke as he'd seen so many times in Esther Williams movies, but he could not move his arms because of the waterlogged jacket.

Ellis felt himself sinking, and he lifted his chin to keep his mouth above water, but the higher he brought his chin, the faster he seemed to sink. The last thing he saw was the moon, then the river washed over his face and eyes and he slipped beneath the surface.

He was under for several moments before a wave pushed him upward a few inches, but as Ellis gasped for air it was water that filled his mouth, and as he coughed he went down again.

His lungs felt as if they were on fire, much like the time David Dushatko had forced him to inhale a cigarette behind Mr. Keifer's shed and covered his mouth and nose so he couldn't expel the smoke from his lungs.

Dizzy and weak, his muscles starved of oxygen, Ellis floated motionless in the water for a few moments. He so desperately wanted to sleep, and he felt himself falling in that direction, but, once more, the instinctive will to survive roared up in him like oxygenated fire, and in a frenzy he pumped his legs again as if climbing stairs. If he climbed fast enough he would finally reach air again. Just one big draw of air, he thought, oh please, all I need is one.

Take the coat off, Ellis.

Yes . . . of course. How silly of me.

Take the coat off, Ellis. Take it off!

Yes . . . yes . . . the coat must come off . . . Is that you, Mother? . . . My lungs . . . I feel as though they might explode . . . this coat . . . it must come off, and then my lungs will be okay. These pants, too. I must shed all this weight, I must become very light. But what shall I do when I return to shore and have no pants? This coat . . . Yes . . . thank you, Mother. I know the coat must be taken off, and I am very warm now so I want the coat off. . . .

And then suddenly it was no longer an issue, the coat no longer felt like some mammal pulling him down, and his urgent, painful need for air was replaced by the most pleasant, warm, electrical tingling that spread through his chest and all the way through his limbs, into his fingers, up the back of his neck and into his toes and cheeks and eyelids. Ellis felt as light as

Spanish moss . . . and he was no longer sinking . . . was he? No, he was indeed moving . . . but where? . . . and how? . . . And this woman, this lovely woman in the pink organza dress is smiling and giving me her hand.

"Ellis! You have come for me," she says.

"Mina?"

"Finally, you are here."

"Mina? Oh, my goodness — Mina!"

"What a gentleman you are. . . . And you have come to be with me. And we will be together forever."

"Of course, Mina," he said. "Of course, I have come for you. It is all I have ever wanted."

Chapter Twenty-nine

Drifting snow had clogged and shut down I-70 from Colby to Salina, forcing Barry south, into the desert panhandle of Texas. He drove for nine hours before finally stopping at a Starvin' Marvin's outside Childress for some gas, a tall cup of coffee, and a barbecue sandwich, which he finished before pulling out of the parking lot, wiping his mouth on the sleeve of his shearling-lined jeans jacket.

As he drove, using the printout of the Cingular bill he'd brought with him, Barry dialed every number in Geena's phone history of the past few weeks. Most of them were retail stores of some kind, though there was one unusual, promising lead: three calls to a Thomas Edison museum or memorial of some kind. Barry asked the woman for the address, which he scribbled onto one of his business cards that he pulled from the glove compartment.

Still, he wondered why she'd waited so long to use the phone . . . or maybe she wasn't there at all. Maybe the cell had been stowed all these months in the bottom of some stranger's bag or purse with six or seven other stolen phones, and this thief would pick one out and talk until he ran out of minutes, then discard it like a bland piece of chewing gum whose sweetness had expired.

Almost hourly Barry tried to call his wife, but each time her phone immediately rolled over into voice mail. It was either turned off or she — or whoever — was talking to someone else. Barry left no message because he didn't know what to say, and he thought an element of surprise would improve his chances.

Somewhere, somehow, he and his wife had lost each other's hands in the storm, and he started reviewing in his mind what he might say to Geena to convince her to take his hand again and start over, because that was what they needed to do: begin anew, from scratch. He knew this now. Perhaps they could go back to school or move to Boulder and open a business. Whatever the choice, he could not imagine making the journey without her.

How could a man even begin to apologize for all that had happened . . . for letting his parents poison him . . . for not supporting her . . . for shutting down, turning to stone after their son died, leaving her vulnerable in a desert to mourn alone? Barry was prepared for Geena to say no. She had left him, after all, and had not called him since. And what possibly could have happened in the past ten months to change her mind?

Somewhere in Louisiana, Barry finally pulled off the interstate, into a Shoney's parking lot. He'd found himself becoming hypnotized by the humming drone of tires on concrete and fatigued from a lack of rest and food. Three times in the last hour he had closed his eyes and drifted off the road, only to be saved by the *kuh-lump, kuh-lump, kum-lump* of the yellow, square bumps glued onto the white line. Nathan used to call them wake-up bumps: *Wake up, wake up, wake up.*

Barry went inside and ate a patty melt with coleslaw, then returned to his truck. He looked in his rearview mirror and noted his red-veined eyes and stroked the three days of beard on his cheek. He noticed that his hair was oily and smelled like sour milk. He opened his mouth and stuck out his tongue — Lord, what organisms had set up camp on this moist terrain of flesh?

"God, what would she want with a man like me?" he said.

Barry scanned the landscape out his windows but saw no motel, and he was too tired to begin a hunt. He vowed to buy some deodorant and a razor and find someplace to clean up tomorrow before driving on into Florida.

He rolled his coat into a pillow and lay down on the seat, curling up into a fermata because he was too tall for the cab. He closed his eyes and began tracing the next day's journey in his mind. Before Barry could even reach Mobile he was asleep.

In her travels with Barry over the years, Geena had developed the theory that each city had its own unofficial freeway-driving speed regardless of whatever was posted. It was purely cultural, in her opinion, created by a mixture of variables: wealth, climate, and location as well as the median age and the election-year color of the state, be it red or blue. Other things mattered as well. If they had a popular symphony orchestra, they tended to drive slower. Cities with large numbers of male-driven convertibles were faster. Geena reasoned they were usually men in midlife, frantically chasing elusive happiness; their children grown and gone, they'd thrown caution to the wind.

Omaha, in a conservative, red state, rarely exceeded sixty miles an hour, perhaps because it was still largely agrarian and people feared they might be recognized if they irresponsibly, ostentatiously whizzed past a fellow motorist. It was also home to Mutual of Omaha, the very presence of which surely set a tone of responsibility and aversion to risky behavior.

Houston drove like mad, eighty to ninety miles an hour. Geena had never seen anything like it except on the autobahn in Germany. And why wouldn't Houstonites embrace speed? From nearly everywhere in the city one could see the glass high-rise headquarters of oil companies that shipped in immense tankers of crude oil just fifty miles south, in Galveston. Houston was home to Enron and a U.S. president who defied U.N. mandates, and it sat in a sprawling state that took two full days to cross.

So here she was in the sluggish freeway traffic of Pensacola, a city she'd never seen, and to pass the time Geena looked about her for clues that might explain why the flow of I-10 was so slow. She'd seen four or five barbecue restaurants, so there was that leisurely Southern thing going on here. Also, she noted the presence of the Pensacola Naval Air Station. Military people might better follow the rules. It also looked poorer than the rest of the Florida Gulf coast, which would put more slow-driving beaters on the road. A few miles back Geena had passed a circa-1970 Chevy Impala sporting four different-sized tires. She watched it in her rearview mirror, amazed that it would go anywhere at all, and indeed there was a barely perceptible back-and-forth tug of war going on as the driver tried to maintain a straight path.

Geena had no destination in mind, but she had missed the West and decided that that was where she would go to begin anew and alone. She also had unfinished business in Sublette. There were some things of her mother's Geena wanted to take with her, and it was unkind to let Barry think indefinitely that she had been killed. She would give him a divorce and a kiss. She would thank him for the good years, then leave, but not before stopping by to visit Dot. Someone needed to tell the woman to her face that she was a toxic mother who was slowly poisoning her family.

Will he marry again? Surely he'll marry again? I can't stand the thought of another woman having him.

Restless, Geena reached for her cell phone in the passenger seat but dropped it a second after picking it up. It was dead. She'd forgotten to charge it before she left and had lost her powering cord for the car.

She then thought of her bedroom at Ellis's house and wondered if he'd found the note and the cashier's check on her bed. Geena had added up all the MasterCard bills and tacked on another five thousand dollars for what she considered to be either penitence or punitive damages. She'd abandoned him and was feeling horribly guilty. Geena had thought of telling Ellis everything, but she was too embarrassed, she'd simply gone too far. It was like sitting next to a stranger on a transcontinental flight, whom you speak with the entire way, dreaming up a different life with different children and a different job. You part and go your own way, your lies shielded by anonymity, but if he were to follow you and discover the truth, he'd be furious because you'd betrayed his trust. You had made him feel stupid and thus had chipped off an irretrievable piece of his core of dignity and his faith in humanity.

Her lies had been too many, too drastic, even for someone like Ellis. He might never forgive her. Or — Geena smiled when she thought this — he would forgive her completely. Anyone who repeatedly painted over rotten wood had a knack for ignoring reality. Oh, the world he'd created with his movies and the Edisons!

Geena wrote six different drafts of the letter, ranging from the very long, full disclosure to a simple, short thank-you note. She wasn't even sure how to sign her name. In the end, Geena chose deception because she didn't want to rattle him.

My dear, sweet Ellis:

I had to leave. It was time for me to go, and I left like this because it would have made me too sad to say good-bye to you in person. I'm leaving a check to help pay for expenses incurred while I was here. You are one of the sweetest men I've ever met, and I'm very proud of you and the life you lead. Love, Irene.

P.S.: I did not have the heart to tell you, but I was fired from the newspaper and there will be no profile of you.

After she loaded up her Excursion for the last time, Geena went back and amended the note just before leaving:

P.S.: If you ever want to talk, you can call me on my cell. The number is 719-345-8465.

As Geena left Pensacola and headed west into Louisiana, one of her favorite old songs by the Go-Go's, *Vacation*, came onto the classic oldies station she was picking up from Baton Rouge. She rolled down all the windows, and the cool spring air filled her car and began to blow her hair around, randomly whipping her face, her neck, her eyelids. To her delight, the loose receipts and other small pieces of paper from throughout the car suddenly became airborne, swooshing about in circular patterns and delicately bouncing off the ceiling and windows like the Ping-Pong balls in the clear Lucite box on the nightly Lotto drawing. Geena breathed in as far as she could, feeling her lungs stretch to their limit.

This lightness! . . . This is what I'm going to put back into my life.

A piece of trash blew out the window, and Geena quickly rolled them up. Silence returned to the inside of the car. She noticed a piece of paper that had come to rest on the floor in front of the passenger seat, blank and rectangular and white. Curious, Geena took her foot off the accelerator for a moment to drag it across the carpet so she could pick it up.

It was a freshman-class photograph of Nathan that had been blown out of hibernation from some dark crevice in the car. It had been taken in October two years earlier. Some of his summer tan still lingered, and he bared most of his large, white teeth in a smile of laughter.

It was the first image of her son she'd seen since leaving home, and Geena was surprised to realize now that she had not once looked at the photographs in her wallet during all these months. This image of Nathan now stirred in her an unfamiliar mix of emotions, different than she remembered from before.

How dare you smile! How could you be so stupid and reckless? Don't you know I'll have to live with this until the day I die?

And also, for the first time since he'd died, a hint of joy, of pleasure from seeing the image of something that had brought happiness for so long. Would it really be possible to someday reminisce without crying? A mother can creep out from beneath her cloud of grief, but how clearly will she truly see? How far does she venture from that point onward? Will she take more risks — or fewer?

I want to forget you, and I don't want to forget you. I don't want the pain anymore, but at least the pain makes me feel alive. What can I find to replace the pain? That's what I need to start looking for . . . but I don't want to live the rest of my life relying on distraction. I want everything to be real . . . not Ellis-real but real-real . . . very, very real.

A twenty-something brunette woman wearing Italian, violet-frame sunglasses passed Geena in a white, two-door Saab. She fleetingly looked at Geena and her contact-paper-covered SUV with a condescending smile born of amusement and disgust.

Smile and laugh all you want, darling. I have seen the bottom, and I have no where else to go but up!

Geena unconsciously sped up. She passed the Saab woman, then another car, and another, and another.

She crossed the Florida border at eighty-six miles an hour, and only outside of Ponchatoula, Louisiana, did she see something that caused her to lift her boot from the accelerator and drift to a slower speed in the fast lane of traffic. In the parking lot of a Shoney's restaurant she saw a copper-colored Dodge crew-cab pickup just like Barry's, and as she zipped past she thought she recognized the silhouette of white mountains on a kelly green background of a Colorado license plate.

There's no way. . . . There is no way in hell.

She took the next exit and backtracked on a frontage road, and as Geena pulled into the parking lot she could read the vanity tag, *REAL-ST8,* the one she'd bought her husband for his birthday three years earlier. The driver-side window was down and from them protruded a pair of legs in blue jeans and the brown leather clogs that had sat in the dark on the floor of Barry's closet, ignored for so long.

Geena's stomach fluttered, her breathing grew shallow. She felt a tickling flutter in her lungs.

Oh, my God, has he come to find me? . . . But why?

She parked ten spaces away and dodged into the Shoney's bathroom, where she brushed her teeth and put on lipstick. She'd left her blush for Ellis, so Geena dabbed her cheeks with the lipstick and then licked the tips of her fingers and rubbed it in. She ducked into a stall to pee, but when she reached for the toilet paper she discovered the tube was empty. With her pants around her knees, Geena waddled out of the stall and in and out of two others before finally finding a roll that had not run out.

When Geena returned outside, the pickup was gone and in its place was a new, periwinkle blue VW bug.

Geena ran to her car, climbed inside, and sped from the parking lot, her rear tires leaving black screech marks on the concrete.

North or south? North or south? . . . South . . . I'm an optimist.

It took her seventeen miles to catch him, but right after the turnoff to the causeway to New Orleans, Geena spotted Barry's truck. He seemed to be driving at least ninety, and she sped up to close the gap.

Finally they were side by side. Geena meant to honk but she could not stop staring, absorbing this man who looked both familiar and different. She noted his longer hair — it had even started curling upward under his neck — and the uncharacteristic shadow of beard.

He looks like a country western singer. Oh, Barry! Oh, my God! Please tell me it's him, Barry, the husband, I want . . . not Nathan's father.

Barry finally noticed the Excursion lumbering next to him. Alternating his glances between the road ahead and the driver beside him, he watched Geena lower her dark glasses farther down onto her nose, then give him a fluttering wave and a crooked smile of someone who's just been caught in a little white lie.

For the longest time he was stone-faced, as if afraid to recognize what he thought he saw — this woman in the crazy patchwork Excursion who looked like his wife — and then Geena stuck out her tongue at him, curling it upwards from the sides so that it was U-shaped. Barry had never been able to do this, and Geena always teased him for it, said it was a sign of royalty and he, thus, was not worthy of her.

Barry finally broke into a full smile and started to shake his head, and Geena felt her insides twitch. A viscous warmth spread like runny, broken yolks, through her body, starting in the womb and somewhere behind the breasts and then running out to her arms, up to her scalp.

This is how I felt twenty years ago.

Barry ascended the next exit ramp and pulled to a stop on the shoulder of the road. Geena pulled in behind him. They got out of their cars and began walking the ten yards to each other, both with the determined, focused gait of someone who has honed in on something that needs immediate fixing.

By the time she reached him his arms were open, and Geena fell into them and buried her face in his chest, grabbing handfuls of the folds of his shirt on his back.

Crying, she looked up at her husband, and he took her face in his hands and kissed her, and at one point when he thought she was pulling away, he gently grabbed at her bottom lip with his teeth. A trucker gave them a double blow of his horn as he passed.

Finally they separated and reached for each other's hands, breaking the connection only to occasionally touch a cheek, a forehead, to squeeze an arm, as if testing to see if this person before them was tactile or illusion.

"What do I say?" he asked.

Geena shook her head.

"I'll say anything you want me to," he said.

"Kiss me again."

When they parted, Geena gave a deep breath and patted her chest. "Okay," she said, "let's get this over with. Yes, there is something I want you to say. I want you to tell me you're sorry for blaming me for Nathan's death. I'm still mad about that, Barry, and it's gonna be a hard one to get over. . . . But I can get over it."

Barry looked away from her and at something on the horizon. Geena could see tears welling in his brown eyes. He swallowed hard and his chin grew tense. What was it about men that made them use their chins as dams, tenuously blocking emotions of great pressure?

He began nodding as he wiped his nose with the back of his hand. He looked down at his clogs and then, finally, again, into her eyes.

"If you never forgive me, I'll understand."

Geena squeezed his hands. "I think we're even now," she said.

He looked at her with renewed urgency and curiosity. Again he wiped his eyes.

"No, Barry, I wasn't with someone else. . . . not like that, anyway."

"We can leave Sublette."

Geena looked at him. She cocked her chin, squinted her eyes.

He wants me back!

"You would?" she asked.

"Is that what you want? We can start over somewhere."

Geena shook her head. "No, darlin'. . . . I want to go home. I want to have another child. I want twenty-four more children, Barry."

"You always wanted just one."

"I never wanted more than one because I wasn't up to any more battles with your parents. . . . But I am now. And let me tell you this: If that woman tries to cut off my feet again, I'm going to scream so loud she'll run and hide under the bed."

Geena followed him to a Ford dealership in Baton Rouge, which he'd phoned ahead of their arrival. As a salesman looked under the hood to help calculate an appraisal for Geena's SUV, Barry opened up the back hatch, and when he lifted a plaid wool blanket and two beach towels, he found a mailbag, sheared in half and filled with envelopes.

"That's mine," Geena said. "I want to take that with us."

Barry shook his head. "I don't even wanna ask."

"Oh, but you'll soon know," Geena said. "Because I'm going to tell you everything."

Chapter Thirty

Unlike the millions of snowbirds who would eventually succeed him in Fort Myers, Thomas Edison found it impossible to live a retiree's life. Just as the warmth of the sun pulled people south, the nagging, elusive mysteries of the invisible-physical world continued to drag Thomas from his bed at Seminole Lodge each morning and into his laboratory.

While he was able, he walked there himself with the help of a cane, self-consciously shuffling across the flat stones of McGregor Boulevard at seven in the morning each day. In his last few years on this earth, an attendant would push him in his yellow wheelchair that Mina had bought him for his eighty-third birthday. Tourists lined McGregor each morning with cameras at the ready, waiting for the old man to be wheeled across, and when he did, murmurs and the sound of clicking shutters would rise from the crowd as the inventor, Garbo-like, slouched and tried to hide beneath a linen duster and old, floppy strawhat. He cowered behind his arms so he could not be photographed.

The only comfort that Judith found in Ellis's death was that he had not endured such an ignominious ending. As a historian, she knew very well there were two ways to pass on. Like Kennedy and Lincoln, you could abruptly die in mid-mission, leaving people wanting more and always thinking that your best work had not yet been realized. Or, like Reagan and Nixon, your persona could slowly dissolve, growing smaller and smaller in footprint until, in the end, your presence seemed more vaporous than corporeal.

Three days after his body was found floating in Cinnamon Cove by two jet-skiers, the director of Edwards-Schreivogel Funeral Home finally called Judith because no one had come forward to bury him. They could find no living relatives, and there appeared to be no will — at least Lee County sheriff's deputies could not find one in the house or at any local attorney's office.

It was Judith and her son Tim who combed through Ellis's belongings on

Wilna Street, with some of it going to Goodwill and the rest destined for the city dump. She'd hoped to finally locate the source of Ellis's inexplicable, intimate knowledge of Mina Edison but found nothing.

Yet she did relish this chance to deconstruct the personality of her guarded, old friend. Judith smiled at the metal Band-Aid box of credit cards and slipped it into her purse. And underneath the guest room bed they discovered a collection of unopened, unnecessary countertop kitchen appliances. Though he rarely cooked, Ellis found great satisfaction in witnessing on late-night infomercials the seemingly magical transformation of food from its raw undignified state into something savory and desirable and complete.

It was next to the George Foreman rotisserie that they found Geena's note and check, which had been blown off the top of the bed by the ceiling fan. Judith wondered how long she'd been gone and why Ellis hadn't said anything. Though the autopsy showed no head trauma or poisoning or strangulation, the coincidental timing of her disappearance and his death-by-drowning bothered her. She wondered more than once if she should call the telephone number on the note. But she did not.

On the Sunday night after the funeral, after Judith and Tim had boxed up the dishes in the kitchen (she helped herself to four chartreuse-colored Fiesta Ware plates), they decided to drive to the Banana Leaf Café for a late dinner. Judith took pleasure in seeing Ellis's table-reserved sign still on the wall . . . and even more pleasure when the waitress wouldn't let them sit there.

It was dark when they returned. After turning the corner, onto Wilna, she immediately noticed something askew.

"I thought I asked you to turn off the lights," she said to her son.

"I did."

"You did not."

"I did so, Mom!"

Judith parked at the curb instead of pulling into the driveway. They walked around the house, to the unlocked back door, and crept inside.

"Stay in here," Judith whispered to Tim. She found a hammer in one of the kitchen drawers and began to tiptoe down the hallway.

Inside Ellis's bedroom, rifling through the shoe boxes on the top shelf of the closet, was Mary Jayne Hartupee. Judith quietly reached into her purse and pulled out the folded pile of Tim's thank-you notes he'd written for his birthday party the previous week.

When Judith loudly cleared her throat, Mary Jayne screamed and dropped a shoe box to the floor.

"Oh!"

"Can I be of some assistance?"

"You scared the bejesus out of me!"

"It's only fair, Mary Jayne, you frightened me as well. May I ask what you're doing here?"

She faltered a moment, then recovered, lifting her chin twenty degrees and breathing in so as to puff out her chest. Judith had often seen Ellis do the very same thing when challenged. She thought of the famous anecdote about two fraternal twins somewhere in the Midwest who were separated at birth, and when the two men were reunited thirty-three years later they discovered that each held his beer can in the same odd manner, wedged between the pinky and thumb, as if he preferred to drink from a mug but had to make do without.

"I should ask you the same thing," Mary Jayne said.

"I'm liquidating Ellis's estate," Judith answered. "It seems there was no family around to take responsibility for burying their own kin. Or is there?"

Judith held up the handful of letters. "Are you looking for these, by chance?"

Mary Jayne's lips grew taut, forcing the blood from them. "Those letters are mine!" she said.

"No, they are not. I believe they belong to your . . . father." Judith refolded them and put them in her purse.

Mary Jayne stepped down from the stool and brushed at the dust on her long-sleeve black sweater. "No one would believe you anyway," she said. "They'd say they were fake."

"Maybe so, maybe not. But is it a chance you're willing to take, Mary Jayne? These letters have some very insightful details. Have you read them?"

"Have you?"

"Of course. All of them."

Feeling suddenly exposed, Mary Jayne buttoned her black sweater. She began to say something, then hesitated, stormed out of the room, out onto the porch, down the sidewalk, and started walking toward McGregor. Judith wondered how far away she had parked her car.

"Would you like a ride?" she yelled. But Mary Jayne ignored her.

As Judith watched her grow smaller, she wondered where Ellis had hidden the real letters and if they would ever turn up. Perhaps they had never existed in the first place. She knew that Ellis, all alone in the world, would find comfort in knowing he had a sister with him on this earth, albeit one he could not openly claim and embrace.

Judith smiled to herself. Perhaps she'd been too hard on him all this time. How many people truly lived in a world free of fabrication, certain of the difference between the unreal and the unrealized?

Chapter Thirty-one

22 March 1944

As I walked through the gardens today, I wondered if I am making a horrific mistake. Such joys that I will miss! The dove orchid, and the mule-ear, the plumeria on the east side of the guesthouse with blooms the color of butter. And who can ignore the Barbara Karst bougainvillea and the mango alee, all these dear friends that Thomas and I have gathered from around the world and brought here, to live in the warm, sandy soil of Fort Myers. Who would have ever imagined I would fall in love with this crude, wild place!

I now look out at the royal palms that line McGregor, brought from Cuba and planted and nurtured by Thomas and myself. I believe we have made a mark here, creating a feeling of civilization by placing rows of trees on the busiest thoroughfare in town, equidistant from each other, in a manner that only man can do when he intervenes to tame nature. To walk or, as so many now are doing, to drive down McGregor is to be comforted by the reminder that man can and does indeed control his environment and his destiny.

I now see a child walking down the sidewalk. It is Irene Norton's odd, sweet boy. I believe Ellis is his name. Such unusual, excellent posture for a child! What legacy do Thomas and I leave him? What impact does one human truly have upon another? I have helped to beautify the city and to build a new train depot, and, lastly, I leave Seminole Lodge to the people of Fort Myers to be used as a museum. This brings me great sadness, but I no longer feel comfortable here by myself. I want to be closer to my doctors and Charles and Madeleine and Theodore.

Against Charles's wishes, I have decided to leave everything. The only personal item I wish to take is the journal from my first few years here as Thomas's new, uncertain wife, but I cannot remember where I hid it. I wish I had buried or burned it as intended. I can only hope that when it does surface it will be discarded as trash or, at the very least, put in proper perspective. I was young and as lonely as the man on the moon.

It hurts me to abandon this home, never to return. It has become a large part of me. To comfort myself, I will fool myself. I will tell a little lie as women so often do to endure the more difficult times of life. I will pack up next week and leave everything as if I plan to return next winter. If I do not shutter and lock away this part of my life, I can always revisit it in my dreams. When I am old and wheelchair-bound in snowy West Orange, I can once again take the train south, down the Florida peninsula to the edge of the world.

Forever in my mind I will walk up the stone path, into the house, and throw open the shutters to receive the cool river breeze. I will cut a snack of papayas and star fruits, and I will rock in the shade of the porch in my white-wicker swing. I will listen for the screeching of the parrots overhead, the creaking of the bamboo, and the footsteps of my eccentric, restless husband, coming home.

All This Belongs to Me

A READER'S GUIDE

A Conversation
with Ad Hudler

Ad Hudler sat down to discuss his new novel, *All This Belongs to Me,* with journalist Drew Sterwald over a bottle of sauvignon blanc in the writer's home on the banks of the wide Caloosahatchee River, just a mile from the Edisons' historic winter home in Fort Myers, Florida. Sterwald and Hudler met seventeen years ago when the latter worked as a features reporter at *The News-Press* in Fort Myers, writing stories about shoes found on roadsides and other offbeat subjects. The two have been low-maintenance friends ever since, picking up the thread of each other's lives through several moves and numerous life changes. For this interview they passed a laptop back and forth as they watched the sun set on a warm, humid winter evening.

417

Drew Sterwald: In any novel that involves historical figures, the author often blurs the line between fiction and fact. What in your book about Thomas Edison's life is true, and what is the product of your imagination?

Ad Hudler: Most of the details about Mr. Edison himself and the estate in Fort Myers are true. He did indeed have a strange obsession with milk, and he did in fact try to invent a machine that could communicate with the spiritual world.

DS: What about the test tubes containing the famous inventor's final breaths? Did you make that up? It sounds almost too "out there" to be true.

AH: As far as I can tell from my research, there was indeed a group of test tubes sitting beside his bed. And when he died, his son, Charles, told the attending doctor to seal the tubes with paraffin. One of these is supposedly in Henry Ford's museum in Michigan. The others inexplicably disappeared. I thought it would be fun to unearth them for the novel.

DS: And what of Mina's life? How much of that is true?

AH: The details of her physical life in Fort Myers are, for the most part, true; she did have one of those fat-burning saunas in her room that was powered with bright lightbulbs. I can't say the same for her private emotions and thoughts — the journal entries are pure fiction.

DS: Really? The voice you give her sounds so authentic for a woman of that period. How did you develop that?

AH: I read many of her letters and travelogues, and I tried to replicate her voice as best I could. I tried to imagine what it would have been like to be married to a workaholic inventor who was known to "check out" for hours and days at a time. Maybe he truly was an attentive husband for the young bride, but I doubt if that was true — and thank God because he wouldn't have invented so many wonderful things had he been lovestruck.

DS: Having visited the Edison estate countless times, I'd say your depiction of the place is pretty accurate. I always enjoy the gardens, but I get a kick out of seeing Edison's dentures, too.

AH: It truly is one of the most interesting historic homes in America, rich in its abundance of artifacts. (His shoes really do lie beside the cot in his laboratory. And Edison really did plant the first of the now famous royal palms lining McGregor Boulevard, which gives Fort Myers its nickname, "City of Palms.") I live just about ten blocks from the estate, and I ride my bike past it every time I go to the post office. Edison's home has been undergoing a huge restoration project after decades of neglect, and it's given the staff a chance to make the estate more historically accurate. The flora is especially fascinating, and the 2004 hurricanes toppled mainly exotic trees that shouldn't have been there in the first place. You can learn more about the place at www.edison-ford-estate.com.

DS: In the novel you ignored any and all references to Henry Ford, who befriended the inventor and moved into the house next door to him in Fort Myers. They're known as the Edison-Ford Winter Estates. Why did you completely ignore the Ford part?

AH: Ford's home was added years later to the tour, and I thought it would be distracting to include it.

DS: The Court of Edisonia is another detail that sounds too odd to be true, though you and I and anyone else who lives here knows it's real. Were you worried that the old guard of Fort Myers, which takes these traditions quite seriously, might think you're poking fun at them?

AH: I'm simply describing reality. If you find that funny, you need to ask yourself why.

DS: Well put. That kind of local color plays a big role in *All This Belongs to Me*, as it did in *Southern Living*, your novel about the modern-day South. How important are these quirky, parochial details to your work?

AH: Very. Without trying, I find that the settings for my novels almost become characters of their own. I think a sense of place is critically important in the experience of reading a novel.

DS: I think it also gives your books a cinematic quality that readers find easy to relate to.

AH: I find that interesting because I don't

watch television, and I don't enjoy most movies. I know it's kind of strange, but I don't like live entertainment in general. I don't know why. My wife says it's a control issue; I have the power to put down a book and stop reading, but I can't leave a theater or ask the actors or musicians to stop.

DS: But I know you're an avid reader. What do you like to read?

AH: Newspapers. I'm married to a newspaper publisher. My father is a newspaper publisher, as was his father and *his* father. My first job was as a print journalist. You'll notice that all my books have references to newspapers, and my next novel will include a retired newspaper editor. I love newspapers — in fact, many of the ideas for my novels come from the smallest of headlines — because they're nothing less than the daily diary of the human race.

DS: *Househusband* was largely autobiographical. In *Southern Living*, you got inside the heads of three totally different women. Who is your alter ego in *All This Belongs to Me*?

AH: While we were waiting for a bus one

time in Central America, stranded in the middle of nowhere, a friend of mind decided to play a game to pass the time. She said, "I have a theory that we all are stuck at a certain age in our mind, and that we identify with that age no matter how old we become. What age would that be with you?" The answers for our group of middle-aged friends ranged from twelve to thirty-six. The answer for me was easy: "I'm seventy-six years old. I've always been a fastidious, crotchety old man." So, the secret is out. I am Ellis Norton. Ellis is who I would be if I had never been married and lived a life alone. To not like Ellis is to not like me. In fact, Ellis is just as autobiographical a character as was Linc Menner in *Househusband*.

DS: Humor plays a key role in your writing. Will that always be so?

AH: I don't know. My agent said that *All This Belongs to Me* was different from my other novels in that it was "smile-funny, not laugh-out-loud funny." So maybe there's an evolution of some sort taking place. I know it's in me to write a deeply serious novel — and I'm sure I will some day — but the genesis of it hasn't yet bubbled to the surface.

To date, I have escaped tragedy in life. My friend Luanne calls me the "boy in the plastic bubble." When something awful does occur — and it will — I'm sure it will change the tone of my novels. Humor is only possible when a person's emotional and physical needs are being satisfied. Humor is a luxury.

Reading Group Questions and Topics for Discussion

1. Knowing what you know about the evolution of Ellis, what would have happened to him had he lived?

2. Chance plays a large role in the novel. Does Geena's serendipitous reunion with her husband cross the line between believable chance and artistic contrivance?

3. Is Judith a protagonist or an antagonist?

4. During the novel Geena moves out from a cloud of grief to a clarity of living. What were key moments that pulled her back into reality?

5. In the course of the novel, Geena does some very unscrupulous, mean things, such as using Ellis's credit card for expensive pedicures. Could you, would you have done the same thing in the same situation? How

did she justify such behaviors? How aware was she of her actions? And did this awareness change over the course of the novel?

6. How does Geena deal with grief over her son's death? At times she uses humor, other times anger, at other times conspicuous consumption. How and why would retail therapy help Geena? How does it help you?

7. The author has described this as "a love story of sorts." If that's true, who are the characters in love?

8. How did Ellis's relationship with his mother influence his dealings with other women?

9. A subtitle for the novel could be *A Tale of Identity Theft.* Besides the obvious credit-card scam, what are some other examples in the novel of one person stealing or borrowing another person's identity?

10. After a lifetime of little change, Ellis begins to grow for the first time in his life. Discuss the women in his life and the roles they played in enabling him to grow.

11. What did Geena get from Safe-T-Man? Should every woman have a Safe-T-Man?

About the Author

Ad Hudler is a stay-at-home dad and author of the novels *Househusband* and *Southern Living*. He lives in Fort Myers, Florida, and has visited the Edison home many times.